DAY NOT PROMISED

BY

PAT SIMMONS

This novel is a work of fiction. References to real events, organizations, or places are used in a fictional context. Any resemblances to actual persons, living or dead, are entirely coincidental.

ISBN: 978-1-7338316-6-6

Developmental Editor: Chandra Sparks Splond
Proofread by Lucky Author's Gill Donovan
Final Proofreader: Darlene Simmons
Beta Readers: Stacey Jefferson, Evangelist Charlotte Townsend
Interior Design: Kimolisa/Fiverr.com
Cover Design: Germancreative and designerzone_lk on Fiverr.com

Praises for Pat

4 STARS Surrender to Salvation

Queen is the perfect example of a person fighting the call of salvation. She needed God's salvation but wanted to do her own thing. Until she couldn't hold out any longer. Phillip had the patience of Job with the church and Queen. Great read, Pat.- Juanetta P. Frazier on *Queen's Surrender*

5 STARS Bible…

Loved it! The thing I love most about Pat's books are that they always refer to scripture. So I know in advance, to have my bible next to me while reading her books. Absolutely loved it! — Amazon reader on *In Defense of Love*

5 STARS Get Your Priorities in Order

While reading this book, this is the one statement that kept coming to the forefront of my mind. In this life we are going to have trouble, but are you mentally ready for this life's trials and tribulations if and when they hit? We never know when something could happen. Placing God at the forefront is to me the best place to start this road called 'Adulthood' Take the journey with Darcelle and Evanston this Christmas season and learn how placing God, love, and family in the right order can make your life worth living and your heart more giving. Merry Christmas!!! –Amazon reader on *Christmas Dinner*

5 STARS Redeemed!

What a blessing this book has been to me! The theme of ex-felons being given the good news of Jesus Christ. Redemption is an amazing theme that was beautifully written in this book. Confession of sins was paramount to redemption and justification. Postpartum depression was a theme most delicately conducted. –Amazon reader on *Crowning Glory*

DAY NOT
PROMISED

Chapter One

May the Lord keep you from dangers seen and unseen.
The weapons of our warfare are not carnal but mighty through God to the pulling down of strongholds. —2 Corinthians 10:4 KJV

Three died, but I survived.

Omega Addams couldn't erase the images that held her mind captive in a headlock. Angels. Demons. Dead people. Was it real or a nightmare? A simple detour home had proven deadly.

Stopping to get gas after leaving work in Midtown St. Louis had put her in the crossfire of a gun battle.

Who robs a gas market on the first day of a work week? Didn't crime happen after dark on the weekends?

Wrong place.

Wrong day to gas up.

Bad timing.

Omega chided herself for not filling up her tank on Sunday as her parents taught her when she learned to drive.

The cracking sound of bullets from inside the convenience store grew louder as the robber—a short white guy—scurried outside while shooting like a madman.

Rapid fire didn't discriminate as it marked unfortunate targets. Bodies collapsed onto the ground like in a video game while others ducked for cover. Officers said three people were deceased.

Not Omega. She was spared.

She was too stunned to move to save her life.

That's when intervention came into play. Without warning, an innocent bystander body-slammed her to the ground. His name was Mitchell Franklin.

He took a bullet for me.

It didn't end there. It wasn't her imagination. Omega saw two angels—too tall to be human beings. Unlike the movie and photo portrayals, they didn't have wings. The pair became a shield to stop more carnage.

"Hey, hey." Her baby sister, Delta, snapped Omega back to reality, shutting down the instant replay button in her mind. The more Omega tried not to think of what happened hours earlier, the more she wanted to make sense of it.

Delta waved Omega's entry key card at the sensor on the security gate to open, then parked the Kia SUV in its designated spot. On autopilot, Omega unbuckled her seatbelt but didn't move to get out.

Her younger sister by two years walked around to the passenger door and guided Omega out like a child and helped her up the stairs.

Punching in Omega's security combination, Delta unlocked the stained-glass front door of her condo. "You're safe."

Yeah, that's what the officer had said when he took her statement. Traumatized but unhurt, Omega refused medical attention.

"Miss Addams, you're done here. You've given us your statement. Call someone to get you," Officer James suggested. "Your vehicle is okay, but you're in no condition to drive yourself."

I'm not? Omega's attempt to recharge her brain to think failed. Her parents weren't an option. They lived hundreds of miles away in Texas. That wouldn't stop them from taking the next flight out of Dallas. And they wouldn't come alone.

Eric and Glenda Addams were active members of the Black Greek letter organizations. Many of their fraternity brothers and sorority sisters were like aunts and uncles to Omega and her siblings. Out of solidarity, they would show up too.

Omega ruled out her big brother Randall. The less he knew, the better for her. He gave a new meaning to overprotective. At least he had a more common name. Their mother had found Omega in the list of baby girl names. Since her father pledged Omega Psi Phi Fraternity, Inc., her name was a tribute to him. Delta—the obvious name choice because their mother was a member of Delta Sigma Theta Sorority, Inc.—was two years younger than thirty-five year-old Omega.

In a daze, the police officer had studied her until she blinked.

"Miss, are you sure you don't want medical treatment?"

"Yes—I mean no—I'm fine. I'll call my sister. Omega pulled the phone from her purse, but her fingers were too shaky to tap on the phone icon.

"Let me help you. What's her name?" Officer James held out his hand.

"Delta."

He scrolled down her recent calls and located the name.

Officer James identified himself and repeatedly calmed her sister down as he gave a recap of what happened at the location. "Miss Addams has a few bumps and bruises but is quite shaken, as you could imagine." He frowned, glanced at the phone, and grunted. "She's on her way."

Delta arrived twenty minutes later from Northwest County to Gus' Gas Mart in a rideshare.

The two sisters hugged and cried thankful tears. Delta composed herself first, then coaxed Omega to get in the car, and her sister sped away. But not fast enough.

Repeatedly, Delta assured Omega that she was safe from harm. *Not after tonight*.

As a single professional living alone, Omega moved to Brentwood's gated community because of the low crime rate, diversity in the ethnic populations, and proximity to shopping, dining, and entertainment. In less than a ten-minute drive, her out-of-town guests could visit the many free attractions in Forest Park, including the world-famous St. Louis Zoo, the Art Museum and Missouri History Museums in Forest Park. Her idyllic bubble was no longer safe.

Inside the foyer of her condo, Delta flicked on one light fixture after another, illuminating the bay windows in the front rooms. The light blinded Omega at first, then the familiar surroundings comforted her.

To calm her nerves, Omega inhaled the scent from the vanilla fragrance candles. It gave her a headache. "That man wanted to kill me. I was so close to death at thirty-five…murdered." Attempting to flop on her chaise, Omega slid to the floor instead. Delta joined her on the floor and wrapped her arms around her as Omega released another round of tears.

"But you weren't. The police shot that deranged man before he could hurt anyone else. It's over. Now I've alarmed your security, and I'm spending the night. Are you sure you don't want me to call Mom, Dad, or Randall?"

"No," Omega blurted out.

Their hothead brother was the oldest at thirty-nine. The man believed in revenge at all costs when it came to his younger sisters. If there was a hint that someone intended to harm or bully them, Randall would strike first.

"I'll be okay." She trembled despite her declaration. "I can't live my life in fear."

"Right." Delta stood and padded across her hardwood floor to her kitchen, outfitted with top-of-the-line appliances and a custom granite countertop. Four swivel stools were ready to receive guests to sample whatever Omega was in the mood to stir up.

Delta reached into a muted charcoal gray cabinet and grabbed one of her many decorative mugs that featured Black divas in hats or dresses on them. These were a few of many ethnic accents Omega used to decorate her two-bedroom place to create a cozy atmosphere.

It was comfortable. Inviting. And safety was never in question.

What happened tonight wasn't supposed to—not in her area on an early Monday evening. Omega tried to rationalize what she had experienced.

A hint of peppermint tea perforated the air as Delta returned and sat on the ottoman in front of her.

"Here. Drink this."

Omega's unsteady hands accepted the brew.

"How's that lump?" Delta stood to examine the back of Omega's head, which had suffered a blow when she hit the ground.

"I'd rather have a bump or a bruise than a bullet like…" She sniffed and thought about the innocent man who had used his body as a shield to save her life.

They both would have lost their lives if the crazed gunman had his way. "I keep seeing that monster's face. The hate in his eyes as he aimed his gun steady at me and fired."

"Sis, it's okay. You're alive. You need to get some rest. Take tomorrow off to regroup." Delta rubbed Omega's back in a soft, circular motion. The touch was soothing to Omega.

"But I'm not staying home. If my Good Samaritan is still in the hospital in the morning, I'm going to thank him."

"Thank God for that innocent bystander. Was he good-looking?"

"What?" Omega frowned at her sister's attempt to lighten the mood. "I don't know. I heard the paramedics call him Mitchell Franklin. Thank God he wasn't killed trying to save me. I didn't have time to check for a wedding or belly ring or nose piercing. We were getting shot at!" Omega displayed a *duh* expression. "Seems surreal. One minute, I'm minding my own business… Then the next, a bullet ripped through his shoulder and whizzed by my eyes. I've never been up close-and-personal with a bullet. But there's something else. Two angels were standing in front of me protecting us. I think they scared the gunman off."

"Angels, huh?" Delta gave her a goofy look. The childhood expression usually amused Omega. Not this time. "How do you know it was angels?"

"They glowed and were taller than the Alton Giant."

She referenced Robert Wadlow who lived across the Mississippi River from St. Louis in Illinois in the early 1900s. At eight feet, eleven inches, he was listed in the *Guinness Book of World Records* as the tallest man in the world.

"Right. Where did they come from?"

"How do I know? They just appeared. All I saw were swords and shields." Omega strained her brain to remember her true guardian angels.

Delta chuckled.

"This was real. They clashed their swords together like superheroes, and the bullets ricocheted off them before the gunman dropped his weapon and ran…but the police killed him." She rubbed her forehead in irritation as she tried to convince her sister of what she saw.

"I guess near-death experiences make a person hallucinate."

"As sure as my head is aching, my vision is 20/20." Omega touched the knot and cringed.

"Right. I'll get you more ice and painkillers."

Had Omega been hallucinating? Did Mitchell Franklin see them too? Omega planned to ask him tomorrow when she visited him in the hospital. If he weren't there, she would stalk him on social media.

Chapter Two

For many are called, but few are chosen.
—Matthew 22:14 KJV

"My son is a hero." Marva Franklin folded her hands as if she were about to lead the group in prayer, hovering over Mitchell in his hospital room. They weren't religious people, yet they all knew God spared his life.

"Were you scared, Uncle Mitch?" Justin, his five-year-old nephew, asked. His eyes were wide with anticipation.

"No, no." Mitchell's father patted his grandson's shoulder. "Your uncle is two hundred and forty-five pounds of solid muscle. He ain't scared of nothing." His signature yellow toothpick was jimmy-rigged between two bottom teeth.

How had his uneventful day gone from leaving the gym, stopping by his brother's place, then stopping to get gas landed him in the hospital? His head hurt from trying to make sense of it. When Mitchell's pain meds through his I.V. reached his pain point, he drifted to sleep.

Hours later, Mitchell woke up alone in a hospital bed with a roommate behind the curtain. The quietness was eerie as the previous evening's event flooded his mind.

"I wasn't a hero." Someone was in harm's way, so he acted accordingly.

Was he scared? By the looks of him—a bodybuilder and personal trainer—not much scared him in his thirty-eight years.

The gas station robbery was an exception. No one had ever pointed a gun at him and fired. But there was more. His mind was fuzzy, but he had backup, except Mitchell couldn't I.D. them in a lineup. They didn't seem real.

Mitchell Franklin took a bullet for me.

A throbbing headache woke Omega the next morning, followed by a growling stomach.

She heard snoring and glanced around her bedroom toward her sofa. Right. Recalling Delta had spent the night, Omega folded the cover back and steadied herself before standing. Her sister stirred.

"I need to call Hathaway and tell them I'm taking a personal day, then go to the hospital and thank that guy who saved my life."

"If your Good Samaritan is still there," her sister reminded her.

Right. Omega twisted her lips in thoughts. She preferred to thank him face-to-face. If not, then a private message through social media would have to do.

As the director of development and community engagement of Hathaway Health Management, an expanding business empire with a presence in five states, her job was coordinating transportation for the underserved residents in the St. Louis area to health facilities. In other words, a fancy title to make secure rides for people to their appointments.

"You better make that a sick day." Delta yawned.

"I'm not. A personal day could mean anything from running errands to an emergency. Trust me, my coworkers are suspect of anyone who is sick on one day and miraculously cured the next." She dragged herself to the bathroom for a shower and shampoo. Omega blow-dried her hair, careful of the tender spot from the hit to the ground, a constant reminder, then brushed it into a ponytail since April was too cool to air dry.

She could be mistaken for a teenager instead of a thirty-five-year-old in skinny jeans, flats, and a sweater. It would take cosmetics, heels, and suits to transform her. Not today.

After Omega made the phone call, she went through the motions with her sister and prepared omelets. Humming, Delta added juice and fruit to their breakfast menu. The aroma teased Omega's stomach, but her appetite wavered. Suddenly, she wasn't hungry.

"You going to be okay, sis?" Delta wrapped her arm around Omega's shoulder. "I need you to eat."

"If only I could erase last night." She touched the back of her head.

Conceding to her sister's advice, Omega ate silently as she overanalyzed what transpired the night before. When the kitchen was restored, Omega grabbed her car keys to drive Delta home, despite her sister's protest to stay another night.

Omega jutted her chin in the air. "Nope. I'm a big girl. Once I process the madness, I'll be alright."

Delta squinted and rested her hands on her hips. "You sure? Because I will call Mom and Dad without a blink. They and the posse will be here before the end of the day."

The two rarely argued growing up. Their personalities were similar—independent, trustworthy, and outgoing. The sisters knew how to keep each other's secrets. This one was huge. Would Delta betray her trust?

Omega had to change the subject. "That's a cute shirt dress. You should have gotten me one. Although you have longer legs, I would have killed it."

"Really?" Delta tilted her head. "You want to talk about fashion right now? I had this on last night. You can't sidetrack me, sis. If you're struggling, you may want Mom and Dad here."

Although in the morning light, the outfit was cute, Omega's attempt at a distraction didn't work.

There was a no mistaking their resemblance, but Delta had the edge—seductive eyes—while Omega inherited her mother's sweet, innocent smile. Both had shoulder-length hair and a body that had garnered attention by the time they were in their mid-teens.

Their height was two inches apart, the same number as their age difference, except Delta had the advantage at five-nine. Where Omega's skin tone was a golden brown, Delta had darker skin like their father and Randall.

"Sis, if I feel I need family support, I'll call them myself. Okay?" She waited for Delta's nod. "Great. Let's go."

Delta followed Omega into the garage. Her sister noticed a small hole in her bumper. "What is this? A bullet hole?"

"What. Seriously." Omega sighed as she examined the puncture that wasn't there the day before. The police hadn't mentioned it. If she didn't have a newer vehicle, Omega would trade it in so she wouldn't have a constant reminder of the night of horror.

Driving off, Omega left her cul-de-sac later than usual, missing Mrs. Helena Wrighton. She lived at the corner and offered morning sendoffs to school children and professionals as they left the gated community— "Have a blessed day," "Be safe, in Jesus' name," or something uplifting.

Yesterday, as the retired grade schoolteacher shouted to passing cars who honked, Omega now recalled Mrs. Helena's fading voice: "May God send His angels to protect you."

At the time, Omega gave little thought to the cheerful adieu. Some say, "Good morning," others, "How you doin'?"

Now, she wondered if the previous evening's misfortune had been a coincidence—or did Mrs. Helena have a sixth sense or something?

The older woman had been a fixture before Omega purchased the condo four years ago. Mrs. Helena was a shoo-in for a stereotypical store greeter, with her warm smile, silver short hair, and friendly eyes. If Mrs. Helena said, "Have a good day," it was a given the neighbors would.

Monday evening was anything but that. One minute, Omega monitored the gallons her tank gulped down. The next—chaos.

A stranger appeared from the other side of the pump and tackled her. Although his weight was suffocating her, she fretted as blood trickled from his wound.

"Hello…hello." Delta nudged her. "You sure you're okay, because you just missed my exit."

"Oops." Omega glanced over her shoulder. "Yeah. I guess I did. Sorry. I'm still in processing mode." She turned on her signal and took the next exit to reroute to Delta's house.

"Do you think it's a good idea to visit this guy while you're dealing with flashbacks?" Her sister stared, waiting for an answer.

"I've got to go, Dell. He risked his life for mine. I owe him a visit." Omega sighed and gripped the steering wheel.

"Since you're going to the hospital, check out your bodyguard in the daylight and see if he rates a ten on the fine scale." Delta grinned.

"Seriously!" Omega eyed her sister.

"Just sayin.' We're both single and cute. You're prettier than me with your widow's peak in your hairline—I'm jealous. Anyway, guys check out your figure when we're together before they even look at me."

"I told you I would look better in that shirt dress." She snickered, and it was genuine. "Stop trying to write a love story out of this. Three people died, plus the gunman. That was somebody's wife, mother, sister, husband, son…" She choked. "Their loved ones are planning funerals. Keep talking this nonsense, and I'll take you to the hospital with me," Omega said, knowing Delta avoided medical attention at all costs, even urgent care and emergency rooms.

It wasn't that Delta had a fear of doctors. After hearing horror stories about medical mistakes from documentaries, she didn't trust them. It would be a twist of fate if she married a doctor.

Minutes later, the sisters parted ways at Delta's house after tight hugs and "Call me's." Taking a deep breath, Omega drove back to the highway for St. Louis University Hospital in Midtown. Although the gas station wasn't far from the hospital, Omega avoided that intersection.

Reliving the memories highjacked her mind and didn't set her free until she reached her destination.

Inside the hospital lobby, she asked for the room of Mitchell Franklin—the man who saved her from certain death.

"Room 323. Take the elevators to your right to the third floor." The kind woman pointed in the direction.

Omega exhaled. So, he was still there. She frowned. "Is that a good thing or bad?" she mumbled.

At least his injuries weren't so critical that he needed to be in the ICU. She detoured toward the gift shop and debated whether her hero would prefer balloons or flowers. She opted for the latter.

A memory hit her at the checkout counter. Everything happened so fast—screams, yells, bodies—she couldn't remember what he looked like. "I thought he was dead." She choked the words out as onlookers gave her curious expressions.

She paid and left. Other images intensified as she pushed the button and the elevator doors opened. She tapped the floor number and leaned against the wall to wait. After the gunman robbed the store, it felt like Omega was his target.

Why was the man shooting at her? Did he want her new Kia for the getaway vehicle? It was the vehicle of choice—Kia and Hyundai—because they could be started with a USB. Of course, Omega didn't know that when she bought it.

If the man wanted her SUV, Omega would freely give it up—no questions asked. With nowhere to run, she had shut her eyes and waited for her demise.

Open your eyes, God had commanded her.

She complied and didn't know what frightened her more, the gunman or the giant angels.

"Whew." She shook her head and stepped off on the third floor. She located Room 323 and knocked on the ajar door. "Hello."

"Come in," a strong and alert voice answered.

Good sign. "Hi, Mitchell." She poked her head inside, walked two steps, and waited for his response. "I'm Omega Addams."

Neither recognized the other. He frowned. She stared. Bruises marred his brown skin—on his cheek and forehead. They both had hit the ground hard.

"You shielded me last night.... At the gas station."

Realization brightened his eyes, but Omega remained rooted in place. Besides being her hero, she didn't know the man.

"I'm sorry you got hurt because of me. Are you going to be okay?" Omega didn't let him answer. "I wanted to say thank you." She stuck out the vase of colorful flowers.

"How are you?" Mitchell leaned forward and cringed. His shoulder was bandaged under his hospital gown.

Omega moved to help, but he stopped her, so she swallowed and rubbed the back of her head. "I got a big bump, but I'm alive, thanks to you."

"You give me too much credit. We were at the wrong place at the wrong time, but I'm glad you're okay."

"What about you? I saw that bullet rip through your shoulder."

"I got hit twice." Mitchell downplayed his injuries with a shrug that made him suck in his breath. "That dude must have been high or deranged, but my body is conditioned to survive an impact," he boasted, patting his chest. "One bullet exited, but the other they had to remove."

Judging from the size of this guy, the man's muscles were solid and built to withstand anything…except a bullet. "Does that mean the doctors are letting you go home today?"

"I wish." He pouted, then recovered. "I was running a temperature this morning. They want to make sure I don't have an infection before releasing me."

Omega exhaled in relief. "Do you remember anything odd about last night?"

"Besides getting shot?" He grunted. "That was odd enough for me."

"Right." Omega nodded and gnawed on her bottom lip. *I'm the only one who saw angels and heard God speak.* With nothing more to say, she thanked him again. "I'll be back tomorrow to check on you."

"I don't plan to be here. I have a business to run." He scowled his displeasure.

Not only was Omega the cause of his injury, but his livelihood was taking a hit too. She owed him a visit as long as Mitchell Franklin was in the hospital.

Chapter Three

Lord, I pray, open his eyes that he may see." Then the Lord opened the eyes of the young man, and he saw. And behold the mountain...

—2 Kings 6:17–20 KJV

With confidence and a living-life-to-the-fullest persona, Omega Addams would return to work today.

She refused to let the gas station robbery and shooting be a stronghold on her, even when it popped up on the news, profiling the shooter. The trip to see—or meet—Mitchell in the hospital caused Omega to sleep better.

Omega was preparing breakfast when Delta checked in. "Hey, sis."

"Whoa. This is a different woman from yesterday."

"Yep." She sipped her coffee and glanced out the window to the community's common ground area, where the children played on swings and sliding boards or fed the geese. "I'm good. I don't want to talk or watch instant replays on the news. They interviewed one survivor, and I turned it off. Besides us, no one else—family or friends—needs to know I was a victim of a crime."

"High five through the phone. So how was the warrior? Is he going to be okay?"

"Yes, we've officially met."

"Was he cute?"

Omega groaned. "Would you back off on the romantic stuff? How cute can someone be in a hospital gown? Mitchell Franklin is alive and well, so I'm thankful. I plan to call the hospital before I leave, see him if he's still there, then head to work."

"I'm glad you're okay, sis."

Instead of finishing her coffee, she poured it down the sink and rinsed out the cup. "I'd better go if I want to stop before going into the office."

Omega ended the call and gathered her things. She couldn't imagine what the families of the store owner and two customers—one inside and one outside the store—were going through.

She was a bullet away from taking her last breath. It was a stupid question she had some nerve to ask, but why not her?

Your neighbor knows. God's voice was unmistakable.

Why was the Lord talking to her? What neighbor?

The bump on her head had caused her to become delusional. Omega dismissed her wandering thoughts and called the hospital to verify whether Mitchell was still an inpatient. He was. Had there been complications?

Because she left earlier than usual, Mrs. Helena wasn't at her usual spot yet, waving to neighbors. She had the sweetest smile and eyes that seemed to laugh.

Mrs. Helena wasn't an older woman on a cane but a vibrant childless widow. That's why she doted on the neighborhood children. Since moving to the community, Omega never had more than a five-minute chat with the woman.

At the hospital, Omega purchased balloons at the gift shop and headed to the elevator.

She stood outside Room 323, knocked, and slowly opened the door. With a smile, Omega entered when she didn't hear any objections. "How's my patient—" Mitchell wasn't alone. His guest was a voluptuous woman—tall with big feet and long toenails. She was thicker than Omega's size ten. *This isn't a competition, so why am I comparing notes?* "Oh, I'm sorry. I—"

With fists on her hips, the visitor squinted. "Who are you?"

"Omega Addams. Mitchell shielded me from getting hurt."

"Oh, so you're the chick who almost got my boyfriend killed." She stepped forward.

She better not touch me, Omega thought as she stood her ground. She didn't need her brother for backup. At thirty-five, she didn't want to fight, but self-defense tactics would be applied if necessary.

"Hold it, Farrah." Mitchell squeezed his lips as he shifted in the hospital bed.

The women watched as he swung his legs over the side of the bed.

"Drop the drama. I'd have done it for any stranger."

"Humph." Farrah looked Omega up and down. "Especially the pretty ones, huh?" She snatched the balloons. "I'll take these for my honey. You can leave now. He's getting discharged today, so you can stop stalking him."

Stalking? Omega ignored her. Besides, Mitchell's discharge would close the dark chapter of what they experienced so they could move on as survivors.

Something has to change, Caylee Price thought as she decided to make a career move from a stripper to…anything else.

At twenty-four, Caylee was a college dropout, one year shy of a fine arts degree. She slipped into high heels when her dad died and worked crazy hours to care for her younger sister. Plus, she didn't have a car anymore. It was repossessed.

Caylee felt alone. No friends, little money, and a teenage sister, barely eighteen, whose dream of being a New York model had to happen.

April making it big was Caylee's success story too. Feeling sorry for herself, a tear fell, then another.

End it all, a voice whispered into her mind.

How? She didn't own a gun. Caylee wasn't a fan of knives. What was the best poison that would make death quick?

Stand in traffic, the same voice helped guide her on a method of choice. *Your bus will hit you. The impact will be instant death.*

Caylee glanced down the street. Number 114 Botanical Garden should be there in ten minutes.

Omega thought the chapter was closed on the shooting when she left the hospital. It reopened her emotional wound when she stepped foot into her office.

Employees were collecting donations for Kennedy Kline. She was part of the Hathaway Health team and had lost a cousin, who grew up with her as a sister, in the shooting.

I was the last one to see him alive. She swallowed back heartache.

Any other time, the news of a death from a coworker's family reminded them how fragile life was and none of them was untouchable.

No need to let them know Omega had been there and survived. Holding her tongue, she added to the money pot to buy flowers for Kennedy's family.

Throughout the day, her mind hit replay about the gas station robbery. Omega couldn't shake it. Whether she watched the news or not, Hathaway Health could be like a newsroom when it came to any horrific happenings in the city.

By the end of the day, the incident was old news, replaced with the breaking news of a fast-moving tornado that ripped through a warehouse in the Metro-East in Illinois.

Six workers died in the horrific tragedy.

When Omega left the office, the rain cleared the way for the sun to fight through the clouds. A rainbow announced its victory.

Still, the mood was sober as Omega drove home. She couldn't help but glance at her fuel gauge numerous times. Omega didn't look forward to stopping for gas at any location. Was there a phobia that existed for fear of pumping gas? If so, she had developed it.

Rolling to a stop at a red light, Omega tapped on the steering wheel. To her left, a young woman waited at a bus stop. A light breeze teased her micro-braids. Omega stared at the tranquil scene.

Even the local traffic was light. Where was the onslaught of rush-hour drivers?

Why the bus rider fascinated Omega was unclear. When the light turned green, she couldn't proceed as if the gear were locked in park instead of drive.

Before her eyes, a battle came into focus and raged behind the bus stop as if it was the backdrop on a movie screen. It was so real as if it were high-definition video.

"What?" Omega blinked. Angels again? It was more this time, an army. She could see them clearly as if she could touch them. A rainbow appeared, and thousands as far as she could see descended behind this woman from the clouds.

There are legions of them at My command, God whispered.

Their opponents came from a dark place, crawling up from the ground. They resembled beasts—wild, savage, and monstrous.

Fierce.

Scary.

The woman was clueless of the danger as the creatures grasped at her.

"No…no. No…God, please help her," Omega's scream was stifled.

You help her. Now! God ordered her.

"Me?" What could Omega do? Gnawing on her lips, she turned the corner, parked, and hurried to the bus stop with no plan.

Omega wanted to grab the young woman and run. Aware of the intense fighting, Omega felt like she was at a museum, watching characters on display in a cage.

Unsure of what to say, she cautiously took her seat next to the woman who was unaware of the battle raging behind them.

"The bus is running late. I hope you don't have to be anywhere soon." The woman checked her phone, annoyed. "I wish it would hurry up."

Should I offer her a ride? Stranger danger was real. Men used women as decoys. Would she be smart enough to decline the offer?

"My name's Omega. What's yours?"

"Caylee. You're the second Omega I know." She huffed.

"Really? I wonder if her parents are Greeks too."

"It's a guy," Caylee corrected her.

"Oh, okay. If you trust me, I can give you a ride to where you're going." *I barely trust you.*

Caylee sighed and leaned against the back of the bench. "I don't even know what trust is. I'm struggling to get away from my old lifestyle, but friends I trusted want to pull me back. After today, it won't matter." She shrugged. "I don't care anymore."

Was this a subtle cry for help? In Omega's role at Hathaway, it was her job to convince people in need that someone cared about their health and quality of life, yet she had no words of encouragement for this young woman.

"Are you a Christian?"

It had been a while since anyone asked Omega. "It's not that I'm not a Christian. I do believe." *Especially after what I've seen going on behind us*. "Why?"

"Ah, just thinking about doing a few things, then I started to talk to God, but I don't think He's listening."

Omega glanced over her shoulder. God's army was winning as they formed a forcefield wall around them, but that didn't stop the beasts from attempting to claw their way toward Caylee.

"I think God's on your side." Omega gave her a knowing look as she bobbed her head.

Caylee blinked. "You think so?"

"Definitely. Last night, I survived a gas station holdup because God sent someone to help me."

"I heard about that. There's been so many. At least police killed the man. One less bad guy in the world." Caylee stared at her as if Omega was a celebrity.

"So maybe I can help you and give you a ride somewhere."

"I'm getting tired of sitting here." Caylee seemed disappointed. "Guess I'll go home."

Both stood as her bus was now in sight. Caylee followed Omega to her SUV. Did she see it? Should Omega point that out?

Caylee lived in the opposite direction of Omega in the city's Shaw historic neighborhood. The older homes had distinguished architectural design that would be too expensive to duplicate now. Even the apartments blended among homes and condos.

Once Omega pulled up on Michigan Avenue, a teenager caught her eye. Her movements seemed well-orchestrated, but natural as if she commanded the sidewalk.

"Oh, that's April, my baby sister." Caylee pointed.

She spun around when she noticed Caylee stepping out of Omega's Kia.

"Caylee! I've got good news to share. A New York modeling agency is interested in me!" She rambled off more details. Omega couldn't keep up.

"April, that's wonderful." Caylee hugged her sister.

"Congratulations," Omega said from behind the wheel through the window.

The sisters separated, and April squinted. "Thanks. Who are you?"

Caylee tugged her sister close to the window. "This is Omega. She gave me a ride home." She nodded. "Otherwise, I probably wouldn't have been here."

"Oh, I saw the bus coming when we left," Omega said.

"I'm glad you came first." Caylee smiled.

"Me too." Omega was about to drive away when Caylee stopped her.

"You saved me from making a wrong decision. Thank you." Her eyes teared. "Things haven't gone in my favor—no job, no car, no future…."

"As long as we are alive, I've learned we have a future. Here's my business card." She fumbled through her purse and pulled out one. "My email is on it. Send me your résumé."

"Ah, I don't have one. My past work experience isn't something Corporate America would appreciate."

Don't judge, don't judge. "Okay. Give me your phone number, and we'll talk."

Caylee lowered her voice as she scribbled her number on a napkin retrieved from her bag. "St. Louis doesn't have the best opportunities for me…and my sister. That's why I've got to get her away from here. Bad influences. I can't wait to see her move to New York."

When April leaves for New York, Caylee will die, God's voice thundered. *The choice is hers.*

What? What did You say? Omega held her breath as fear strangled her spirit. What was Omega supposed to do? Befriend this woman to persuade her sister not to pursue her dreams? *I'm over my head on this one.*

Mitchell saved her life. Now she was supposed to save Caylee. If this was a game of tag, Omega didn't want to play.

She could quarantine herself to keep from running into folks. Omega knew one thing for sure, she didn't have the power to change the course of nature.

This couldn't be happening. Omega must have entered some virtual reality world.

Chapter Four

The LORD had prepared a great fish to swallow up Jonah. And Jonah was in the belly of the fish three days and three nights. —Jonah 1:17 KJV

Mitchell was living his best life. The Franklin family—his parents, two brothers, sister-in-law, and nephew—praised him as a hero, and his girlfriend, Farrah, pampered him like a baby. He was a man, not a baby, and that irked him.

After two nights in the hospital, Mitchell was discharged with instructions to have his primary care physician refer him to a surgeon if he experienced any shooting pains or to return to the ER if he developed another fever.

"Will do." Mitchell knew what exercise regimen to put his body through to ensure his complete recovery as a part-time physical therapist, bodybuilder, and personal trainer turned franchise owner of a neighborhood gym.

Kings and Queens Fitness was his baby. What would it look like if he couldn't get his own body back in shape? The gym was where he met Farrah Williams, not the love of his life, but she was trying hard to fit the mold. She was no different from the other women who flaunted their bodies while at his place of business, but Farrah played hard to get, and Mitchell enjoyed the chase.

The two hadn't dated long before Farrah switched tactics from being coy about their relationship to demands—not hints.

Marriage.

Starting a family.

Not so fast.

It was too early for Mitchell to know whether she was the one who couldn't get away.

Farrah wasn't interested in that conversation.

Omega Addams had asked him if he saw anything. Who names their child a Bible reference about God? Mitchell's story was his mind had played tricks on him as part of a near-death experience. He was sticking with that story. All Mitchell wanted to do was fade quietly back into his own life.

The media and Farrah had other plans. He suspected his family or Farrah had contacted the press and sung his praises. Now, Channel 12 called him twice to interview a gas station hero. No way. He didn't call them back.

Mitchell saved one life—and he would do it again. Nothing heroic like rescuing a child from a house fire or being a hostage negotiator. He had done neither.

When he returned to the gym the following week, his staff and patrons gave him a hero's welcome. All the attention was embarrassing.

He shook hands and accepted pats on the shoulder—the good one—declining to talk about it. After greeting all his staff, he climbed on his favorite treadmill for a few minutes. Four days without exercise was a setback.

Hours later, his shift manager, Steven Cross, walked up to Mitchell. "Man, good to see you. Amazingly, you survived the shooting. A lot of people were hurt."

"God did it. I owe my life to Him." Mitchell almost dropped his weights. Did he say that? Had his ears deceived him?

If you don't praise Me, the wind, the rocks, the birds will cry out in praise, God whispered. *Read Luke 19:40.*

Fear struck Mitchell who flopped on a nearby workout bench. First, the possible angel sighting; now God put words in his mouth. Yikes. What was happening to him?

"Yeah. I'm pushing myself too fast and didn't realize what I was saying." He released a weak grin.

Confusion must have plagued his face because Steven sat too. "You know, I've been thinking about getting my life together. I owe Him my life without being in the crossfire of a gun battle." Steven bit his lip. "What church are you attending?"

"Ah, I'm not really into church now." How had this conversation become a witnessing campaign?

"But you're going now, after what happened to you, right?" Expectancy was in Steven's eyes and voice.

Mitchell didn't know.

Be ready always to answer every man that asks you a reason of the hope that is in you with meekness and fear, God whispered. *Read 1 Peter 3:14–15.*

"Thanks, man, for encouraging me to get right with God." Steven grinned, stood, and moved to a leg curl machine.

Did he? Mitchell closed his eyes and huffed. "Lord, what did You say?"

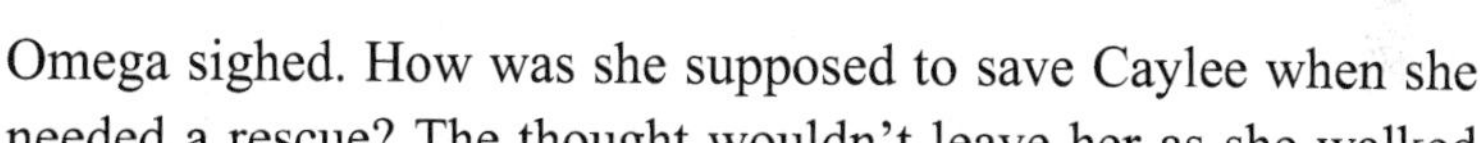

Omega sighed. How was she supposed to save Caylee when she needed a rescue? The thought wouldn't leave her as she walked through the door of her condo. Glad to be home.

Later that evening, Delta called concerned about how Omega was coping. "So, how was your first day back at work?"

Shaking her head, Omega closed her eyes. "It was going okay—until I learned one of the victims was related to a woman at the office."

"Oh, no." Delta gasped. "Sorry to hear that."

"I know. Get this," Omega said, stretching out on the ottoman in her bedroom, "after work, I saw a gun battle between angels and demons behind a woman sitting on a bench. It was as real as a movie set."

Delta didn't respond right away, and when she did, an annoyed sigh preceded her. "Not that angel stuff again."

Her sister would be a hard sale, and Omega didn't blame her. "And I heard God's voice again."

"I think you need to have the bump on your head checked out."

"Dell, I'm not hallucinating. I know what I saw and heard."

"Yeah. If you keep talking about this craziness, I will have to tell Mom and Dad, and they will make sure you go to the doctor."

Omega's heart sank. There was no way to convince Delta that God wanted Omega to keep a stranger from dying. A Moses figure, she wasn't. "Okay. Not another word." Who *would* believe Omega without questioning her sanity?

That night as Omega climbed into bed, she talked with God. "I'm sorry that Caylee is going to die. I thank You for sparing my life, but I don't have any power to keep her from dying." She had heard her share of people say, "speaking it into existence." The outcome proved they didn't have the power either. Omega knew without a doubt that only God had power over a person's birth and death date.

Besides, if Caylee had a dark past....No, Omega stopped herself from giving more thought to it. She didn't want to get involved in the young woman's drama. Hadn't she suffered enough trauma for the week? Omega should take a vacation and convince Delta to come with her. Yes, she needed to get away—and fast.

Unfortunately, Omega couldn't escape. For three days and nights, it stormed in St. Louis. She and most residents were holed up inside their own homes. Some areas had sustained damage from the flash flooding that raged like an angry river, especially near her job.

This was torture. Omega wasn't a homebody. The evidence: She ran low on food essentials. She could only eat so many bagels for breakfast, noodles for lunch, and lettuce disguised as a salad for dinner. At times, she had a bad habit of living on the edge when it came to responsibility.

Omega peeked out the window, hoping for a break to drive to the corner store. She caught a glimpse of the sun through the clouds late Saturday morning. Grabbing her purse, she decided to make a run for it. Omega did a doubletake as she drove past Mrs. Helena's townhouse at the corner of the cul-de-sac. After the three-day deluge, it was an odd sight to see her neighbor watering her flowers.

"What in the world is she doing?" Omega frowned, then recalled the woman had mentioned "let angels protect you" the morning of the robbery. She put her SUV in reverse, backed up, parked, and called out to her.

Mrs. Helena smiled and scanned the sky. "All this rain. We should see some rainbows soon."

Omega squinted. "So why are you watering your flowers?"

The woman shrugged like it was no big deal. "God told me to. Seems strange, but God always makes sense." She pointed to her flower bed. "Although my lawn is saturated, my petunias bed was thirsty. The ground was dry as dust."

Getting out of her vehicle, Omega had to investigate. Her neighbor was right. The rainstorm had soaked the lilies in Omega's yard to the point where they hadn't bounced back to their height again but remained slumped.

Mrs. Helena's garden didn't look soaked.

"That is odd." So many things lately weren't making sense. "Do you remember earlier in the week—on Monday morning—when I was going to work, I waved, and instead of your usual greeting when we leave the cul-de-sac, you said something different about an angel watching over me. Why did you say that?"

Turning off the hose, she studied Omega. "That prayer was for you. The words that come from my mouth have to mean something, or why say them? God had me speak the prophecy to you."

Omega's heart pounded in fear. Why had she caught God's attention? What was so special about her? More whys filled her head. "Did you hear about the gas station shooting down the street?"

"I did. Lord, have mercy." Mrs. Helena *tsk*ed and shook her head. "Those innocent lives."

"I was one of the victims." There was a rumble overhead, but the sun remained in place. "A guardian angel—a man—covered me, then I thought I saw real angels fighting off bullets." She touched the back of her head through her cap. "I probably suffered a concussion from the bump on my head, but there's more…"

Mrs. Helena chuckled. "Oh, I'm sure there is. Let's go inside to chat. I made soup and have fixings for sandwiches." She adjusted her water hose to retract into its holder.

Omega's mouth watered as her stomach roared to life. "I was on my way to the store for groceries and food."

"Looks like our timing is perfect then." Omega walked inside the foyer with parquet flooring and glanced around. The townhouse's layout was smaller and simpler in design than Omega's condo.

Where Omega had two bay windows on both sides of her front door, Mrs. Helena had one large front window where a few plants resided. Omega followed her neighbor back into the kitchen, which seemed to be the biggest room in the house. The décor was something out of *Country Living* magazine with red-checkered curtains, towels, and seat cushions. A metal rooster on the wall served as the timekeeper.

They were settled at a red rectangle table with black legs. Mrs. Helena asked for blessings over their food. "And Lord, help us to remember those in distress and feed their tummies too. In Jesus' name. Amen."

Hmmm. Whenever Omega said grace, she never added a footnote to feed others. Clearly, Mrs. Helena was a faithful Christian. Omega wasn't.

"So, tell me, what else has happened." Mrs. Helena took a bite and waited.

Staring at the white butterflies outside her patio door, Omega didn't know how to phrase it so Mrs. Helena wouldn't think Omega was delusional. She told her about the battle between the angels and demons, then took a sip of her lemonade mixed with fruit juice.

"God told me one sister will die once the other one leaves unless I do something." Omega threw one hand up in defeat. "Am I suddenly an angel? I don't want to be responsible for someone's death or know when someone is supposed to die."

Mrs. Helena didn't seem fazed by Omega's disclosure. "God will never share that with you. The angels don't know when the end is coming. It sounds like the Lord Jesus has chosen you to be an intercessor for those young girls."

"A what?" Omega blinked. "I'm not a strong Christian."

"Not yet, but God is about to change that." Mrs. Helena nodded with a pleased expression. "The Lord has an assignment for you. He saved your life for a purpose. Like that young man kept you from harm, it's your turn to do the same. Jesus has opened your eyes to see the spiritual realm in addition to the physical world, which is a must for a Christian."

Great. Omega's shoulders slumped as she managed to finish off her stack of chips. "I guess it's only fair. A man named Mitchell saved me. So, if I do this, I guess I'm off the hook, and Caylee and her sister can pay—or pray—it forward for someone else."

"I don't know if it works like that. God has His way of doing things." Mrs. Helena took a sip of her tea. "How's your prayer life?"

"Every night before bedtime." Omega grinned in victory. See, she wasn't a heathen. "And I try to remember before I eat if I'm not starving. Does that count?"

"All prayers count if said with a pure heart." Mrs. Helena stood and walked to the stove. "More soup?"

"No. I need to finish what you gave me."

"How often do you attend church and read your Bible?" Her neighbor scooped another serving into her bowl and returned to the table.

Rocking her head from side to side, Omega gave it some thought. "Well, that's hit-or-miss."

Mrs. Helena exhaled, then patted the table with a slow, steady rhythm. "Why don't you come to church with me on Sunday? God talks to us through His messengers—ministers, angels—or His Word in the Bible."

Omega didn't feel she could say no. Besides, if God was calling her out to do this, she needed to know more about being an intercessor. "Give me the name and address of the church, and I'll meet you there."

The woman scribbled it on a nearby paper instead of shooting her a text.

Old school, Omega thought as she finished the last of her homemade vegetable soup. She took the bowl to the sink and rinsed it off. The sun was still out. She had to get out of there. "Thank you for the insight and meal." She rubbed her stomach. "I guess I'd better head to the store since we have a break in the weather."

A boom shook the house the moment she opened the door. A downpour greeted her. Gritting her teeth, she groaned.

Omega chided herself for stopping. She would have been back by now if she ran her errand to the store. She twirled around. "I guess you're stuck with me until the next break in the weather."

"I enjoy the company when my neighbors stop by." Mrs. Helena stood. "Since you're here, let's have a moment of prayer."

The moment turned into a half hour, and Mrs. Helena seemed to pray for everything that came to her mind regarding Omega. One thing she didn't pray for was to teach Omega how to be an intercessor.

Chapter Five

Be careful for nothing, but in everything by prayer and supplication with thanksgiving let your requests be made known unto God. —Philippians 4:6 KJV

Life was rough. Caylee knew that firsthand. While attending college, she side hustled as a dancer in local plays and musicals, then dabbled in exotic dancing because the pay was good. The network of friends she made was slightly older, had children, and raved about the lucrative tips strippers earned.

The pay wasn't good, but the tips were worth the long shifts in six-inch heels. Some of her associates even sold their services to pay bills. When Caylee complained a few weeks about her rent going up, her coworker, Flamingo—stage name—suggested Caylee try sex work just once.

At twenty-four, Caylee might be poor, but she wasn't stupid, except for investing too much time in an industry that was taking her further away from her dreams. Without finishing her degree, Caylee would have to find another job, but how could she do that without references? Strippers were considered independent contractors.

"Lord, I'm trying to leave that life behind."

Her conscience was clear, noting the difference between prostitutes and strippers. She did not have sex with the patrons. That had been her justification over the years. Until a few nights ago, while dancing, a frightful thought came to her during one of her routines. Instead of disco dancing on stage in Sam's Gentlemen Prefer Black Club, she moved amid the flames that raced toward her. Her movements were no longer her own but were guided like a puppet on a string.

A light flashed before Caylee's eyes. Applause no longer came from men dressed in suits under the guise of business meetings, but distorted creatures growling at her. Her mind set off a warning sign: get out.

One eerie monster-type thing laughed. "Gotcha. Welcome to Hades!"

Hell? Was she dying? Caylee felt perspiration lather her body. "No," she remembered screaming.

She blinked and was back in the club. A standing ovation. The men shouted for more, thinking her out-of-character movements were part of her dance. They weren't. Caylee had never seen a sight like that before, and it freaked her out. She left her shift early and never returned. Her dancing days were over.

Since then, Caylee tried to find a day job. Without a car, she was limited to no more than two bus rides. Now, weeks later, she couldn't shake the image. She was still uneasy the day she met Omega at the bus stop. Honestly, she was glad for the company.

She hadn't had that eerie out-of-body experience again. If only Caylee could understand why she experienced it in the first place.

"Sis, you've been quiet all weekend. You okay?" April asked with concern in her eyes.

Caylee reached over the sofa and hugged her. "Looking for another job isn't easy. I'll return to school as soon as I get you off to New York for your big gig. That way, I can stay in the dorm."

"Sounds like a plan." April grinned.

"In the meantime, I've heard about some housecleaning gigs to pay the bills."

"You sure you don't want me to help with the money I make at the fashion and event shows?"

"No. Invest in yourself—clothes, hair, makeup for updated head comps, and classes. New York is going to happen. I can feel it." Caylee couldn't help but be proud. Her sister would succeed by any means necessary.

"Church?" Omega's sister, Delta, wasn't happy about it. "What about our weekly Sunday brunch?"

Unless either of them was sick or out of town, Sundays were reserved for sister time—all day. It had been that way for years. "You can always go with me, and afterward, we can do brunch."

Delta uttered some choice words that shouldn't be said on a Sunday, but Omega held her ground and would have to make it up to her sister. "My neighbor invited me when I told her I was involved in that gas station shooting."

"Oh, wow. I get it. That robbery put the fear of Jesus in ya."

"You have no idea." Omega shook her head. Her life hadn't been the same since Monday.

"Oh, but I do. Remember, I came to get you at the gas station. I'm glad you're okay, so..." Delta paused. "I'll excuse you for today. Maybe our knucklehead brother wants to treat his baby sister."

"Good luck. Randall and Tally probably have their day planned out, and you'd be the third wheel."

Delta laughed. "I'm the baby sister. Do you really think I care about being a party crasher? I'll call him anyway. I'll let you go. Try not to fall asleep at church."

"Right. Bye." Sleep eluded her some nights.

During the next hour, she hurried through breakfast, showered, and donned a springy dress for church since the rainy days had yielded to a gorgeous Sunday.

Ready, Omega entered the church's address on her phone's navigation. This was different. She couldn't remember the last time she was physically inside somebody's church. Most of her friends didn't go to church but watched short inspirational clips on social media.

Omega was ashamed to admit it, but she hadn't put that much effort into social media sermons either. She did have a coworker who posted the thought of the day on her office door. That served as her daily dose of inspiration.

Yet, Omega was looking forward to this church visit. Would the sermon provide clues to what God wanted her to do? She half-expected to see an army of angels or to hear God's voice thunder again after Mrs. Helena's prayer the previous day, but nothing.

Her neighbor's words had been simply, "Lord, show Omega what Your will is, and give her strength to carry it out, in Jesus' name. Amen."

Omega hoped the preacher would do better and break down instructions for God's assignment. She felt like this was a plot for an action-packed movie.

"Without a doubt, I heard God say when April leaves, Caylee will die." Not only was it a burden to know when the woman was going to die, but to *know* she was going to die.

She shivered as she followed the GPS directions to Christ For All Church. The tip of the steeple caught Omega's eye from Highway 40 as a beacon that drew her once she exited the highway.

The powder-blue stone edifice boldly greeted visitors on a freshly paved and yellow-striped parking lot. It wasn't intimidating, but had a welcoming effect, especially with the colorful flowers that bordered the front entrance.

Inside the foyer, two teenage girl ushers smiled and welcomed her. They were polished in navy skirts, white tops, and powder-blue blazers. She spied young male ushers in the distance in the same uniform, but in pants. Omega returned their smiles and informed them that she was a guest.

One girl with long cornrows giggled. Her name badge read Heather. “We know. You’re a new face.”

Right. Newbies stand out. “Mrs. Helena Wrighton invited me. Do you happen to know where she sits?”

“Yes,” answered the girl with remarkably flawless skin. She wore an afro puff on the top of her head, giving her more height. “On the front row.”

Omega stepped back. “I’d rather find a seat away from the front.”

They nodded at her request, and Bailey, the taller girl, instructed Omega to follow her. The inside of the sanctuary was a contrast to the soft, calming blue exterior. The stadium-style seats, carpet, and front stage were in bold blues, burgundy, and splashes of yellow accents. Accepting her seat in a long row with five or six others, Omega acknowledged them with a nod.

As the minister welcomed family and friends, he identified himself as Pastor Rodney. Omega didn’t know if that was his first or last name. He tapped on his tablet. “Do you have a safe place?” The pastor paused and waited for a response.

“I heard many of you say, ‘Yes, in the presence of the Lord, or under the shadow of His wing.’ I’m sure most of you heard about that shooting at the gas station earlier this week.”

Omega held her breath. She had lived through it.

“Three people lost their lives; others were injured…” Pastor Rodney listed other calamities around the country and the world last week. “What are we supposed to do?”

“Pray,” a woman shouted not far from behind Omega.

“Yes.” He nodded. “We have to pray for one another. We don’t know what they’re going through or about to face. When you pray, your wants and needs should be last. Intercede for someone else.”

Got it. Omega could pray for Caylee. The thought to kidnap April did cross her mind as a drastic measure.

"Spiritual warfare is real. The Bible tells us in Ephesians to put on the whole armor. I don't care how many police are on the streets or troops on the ground, it's God who fights our battles…"

Was God fighting a battle for Caylee that day? Omega wondered.

"When you think of weapons, the first thing that one might think is firepower, but not for the saints of God." The pastor shook his head. "Second Corinthians ten and four says, *'The weapons of our warfare aren't worldly, but mighty through God to the pulling down of strongholds.'* Demonic forces are the strongholds that cause destruction, even death. We never know what strongholds others are going through—your siblings, parents, coworkers, cousins, and on and on. That's why Jesus wants us to pray as an intercessor for others. We have to tap into the spiritual realm with God, and He will direct our paths…"

The weapons of warfare—the ones she saw in those visions—looked mighty. What Omega could only describe as a forcefield had certainly kept the bad people at bay the night of the gas station shooting and another time from Caylee.

When Pastor Rodney mentioned intercession, Omega developed tunnel vision to the pulpit as her surroundings faded. If Omega was honest with herself, her prayers were generic: world peace and blessings to family and friends.

"Intercessors are prayer warriors. They pray long and hard. They pray when God drops names in their spirits. They pray earnestly." Pastor Rodney continued to preach about intercessors four times—Omega counted—for another thirty minutes. He ended his sermon by closing his Bible.

"Are you a warrior? I want to invite those outside the safety net of God to repent of your sins and take the next step toward your salvation. Walk down the aisle for prayer. Tomorrow is not promised, so get your soul right with God today."

If Mitchell hadn't saved her, the bullet would have shot Omega through her heart or head. Dead. This could have been her funeral this man was preaching.

Pastor Rodney looked both ways. "I don't see enough movement." He frowned and turned his head from left to right. "What part didn't you hear? Twenty-four hours isn't promised to us. The Bible says for us to repent—the day we hear His voice, harden not our hearts—and be baptized in the name of Jesus. That's the water baptism, and the Holy Ghost is fire baptism that will enter your soul. Save a life today, not by giving blood, but your soul by allowing Jesus' blood from the cross to cleanse you from your sins. Hell is a place reserved for sinners. You don't want to go there. Trust me."

He said it as if he had been there and back.

Without her mind giving her body a heads-up, Omega stood and followed others to the front. Soon, she was sandwiched in. A tall, dark-skinned minister stepped up to her.

"Would you like prayer, sister?" he asked. The man looked about the same age as Randall, thirty-nine-ish.

"Yes. I've repented in my heart just now. Can I get baptized?"

He smiled. "You sure can. God will wash away your sins, something that can't be seen with human eyes. The baptism of the Holy Ghost is God's doing too. Your eyes will be opened to the spiritual world in addition to the present."

After he prayed, Omega was excited to see a familiar face. Mrs. Helena and another woman—both in white attire—greeted her and explained they would help prepare her for the baptism.

"I'm glad to see you here," her neighbor said.

In a small room, the ladies instructed Omega to change out of her church clothes and don a white gown, robe, socks, and swim cap as the pair tag-teamed, singing church songs. Once dressed, Omega was led to the pool, encased by elaborate stained-glass windows behind the pulpit.

Once she stepped into the water, a minister instructed Omega to cross her arms over her chest as he gripped the back of her robe with one hand and lifted his other.

"My dear sister, upon the confession of your faith and the confidence you have in the blessed Word of God, I indeed baptize you in the name of the Lord Jesus Christ, the highest name we know on Earth, for the remission of your sins, and Acts two says you shall receive the Holy Ghost. The evidence will be the heavenly tongues that will flow from your mouth." The minister submerged her.

Omega resurfaced with a bounce. She opened her eyes and saw two angels in the water with her. Instead of swords drawn, it was as if they were dancing.

There is joy in the presence of the angels over one sinner who repents, God whispered. *Read Luke 15.*

Really? Angels were excited about her salvation? That made Omega smile. She lifted her hands. As the minister guided Omega out of the pool, a heavenly language exploded from her mouth. Those around her rejoiced.

An electrifying sensation coursed through her veins. She couldn't wait to tell Delta. Her sister would never believe what happened though.

She couldn't stop crying tears of joy. It was indescribable. This foreign experience evoked peace, jubilation, and supernatural strength at the same time. Was this necessary in preparation for God's assignment? Despite the joy, Omega had no idea how to keep someone from dying.

Soon the deacons began to shut off the main lights in the sanctuary as a subtle hint for everyone to go home. Omega didn't want to go.

Mrs. Helena gave her a hug. "We'll talk soon. You know where I live if you need me."

They said their goodbyes in the church parking lot. During the drive home, Omega was in awe as her mind tried to reconcile what she had experienced. God's presence accompanied her home.

Delta called as Omega rested her keys on her kitchen counter. "So, was it worth passing up brunch? You know the fresh fruit alone is worth it."

Oh, taste and see that I am good, God whispered.

Still high on Jesus, Omega tried to explain to her sister what had happened but couldn't get through the conversation without God's presence taking control of her words.

"Sis, I don't know what you've gotten yourself into, but you're scaring me."

"God is real," Omega said. "He's real in my soul."

"I don't doubt that, but all this… Is the mumbo jumbo necessary?" Delta sounded annoyed.

"The Bible says it is in the Book of Acts that the disciples spoke in tongues when the Holy Ghost filled them. When I heard myself, I felt connected to Him. It's kinda of cool. You have to come to church with me—"

"Oh, no. You're not sucking me into that. Ah, I'm good." Delta hurried to end their call.

Lord, help me to win my sister and family over, Omega prayed. As the older one, Delta copied Omega in fashion, education, and activities.

Could Omega influence her baby sister to follow her to surrender to Christ?

Chapter Six

For if you live after the flesh, you shall die. But if you through the Spirit mortify the deeds of the body, you shall live. For as many as are led by the Spirit of God are the sons of God. —Romans 8:13–14 KJV

"This is what addiction feels like."

Omega couldn't conquer the craving to feel the Lord's presence and hear His heavenly language. She guessed God had her praying for people she didn't know—an intercessor. It was exhilarating in a way.

On Monday, during Omega's morning drive to the office, she hummed unfamiliar tunes, without the accompaniment of the radio. When she arrived at work and parked, Omega glanced toward the clouds.

Last night, she had read in her Bible that Jesus would return by splitting the clouds. "Wow." Shaking her head, Omega knew she would never look at life the same again. She waved, knowing the Lord was watching. "Hi, God. Thank you for saving me."

Light on her feet, Omega felt like dancing—no partner needed—as she continued toward the entrance. Once inside, she greeted her staff full of joy.

"Boss, you are glowing." Bobby Truman, head of Hathaway's graphic department, squinted. "What a difference a weekend made for you. Something happened—engaged, pregnant… Don't tell me you got a new job and you're giving your two weeks' notice." He seemed eager for the scoop.

"Better." Omega grinned. She didn't know if she would start praying in the spirit or not. "I got saved!" She danced in place. "Do you realize you're a sinner?" She didn't give him time to answer. "I didn't. I mean I thought I was as good as the next person, but I repented anyway. I asked God's forgiveness for everything I've done, even stuff that I hadn't realized. I got baptized…" She paused and waved her hand in praise. Was Bobby ready for the vision of the angels in the baptismal pool?

"Whoa. Whoa." He stepped back. "You're over the top this morning." He twisted his lips in amusement.

"Yes, I am." She lifted her hand, forcing Bobby to meet her high five.

Omega couldn't wait to share the news of her salvation with Yolanda, a soft-spoken practicing Christian who never engaged in office politics. What inspiration of the day would she post on her office door?

She was a silent witness who intimidated many, including Omega. She didn't understand her hunger for God—until now. Coworkers respected her privacy if they glimpsed a Bible in her hand at lunch.

Sticking her head into the finance manager's office, Omega pouted when Yolanda's desk was empty. She was usually the first one there. Omega twirled around and asked her assistant. "Where's Yolanda?"

"She's running late," Reba Stewart said, "that was about thirty minutes ago, but she should be here any minute. Anything I can help you with, or do you have a message for her?"

Reba was short, petite, and could be a double for her brother Randall's girlfriend Tally. Not a churchgoer like Yolanda, Reba had repeated some of Yolanda's religious sayings. It was amusing because it lacked conviction.

"Yeah. A big one, but I'll wait to deliver it myself." Omega returned to her office. She had to follow up with requests from churches and social agencies about Hathaway's services.

Twenty minutes later, she heard Yolanda's voice booming outside her office.

"About time you got here," Omega mumbled cheerfully as she stood from behind her desk.

Then it struck her that something was off. Yolanda never raised her voice, even when she was annoyed. Omega went to investigate the woman's cause for such a disturbance.

"It's time to get right with Jesus! All of you!" Yolanda screamed at the top of her lungs while Bobby, Reba, and Gerri Newsome—the human resources manager—looked on. "Don't delay."

"Yeah." Omega grinned and nodded.

"He's tired of our foolishness. You have been warned, every last one of you." Yolanda pointed, making eye contact with many but not Omega, then she pivoted and walked out into the lobby instead of her office.

Omega's jaw dropped.

Speechless.

She exchanged bewildered looks with Bobby, Gerri, and Reba. Surprisingly, no other employees came to find out what was going on.

"What just happened?" Reba asked.

After Omega closed her mouth, she shook her head. "I have no idea." Yolanda was Omega's new shero up until a minute ago. The woman had snapped, but Omega needed Yolanda to be her prayer buddy.

"Where is she going?" Bobby asked. "I sent her an invoice from a vendor this morning to be paid." He didn't look happy about it.

"I don't know. Maybe she's having a bad day. I'll go out into the lobby and check on her," Omega said, but Yolanda was nowhere to be seen inside or outside in the parking lot.

Whatever Yolanda was going through, Omega figured she had to pray. She returned to her office and looked up Yolanda's cell in the employee directory to make sure her coworker was alright. When Omega called, it defaulted to voicemail.

Bobby appeared in Omega's doorway with his arms folded. He moved his lips as if he were chewing on a toothpick. "You have to watch out for those quiet ones. That chick's crazy." He grunted. "People always trying to beat people up with the Bible. Ain't nobody got time for that."

Bobby was right. They all had a lot of work to do. Omega would analyze her coworker's behavior later. First, it was May already, and Bobby was working on a new campaign about health initiatives for low-income residents during the summer months, and Omega had a conference call in an hour.

Regrouping her thoughts, Omega answered emails. She didn't stifle the smiles that popped up whenever she thought about angels, heavenly tongues, and becoming a prayer warrior. She wanted a praise break—a few minutes—where she could raise her hands and pray to God to feel his presence. She had spied a small Bible on Yolanda's desk and a highlighter she used sometimes when reading. Omega would be a copycat.

Until then, she downloaded a Bible app.

It was late afternoon, and Omega was in the human resources manager's office, when Yolanda's daughter, Dana, called. Gerri frowned and looked at Omega, then put the call on speakerphone.

"Mama's dead." Dana wailed.

Gerri blinked as Omega sucked in her breath.

Had she heard right? What happened, was the first question Omega had but couldn't ask.

"Oh, I'm so sorry, Dana. What happened? I know she was acting strange when she came to work earlier," Gerri consoled the daughter.

Silence.

"She never made it to work. Mama died in a pileup close to home this morning. I called Reba but got her voicemail. I couldn't leave this message. I had to talk to somebody."

"I understand," Gerri said, but her bewildered expression showed otherwise.

Omega's heart plummeted to the floor. She didn't know what to think. Had Yolanda's appearance been another vision? This time, Omega wasn't the only one who witnessed the supernatural phenomenon.

How terrible. Yolanda's death not only was Dana's loss and the company's, but Omega's too. She'd looked forward to seeing Yolanda's excitement about Omega's salvation experience. An agonizing pain spread throughout Omega's chest. She needed Yolanda to help her grow as a Christian. Now that would never happen.

Time to start praying, God whispered.

Gerri offered her condolences. "Dana, I know how much she loved you. If you need anything, let me and the company know…"

Jesus, thank You for allowing Yolanda to come into our lives—my life. She is gone too soon for us, so please comfort her parents and daughter, in Jesus' name. Amen. God's peace seemed to descend on Omega immediately.

After Gerri ended the call, she closed her eyes and rubbed her forehead. "I know what I saw earlier. Yolanda was alive and real this morning as she was any other time," she mumbled.

Omega wasn't so sure. The warning was real, but Yolanda wasn't. It had to be a vision.

"How am I going to tell my staff Yolanda is dead and was supposedly dead when a handful of us saw her right here this morning?" Gerri looked to Omega for answers.

She shrugged. "Since the Lord saved me this Sunday, I'll be praying for all of us to make sense of this." Omega planned to stop by Mrs. Helena's house after work and get her opinion.

"I'm going to send an email out to everyone to meet in the breakroom, and I need you to stand with me as I deliver this heartbreaking news. If you're going to church now, God might have tagged you to give us daily inspirational thoughts."

"I don't know about that, but I'll try and be a light the best I can." Omega exhaled and straightened her skirt. She left, wondering, *Lord, what can I add?*

Omega slowed her steps as others rushed in. As she was about to take a seat, Gerri motioned for Omega to stand beside her.

All eyes were on them. Gerri inhaled, then released. "Thanks for coming." She paused. "Omega has an announcement to make," she choked out and stepped away.

Me? Omega tapped her chest and squinted at Gerri, then faced her coworkers. Sadness struck her as she fumbled with her fingers. "We have some bad news about Yolanda."

"Did she snap again?" Bobby twisted his lips in annoyance.

"She's dead." Omega braced for their reaction in three, two…

Gasps. Stunned faces, then outbursts of disbelief.

"Did she…she killed herself?" Yolanda's assistant, Reba, asked.

"Huh?" A coworker frowned.

The odd question was evidence that Reba had indeed saw the same vision and thought her boss was unstable.

"No. She was killed in a car accident this morning—" Omega stuttered— "on her way to work."

Pandemonium exploded among the employees.

"I saw her! She came in here yelling," Bobby squinted at Omega as if she were lying or his eyes were lying.

"That can't be true." Reba shook her head.

"I know," Gerri mumbled, then gnawed on her lip.

"Y'all acting like you saw a ghost." Karla, a public relations intern, jumped to her feet and pointed at Bobby and Reba. "I'm sorry, Miss Addams and Miss Newsome. Friday was supposed to be my last day. This place must be haunted. Eerie." She shuddered. "Can't stay. I hope this won't affect my grade."

"It won't," Gerri spoke up.

"I'm going to need a mental health day, if I'm seeing and hearing ghosts," Bobby said.

Gerri touched her forehead. "I think we all do. Let's close the office out of respect for Yolanda, and if your position allows, you can work from home tomorrow. If not, come to work late. Finish up today and go home."

Omega joined the others and headed to her desk to pack up. Her first stop: Mrs. Helena's house.

Seeing angels was hard to believe, but this…the walking dead?

Mrs. Helena sat on her red rocker on her porch. As Omega approached her neighbor, she heard nature music play, entertaining a row of birds perched on a tree branch, as she approached.

"Join me." Mrs. Helena pointed to the twin rocker on the other side of a small wicker table.

"Okay." Omega sat with a perfect view of the comings and goings of the neighborhood.

"What's on your mind, dear?"

"My life is becoming weird," Omega said, then recapped what happened. "My company lost a coworker today. But instead of mourning her loss, I'm trying to make sense of her speaking from the grave. This is too much. I'm not sure how to describe it. I've seen angels, demons, and now dead people. Plus, someone is going to die unless I do something." Omega threw up her hands. "How do I navigate through this virtual reality or the spiritual realm?"

Mrs. Helena stopped her rocker and leaned forward with an intense expression. "By listening. You are His sheep now, and

His sheep are able to know their Shepherd's voice. God sends visions to get our attention, not dead people to deliver a message. He has angels for that."

"You're telling me that really wasn't Yolanda?" Omega frowned. "It looked like her and sounded like her to me. She was more intense than I've ever seen her." She shrugged. "Her daughter said she had died that morning, so Yolanda's an angel now?"

"No. Angels are heavenly beings. If she had God's Spirit, she'll rise with a new body, but not as an angel. You have seen them a couple of times now. There's a passage in Luke 16 that talks about the dead." She got up and walked into her house.

She reappeared with a large white hardcover Bible with long red ribbons serving as bookmarks in her arms. Mrs. Helena took her seat, opened it, and started reading aloud at verse nineteen about the rich man and the beggar. "It goes on to say, *'There is a great gulf fixed: so that they which would pass from hence to you cannot; neither can they pass to us, that would come from thence. Then he said, I pray thee therefore, father, that thou would send him to my father's house: For I have five brethren; that he may testify unto them, lest they also come into this place of torment. Abraham saith unto him, They have Moses and the prophets; let them hear them. And he said, Nay, Father Abraham: but if one went unto them from the dead, they will repent. And he said unto him, If they hear not Moses and the prophets, neither will they be persuaded, though one rose from the dead.'*

"If your coworker has God's Spirit, Yolanda will rise in the first resurrection—the rapture. That's a discussion for another day." Mrs. Helena closed the Bible.

"There's so much to learn. I'm overwhelmed. Yolanda's—I mean the angel's—message to all of us was to get our act together with God, or else?"

"We can't accuse God of not warning us. My prayer is that your staff takes heed as you have." Mrs. Helena studied Omega.

"I wonder if God sent an angel to warn Caylee." Omega gnawed on her lip.

Mrs. Helena tilted her head and gave it some thought. "I think God sent you to intercede on that young woman's behalf by praying."

"Pray. Sounds like I need to go home and get on my knees." Omega stood. Her shoulders slumped with the weight of the world. As she stepped off the porch and headed to her car, Mrs. Helena called out to her.

"God will send you re-enforcement. You wait and see."

Since the robbery, the dreams kept coming.

Every night.

Mitchell got a glimpse of heaven, angels, and figures in the Bible he had read about long ago. The bird's-eye view of palaces would rival those in Asia or Europe. The people who moved about were of one kind. Their features were indistinguishable.

That was last night. Today, Mitchell thought he spied angels again a few times. Instead of being engaged in battle as they were during the gas station robbery, they were escorting—children, women, the elderly—to safe places.

Why were his eyes opened to this spiritual portal? He had been wracking his brain for answers.

His girlfriend continued to complain that Mitchell's focus wasn't exclusively on her—or them. "You've changed since the shooting." Farrah pouted at dinner after they attended a Saturday evening play. Earlier, he had taken her shopping for lingerie. "I don't know if I like it."

"Babe, I'm glad to be alive. Escaping death was my wakeup call." Mitchell cut into his medium-rare steak, then chewed. "Since then, I can't help but reflect on my life and death."

She rested her fork. "Mitchell, would you stop overthinking what happened? You're a hero, yet you don't want anyone to know it. I'm proud of what you did, and I want everyone to know it. Since you were discharged from the hospital, I feel like you're pulling away from me."

Farrah leaned forward and forced him to look into her eyes. "You got shot, you survived, so can we move on? It's no big deal if you won't tell the media your side of the story." She sat back and folded her arms.

Whiners annoyed Mitchell, and that's exactly what Farrah was doing. She wanted to go out, and he took her. She wanted more of him mentally. He didn't have it to give right now.

"Listen," he said, attempting to keep his tone gentle, "I'm healing physically, but mentally and spiritually, I'm shaken. You want me to get over it, but I can't. I started having dreams…"

She huffed and rolled her eyes. "Do you need to see a psychologist?"

They'd had disagreements, but they were minor. This discussion was evolving into an argument, and Mitchell was getting more ticked by the minute. "Can you let this not be about you for a moment? I don't need attention from any reporter, and I don't need your sympathy, but it would be nice to have your understanding." He looked for their server and asked for the check.

"I'm not finished eating." Farrah jutted her chin and shifted in her seat. When Mitchell ignored her, she cleared her throat. "We've had a nice outing. Let's not spoil it. This is no way for us to build a relationship."

As Mitchell studied her, he realized she was not the one for him. "A relationship is a give and take. This isn't what I want."

Farrah chuckled. "You're just being emotional, and I'm sorry if I hurt your feelings." She sounded anything but repentant.

"I'm not the same person anymore." Mitchell slipped his credit card into the folder for the server. "I keep dreaming about heaven as if God is calling me."

She gasped, and her eyes misted. "I hope not. I was sick to learn you were shot. I love you, Mitchell, and I've had these feelings for a while."

Love?

Farrah waited for him to respond.

"So soon? We've only been seeing each other for a couple of months. I don't share those feelings." Mitchell believed in honesty when dating women.

Been in love once.

It didn't end well.

Mitchell had proposed to Regina, and she had said no. He was in no hurry to ask any woman again anytime soon.

"Will you ever be?"

Opening his mouth to say one thing, Mitchell was surprised by what came out. "Finding a wife is preferred over a woman finding a husband." It was the truth, but he hadn't planned to verbalize that.

She squinted and twisted her lips. "What are you saying, Mitch, that you don't look at me as wife material?"

He groaned. Another argument was brewing, and Mitchell didn't want to engage. He took her shopping, to a play, and now to dinner. He realized he was just going through the motions. His heart was far from wanting to spend time with Farrah, or any woman at the moment. "I've got to get myself right with God. Are you in with me, or out? Yes or no."

"What kind of question is that? I signed up for a relationship, not going to church." Farrah's defiant look revealed the truth. "No."

"A relationship with God is exactly what's been missing in my life."

Saturday night went downhill from there and never recovered. Mitchell told her it was best they both moved on. Farrah's response was they needed only a cooling-off period.

Chapter Seven

Precious in the sight of the Lord is the death of His saints.
—Psalm 116:15 KJV

No one from Hathaway Health Management could bring themselves to attend Yolanda's funeral, including Gerri. As the human resources manager, her presence meant she represented the company. Not this time. Bobby commented they had seen her alive and dead already. Reba was withdrawn.

On Friday morning, Omega represented the company at Yolanda's homegoing. She was as bewildered as her coworkers, but she was becoming accustomed to these visions. She was no longer afraid of what she saw—just confused.

During the eulogy, Omega learned about the deceased's personal life.

"Yolanda knew how to turn situations that seemed hopeless around through prayer. It was as if God listened…." Dora Carr, the woman on the program, seemed to chuckle at unshared memories. "And she didn't have to open her mouth. When she did, one word made the difference—Jesus."

Omega straightened her long black skirt and perked up. How did Yolanda become a prayer warrior? God listened to her, and things changed. If only she had lived a few days longer, Omega could have told her about Caylee and April, and God would have answered her prayers to reverse the death sentence.

Family and friends spoke highly of Yolanda's character, to which Omega could attest.

"Even in grade school, Yolanda was the peacemaker," Sara Watkins, a childhood friend, told the packed mega church. From outward appearances, it didn't appear the two were compatible. Where Yolanda looked wiser and dressed more conservatively like Omega had been trying to do since the day she received the water and fire baptism, Sara was painted with tattoos up one arm and down another leg. A tooth or two was missing, and her hair was red. The women had chosen two different paths, Omega thought.

"She had a good sense of humor but never played about God or her salvation. Yolanda had been a silent witness to me for years before I asked her why she viewed things differently and didn't follow the trends. Her answer was she saw the good and the evil."

Omega's heart pounded. Had she replaced Yolanda? If so, Omega wasn't ready. She had a lot to learn.

"Yolanda told me she could see the consequences of sin. What one person may label as fun—as I had for so many years…" Sara bowed her head and took a moment to reflect, "Yolanda had the sense to know what was going to happen. There was this party a classmate gave…"

Someone groaned behind Omega and mumbled, "Some people don't know how to limit their remarks to three minutes as it says on the program."

Omega didn't care how long people took as they built a character sketch about a woman she worked with every day but didn't bother to get to know. Like many of the staff at Hathaway, Omega was cordial but steered away because she and Yolanda didn't seem to have much in common.

"Anyway," longwinded Sara continued, "Yolanda didn't go, but I did. There was plenty of everything there. Use your imagination. We lost two friends that night because of drinking and driving. The last time I ran into her was a few months ago. She hugged me and prayed. My life changed that very moment when I repented. I was baptized as the Bible says."

Sara had everyone on their feet, clapping at her testimony.

Yolanda had turned Sarah around with a hug and prayer—well, more than that. Could Omega do the same with Caylee and April? She hadn't spoken with Caylee since Omega gave her a ride home.

Two hours later, there wasn't a dry eye in the church from the emotional songs, a video presentation, and an uplifting eulogy. In Yolanda's forty-three years of life, she had been a powerhouse for the Lord.

Suddenly, the urgency of Omega's mission hit her. She would call Caylee today. No more stalling. After the parting view, mourners gathered outside to offer condolences to Yolanda's daughter.

Omega watched from afar. She was about to walk away when Dana called her name as she was about to climb into the funeral car.

"You're from my mom's job, right?" Dana hugged Omega when she nodded. "Thanks for coming."

"Of course. She was a sweet lady. I wish I hadn't taken our time together for granted." Omega sniffed.

"I don't know what God showed you on the morning of my mom's death…let it make a difference in your life."

"It already has." Omega squeezed Dana's hands, then stepped aside as the funeral director instructed everyone to get in their cars if they were going to the cemetery.

Accepting the spiritual torch Yolanda passed, Omega had to make an impact on lives. Caylee was her first assignment. She called her to stop by since she was in between jobs.

"Omega, I didn't think I would hear from you again."

My fault, Omega chided herself. To her surprise and disappointment, Caylee worked a temp assignment and wouldn't be available until Saturday. That was almost a whole week away.

"Sundays are hit-or-miss, depending on whether April has a fashion show or a convention where models are needed. April is working this Sunday on Mother's Day."

"Right." Mother's Day and her parents were coming to town. Omega hadn't spoken with Delta in a couple of days or Randall all week. Shame on Omega for forgetting that. One thing was for sure: She would see Caylee sooner rather than later.

Chapter Eight

Be kindly affectioned one to another with brotherly love; in honor preferring one another. Not slothful in business; fervent in spirit; serving the Lord. —Romans 12:10–11KJV

Mitchell stepped inside the jewelry store and glanced around. He was there for one woman only. If he didn't find anything unique here, Marva Franklin would get a gift card again this year for Mother's Day.

An older woman approached him at the necklace display counter. Christmas red lipstick outlined her smile. Her dark hair had graying roots. "Are you looking for anything special today?" Her nametag read Lana Avon. "Mother, wife, sister, girlfriend?"

"My mom." Mitchell eyed the row of necklaces.

A few days after dinner with Farrah, she called him and pretended as if they hadn't argued, and Mitchell had made up his mind. He was done with their relationship.

God was trying to get his attention, and Mitchell wanted to know why. Farrah could care less. Wait until she experiences a "coming to Jesus" moment for herself, and she might think differently.

That Omega woman had briefly mentioned seeing something unusual when she visited him in the hospital. At the time, Mitchell had played it off. Now he wished he hadn't. He'd search for her on social media and compare notes because something happened with her too.

His mind drifted as the saleswoman showed him one necklace after another, and then he noticed her hands. Each finger bore a ring.

"Looks like you have a nice collection yourself." He nodded to her hands.

She gave him a weak smile. "They all represent memories of my family who are no longer present. Two sisters, parents, husband, children, dear friend, and nieces."

"That's a lot of losses." Mitchell whistled. "I'm sorry."

"I guess I should be happy I only have ten fingers." Her smile didn't lift her cheeks or brighten her eyes.

Pray for her, God whispered.

Now? In public? Mitchell glanced over her shoulder. *Wasn't that something done behind closed doors?* Sadness washed over the woman's face after he asked the question.

"I don't think I can bare another Mother's Day living alone." She choked.

Mitchell began to panic. What did she mean?

Pray! Bind on Earth what I have bound in Heaven.

He rested his hand on top of hers. They were cold. Icy cold as if she were dead already. "Do you mind if I pray for you?"

"Please." Tears formed in her eyes.

"Our Father…"

No, that's a guide on how to pray. Pray for her out of your soul as if she were your mother or grandmother.

More customers walked into the store as Mitchell closed his eyes and made it quick. "Jesus, show her how much she's loved and needed…" He paused. What else? He had nothing more, so he closed, "In Jesus' name. Amen."

Mrs. Avon sniffed. "Thank you, young man. God sent you in here to pray, didn't He?"

With a shrug, he had no idea what God was up to. Mitchell regretted he hadn't whispered a better prayer, but he'd done his best. He quickly made a choice so he could leave and tapped on the glass counter.

"I'll take that necklace." It was fourteen-karat rose gold. Two tiny diamond-studded hearts were fused into one. Knowing his mother liked jewelry, he hoped his brothers Quinn and Nathan didn't buy the same one. It wouldn't be the first time his mother received duplicate gifts from her three sons. And she kept them all—white sweaters and tennis bracelets.

With his purchase in hand, he thanked the woman and left the store. That's when a face came into view amid the other shoppers.

His heart crashed against his chest in excitement. He quickened his steps to verify his eyes had registered the woman. "Omega!"

She was with another woman and a man and recognized him immediately. Omega detoured and met him halfway with the others on her heels. "Mitchell. It's good to see you. You look well."

"Is this the Mitchell who saved you?" the woman who resembled Omega asked. All three had the same shaped eyes, which were gorgeous on the women.

"*Shhh*, Delta." Omega elbowed her and apologized.

"I am." Mitchell grinned as he checked Omega out. He hadn't recognized her beauty while hospitalized, but now up close, she was pretty.

"Saved you from what?" Confused, the man whose muscles were the evidence of consistent workouts sized Mitchell up. He towered over the women but didn't meet Mitchell's height at six-three or solid muscle at two hundred and forty-five pounds.

Mitchell was not intimidated as he answered, "The gas station holdup."

"That robbery not far from your condo?" the man roared and eyed Omega. "What is he talking about? Leave nothing out." He tugged Omega to the side near a rail out of the way of foot traffic.

She looked uncomfortable as she made the introductions. "*Ahhh*, Mitchell, this is my older brother, Randall, and—"

"I'm her only brother," he corrected with an edge to his voice.

"This is my sister, Delta." Her sister hadn't taken her eyes off him.

Sororities and Fraternities? Mitchell had it wrong when he thought it had something to do with the Bible. Although he attended St. Louis University, he was never drawn to the Greek letter organizations.

"We'll talk later, Randall." Omega gritted her teeth and held her ground.

She needed rescuing again. "Can I talk to you for a sec?"

"Sure." Omega lifted her chin at her brother and stepped away for privacy. The concern in her beautiful brown eyes was heartfelt. "How's it going?"

"Physically, I'm healing. My nephew says I'll have a tattoo." He played it off, then frowned. "In the hospital, you asked me about seeing those angels—"

Suddenly, Omega's interest was piqued. "So, you did see them too?"

"Yeah." He looked away, embarrassed for lying. "And God is speaking through me. I've said stuff I know I wouldn't say."

Her eyes widened in recognition. "You're speaking in heavenly tongues too?"

"I don't know." Mitchell was confused.

"We've got to talk," she whispered. "Take my number. Call me when you get a chance, and please tell your girlfriend I'm no threat. I don't want her trying to jump me when she finds out you called me."

Mitchell didn't bother correcting her about Farrah as he punched in her number. His interest in Omega had no romantic intent. He had one question for her: Did she know how to pray?

"You've got some explaining to do, sis," Randall said when Mitchell was barely out of earshot.

Delta looped her arm through Omega's and danced in place. "He is fine. Girl, those muscles. He can protect me anytime."

"And you knew about this?" Randall gave their baby sister an incredulous look and balled his fists like he would punch somebody.

"Yep. Who do you think went to get her from that gas station and drove her home?" Delta had no shame in her grin.

"Do Mom and Dad know about what happened?" He directed the question at Omega.

Ignoring her brother's theatrics, she strolled on and window-shopped for a gift. "They do not, and don't you say anything while they're here. It will only upset them."

"You mean like the way I'm upset now that another man had to protect my sister during a shootout? Should have called me." Randall pounded his chest.

"Trust me, I made the right choice who to call, so tone down your hormones," Omega said.

"Yeah," Delta chimed in. "The police shot the guy, so our sister is safe, thanks to Mitchell. Did you see the size of his muscles? They are bigger than yours, Randall." She laughed, always the instigator.

Delta slipped her arm through Omega's and sped up to put some distance between them and their brother. "Sorry about that. It slipped, but he is fine and not wearing a ring."

Omega stopped and admired the detailed stitching on a red dress, which would be flattering on their mother. "He's cute," she emphasized. "No ring, but a girlfriend."

"Oh." Delta sighed. "Too bad."

"I'm not interested. God has other plans for me. Anyway, I didn't tell you that the second time I went to visit him in the hospital, she was there and rude."

"We both can take her down, you know." Delta grinned.

"Not happening. I'm on the Lord's side now."

Delta groaned and shook her head in disapproval. "I forgot. Too bad, but I saw you give him your number. What was that about? You never know, he might dump the chick, and you two might have a love connection."

Omega shook her head. "Trust me, this is a God connection."

"Don't think I'm going to forget about this," Randall said when he joined them with long strides. "And you know, as the oldest, I'm good at blackmailing my little sisters to keep quiet. Not the other way around. You have nothing on me."

Tuning her brother out, Omega walked into the store to buy their mother the dress. Girlfriend or not, Omega did hope Mitchell would call her sooner than later to compare notes. Until then, she had to learn to pray for patience, even though time was ticking.

Sunday became a day of mixed emotions for Omega. Since God had filled her with His spirit a few weeks ago, she couldn't get enough spiritual food, as the church folks say. She craved to hear more sermons, read Scriptures, pray, and talk with Mrs. Helena.

But her closer relationship with the Lord was a source of contention with Delta. She didn't want to attend service with Omega and didn't want to wait until after church for Sunday brunch.

"It's our day, and I don't want to share it," Delta had said stubbornly.

Omega was torn. Not only was Delta her sister, she was her bestie, but Omega held her ground, knowing what she did about Caylee and seeing visions that couldn't be explained. Let her sister pout like a grade-schooler. "You'll get over it."

Despite Omega's boast, she skipped service on Sunday because her parents were staying at Randall's place to celebrate

Mother's Day. Church wasn't on the agenda. Their mother looked forward to her family pampering her with their culinary skills, starting at breakfast.

At sixty-four, Glenda Addams' beauty was timeless. With hints of gray, their mother's hair still had a sandy brown glow. Few could guess her age, and she kept up with fashions that complemented her slender figure. Two years older, Eric Addams had aged well with his trimmed gray beard and a full head of thick salt-and-pepper hair. Her parents looked cute together.

Although she enjoyed their presence, Omega ached to be in God's house. Plus, she had to see Caylee who was with April who was modeling.

Continuing the Addams family's Mother's Day tradition, they had tickets for a matinee jazz performance featuring St. Louis native Denise Thimes at the Shelton Theatre. They rounded off the day lounging at Randall's, getting updates on what was going on in their children's personal lives.

"Randall, when are you going to propose to Tally? You've been dating what, almost two years?" Glenda pried.

He shrugged. "I want to marry her, but something's holding her back. When I bring up the subject, she shies away."

"*Hmmm.*" Their father rubbed his lips in thought and frowned. "The compatibility is there," he said, and they all knew he was referring to Tally pledging AKA and the fact that Randall was an Alpha as if that was enough for a perfect match.

Omega snickered. She had no interest to pledge in college, to the horror of their parents, so she didn't have to worry about a Greek matchup. Their mother turned to her. "Omega, are you seeing anyone?"

Randall cleared his throat, then looked away.

Omega gave him a side-eye. At thirty-five, she still had time.

"Funny you ask, Mom. Omega did meet someone. He's fine. *Ummm, ummm, ummm.* Has more muscles than Randall too." Delta smirked to Omega's annoyance.

Okay, her siblings were double-teaming her. She shot daggers at both. Their father, Eric, roared with laughter. "Him, I want to meet."

Glenda sighed. "My children are in their thirties. It's time you settle down and marry a life partner with whom you can share experiences." She wore a whimsical expression. "I received precious Mother's Day gifts, but a son- or daughter-in-law would be a nice surprise. Nine months after you say, 'I do,' I'll be expecting a bonus gift on my birthday." She scooted closer to their father. Eric rubbed a kiss on her cheek.

"No boyfriend, Mom, but I do have news—good news." Omega grinned.

Delta slapped her forehead and groaned. "Please, not that—again."

"What?" her parents said in unison and leaned forward in expectancy.

"I'm back in church." Omega beamed and pumped her fists in the air. She felt like doing a victory dance. Her happiness was overwhelming.

Eric and Glenda's responses were the same. Quiet.

"Oh, okay. That's nice, dear. One of those church brothers will snag your attention," her mother finally said.

"That's not the plan, Mom." Omega shook her head. "Recently, something happened that drew me closer to Christ. I was baptized in water and the fire of the Holy Ghost. *Whew*." She thought she was about to pray in the Spirit. "God has given me a mission, and I have to see it through."

"You're not going to be one of those overseas missionaries, are you?" her father asked.

Omega jutted her chin. "Dad, I'm going to be whatever God tells me. Souls are at stake." Her audience was quiet, and she didn't know what her family was thinking. But Omega had seen visions. She could no longer stall. Her focus was to sway people to God's will. "We all have an appointed time to die. Heaven and Hell are real."

Eric chuckled. "And how do you know this, dear?" His challenge was the lift of a bushy brow.

"I've seen some things to convince me." She eyed Delta to get her reaction, but her sister seemed disinterested.

At least God hadn't shown Omega any harm coming to her family. For that, she was grateful.

To rid the silence among them, her mother turned to the youngest. "Delta, how is it going with you?" Her eyes sparkled. She hoped for better news.

"I'm availing myself to possibilities. So far, I haven't been impressed with some of the potential candidates."

"Hey, Mom, Dad, maybe the next time you come to town, you'll go to church with me."

"We'll see," her father's reply didn't sound close to a commitment.

Glenda patted her husband's leg. "We're catching an early flight in the morning, so we want to check in on some of our old neighbors, especially the Bradshaws, while we're here. Anybody want to come along?"

Omega and Delta scrambled to their feet and announced they had things to do. Randall threw his father his car keys and grinned. "You young people don't stay out too late."

That earned him a laugh from them all.

After hugs and kisses, Omega left. She called Caylee. "If you and April are back home, I would like to stop by for a visit."

"Come on."

Now that the opportunity was before her, Omega wasn't sure what to say: *Caylee, you're going to die, and God told me to pray for you?* She groaned. "Lord, give me the words."

April met her at the door when Omega arrived at their apartment. "Hi, it's good to see you again. I'm heading down to the store. I'll be right back. Go on in."

This was a good thing. Omega could talk to Caylee alone. She joined watching a movie. "How was the fashion show?"

"April did a fantastic presentation, but I'm exhausted. Cleaning hotel rooms for the past few days is no joke, and the tips aren't as good as my last job."

"Which was what?"

Caylee hesitated as she picked imaginary lint on her oversized T-shirt. "Don't judge me—I've already done that—but I was a stripper."

Omega blinked. She wasn't expecting that.

"I was almost killed one night when I was in the club. A patron tried to rape me. I fought him off…."

"It's okay." Omega patted her hand. So many thoughts came to her mind.

God shut them down. *Do not judge or by the same measure I will judge you.*

Omega swallowed. "I'm sorry that happened to you. I'm not judging, but please tell me you quit."

"Not right away. I needed to pay bills, so I asked God to protect me. A few weeks ago, I saw a vision when I was in the middle of a dance routine. The club was suddenly on fire, and the well-dressed businessmen turned into half-animal creatures. That scared me more than the rape attempt. When I came to my senses, I packed up and was out of there. As an independent contractor, it was my loss." She choked. "The money was good, but I want no part of that life anymore. I want better for my sister and me."

With much fanfare, April returned. That was a quick trip. Omega hadn't even prayed as she wracked her brain on how she could help Caylee's current financial needs.

Yolanda is gone, God whispered.

Right. How could she forget? But she wasn't H.R. "My company recently has an opening. This is a busy time of the year. We could use the extra help. How are your office skills?"

"Really?" Caylee's face brightened. "The basics that I learned in college."

Lord, let Gerri back me up on a temporary new hire. Reba was swamped with more responsibilities since Yolanda's death. Caylee could help with simple tasks.

April bounced on the sofa. "Omega, please help her. I'll feel better knowing she has a decent job while I'm away breaking into the modeling biz in New York."

Caylee squeezed her lips and nodded. "I can't wait for my sister to leave this city. The sooner, the better."

Oh no, you don't. Omega steadied her racing heart. The sisters had no idea what fate waited for Caylee when April went away. *Lord, can you slow down time*?

No answer.

Omega refocused. "It's late, and I have to work in the morning. If you want a job, we offer great benefits after your probationary period. Come tomorrow." She gave her Hathaway's address. "Do you mind praying to receive what God wants you to have?"

The sisters agreed. Omega wasn't a prayer warrior like Mrs. Helena, but she would give it her best.

The trio held hands in the center of the living room in the small apartment. "Jesus, we're here asking for forgiveness and blessings. Send angels to protect them…." As Omega paused for more words to come, April gripped Omega's right hand and screamed.

"Send him back. Omega! Send him back!"

Who? Omega wanted to ask April but dared not to open her eyes. Suddenly, she felt a dark presence behind her coming from the kitchen. Instead of fear overpowering her, God gave Omega boldness as she continued to pray until a powerful language took over. Her arm lifted, but that was impossible since she was holding April and Caylee's hands.

Was it an angel walking through her, commanding the spiritual realm or what? This wasn't the time to figure it out. Emboldened with spiritual authority, Omega allowed God to subdue the spirit and she said, "Back, back, back," and it was as if Omega's spirit forced the demon from their presence until the atmosphere calmed.

Returning to the present, Omega opened her eyes.

April knelt on the floor, crying. Caylee squatted. "What's going on? No one is here but us. Who were you screaming at?"

With a dazed expression, April looked over her shoulder and darted her eyes around the apartment. "You didn't see it? M–My eyes were closed, but somehow, I saw this dark figure, but it couldn't get past you, Omega."

Omega didn't see the vision this time but felt evil in the atmosphere.

April stood, frantic. "Omega, teach us how to pray like that."

"It can't be taught. That was God speaking through me. If you want that power, my neighbor prayed with me and invited me to her church."

"Can we meet her? Is she on the bus route?" April fired off one question after the other.

"I'll talk to her. See you tomorrow, Caylee," Omega said her goodbyes and left.

In her car, Omega gripped the steering wheel. Whew! She didn't see the angels or demons this time in Caylee's apartment, but she felt them. And God overpowered them.

Had she been what Mrs. Helena called an intercessor? She wished God would give her the heads-up next time. Something told her it would be more next times.

Omega remained in awe as she entered her condo. Her body was tired, but her spirit was on high alert, and she wanted the next fix like a drug addict. It was too late to call Mrs. Helena and tell her about it. Her family wasn't an option. They wouldn't believe her. Mitchell came to mind.

She thought he would have called but he didn't. It was Mother's Day. It didn't matter, and she reflected on what just happened. She scared a demon away. "Team Jesus!"

Pumping her fist in the air, she danced around the living room as if she were blasting her latest jam. Before she knew it, tears were streaming down her cheeks. Heavenly tongues buried deep within her belly expelled.

She didn't know how long she had a praise break. Exhausted in a good way, Omega prepared for bed, wondering what God had in store for her the next day.

Chapter Nine

And as it is appointed unto men once to die,
but after this the judgment...
—Hebrews 9:27 KJV

The next morning, Omega spotted Mrs. Helena in front of her house as she waved and bid farewell to their residents, shouting an inspiring sendoff. Omega stopped.

"Good morning, Mrs. Helena. You won't believe what happened to me."

Her neighbor chuckled. "If God had anything to do with it, I will. If you're not too tired after work, stop by and tell me all about it." She waved at others driving by.

"I will." She grinned until she glanced at her gas gauge.

A pang of fear struck her.

Less than a quarter tank.

Why couldn't she remember to gas up on Sundays in the daytime? Granted Omega pumped a few gallons in her vehicle the other day, but she hadn't wanted to stick around until it was filled up. She was still uneasy, but after what she experienced last night at Caylee's, Omega had confidence that God would fight her battles.

But doubt took stabs at her psyche as she drove past the station that had recently reopened after the shooting. Omega wasn't ready to return to the scene of the crime, so she bypassed Gus' Gas Mart and pumped gas at QuikTrip without incident.

She wondered how the Prince sisters' night was. Caylee seemed clueless about the chaos, whereas April recognized something wasn't right.

What is God's game plan? Omega wondered. Maybe April was Omega's focus instead of Caylee. April seemed eager for more of God's power. If she'd surrender, would the Lord bless her with a better job here to help her forget about New York? Omega didn't see that happening. Who didn't want to go to New York?

As God worked out the details of His will, Omega would wait for His instructions. When she arrived at Hathaway Health, Omega recommended Caylee Prince for a ninety-day trial basis to the H.R. manager, hoping everything would work out.

"Thanks for taking the initiative on that. I know Reba needs help, but I can't bring myself to cross the threshold into that office, so yeah, let's give your friend a try." Gerri appeared grateful.

To Omega's relief, Caylee did show up ready to work. While she completed tax forms and listed April as her emergency contact, Omega left her to place a copy of Yolanda Ann Ward's obituary in the break room for whoever wanted to read it. The few times she passed by the room, the program appeared untouched. As if it was taboo, a couple of staff members sat as far away as possible from that table.

Omega imagined they were still in shock. She would have been too if it weren't for the visions she had seen prior to Yolanda's death, and this time she wasn't alone seeing it. No one had mentioned their late coworker's name since that day, but the shock hung in the air, despite the company owner calling in grief counselors. No one could erase what they'd seen or heard.

Back in her office, Omega sipped her herbal tea and began to review requests. Minutes later, Caylee appeared in her doorway.

Gerri stood behind the new-hire and winked. "She's all yours to take to accounting." She patted Caylee's shoulder. "Good luck. I hope you like it here."

Once they were alone, Caylee gushed about the plush office interior and the casual feel. "Wow. Thank you, Omega."

Omega smiled and stood. "It was perfect timing for us to meet. Come on. I'll show you where you'll be working. Caylee trailed Omega down the hall to where Yolanda had clocked in for the last seventeen years of her life. Reba had her back to the doorway, packing up her former boss's items for her daughter to pick up.

In a soft, almost reverent voice, Omega spoke. "Reba, meet Caylee Prince. She's here to help in whatever you need as you fill Yolanda's role, so please be patient with her as she learns new skills."

"No problem." A smile replaced Reba's sober expression. "Welcome. It's nice to meet you. I love your name."

Caylee blushed, thanked her, and listened as Reba patiently gave her instructions.

"You have a good day." As Omega pivoted to retrace her steps to her office, she spied the Hathaway's "poster boy for Mr. Cool" swaggering toward her. Charm with a commanding height made Bobby Truman more arrogant than handsome. His personality won him the unofficial company popularity contest by coworkers.

His downfall at one time was that his personal lifestyle crossed over into his livelihood. He forgot the value of showing up for work on time. Yolanda had held his indiscretions close and prayed for him.

Suspecting something was going on, Omega pulled him aside and gave him tough love as a big sister figure of almost nine years. He had stopped smoking illegal weed until under the guise of medical marijuana the substance became legal to purchase at dispensaries in St. Louis with a prescription.

Bobby had friends who had friends to get those prescriptions.

"What's up, O?" He grinned, then slowed his gait as he passed Reba's old cubicle outside Yolanda's office and backtracked. His eyes widened in appreciation. "Well, hello there." He extended his hand. "Bobby Truman from graphics. If you want to know anything that goes on here, ask me." He patted his chest.

"Thank you." Caylee was cordial. Bobby's charm didn't faze her.

After what she had endured as a stripper, Omega guessed not. She cleared her throat. "Bobby, let Caylee get settled."

"Of course. Caylee and I will have lots of time to get to know each other. I'll make sure you're at the top of my guest list."

"Guest list for what now?" Omega snickered.

"I'm going all the way out to celebrate my twenty-fifth birthday. It's going to be big, big, big, big with an emcee, servers, semi-formal dress attire, and more as things come to mind."

You fool! His soul will be required of him, God whispered. *Read My Word in Luke 12:20.*

Wait? Omega froze as the Lord's word rewound in her head. Not Bobby. Was he going to die too? Now she had two people with a death wish. Lord, have mercy. This was too much.

Chapter Ten

Pray without ceasing.
—1 Thessalonians 5:17 KJV

During the Mother's Day celebration with family, Mitchell's nephew, Justin, stole the show when he gave his grandmother a 3D picture of her holding him as a baby. It brought Mitchell's mother to tears.

But his mind drifted to the salesclerk at the jeweler's. How did she fare on a day honoring mothers when she would be alone?

Before leaving, Justin had to see Mitchell's scar from the bullet. "It's still healing, buddy." And it had been aching all morning.

"Have you made a follow-up appointment with a doctor?" his mother asked. "I'm sure Farrah has you on top of it."

Mitchell groaned. "I will, Mom, but Farrah and I aren't together anymore."

"What?" His mother studied him. "What happened?"

He didn't want to talk about Farrah who had sent text messages asking him to reconsider the breakup. "Let's just say she isn't the one."

"Okay. I can kind of see that, but one day you're going to meet a woman that isn't Regina and who will be the one you won't want to get away."

"Noted." He kissed his mom and shook hands with his father, brothers, and nephew, then left. It was no secret that the Franklin family tolerated Farrah because of him. And he dated Farrah even though she was more into him than he was into her. Big mistake. Mitchell's attraction never grew. His parents were probably thinking, "Good riddance," but would never say it out loud.

On Monday evening, Mitchell left his gym in the hands of his assistant manager to do a mental wellness check on the saleslady at the jeweler's. She had been on his mind all Mother's Day.

When Mitchell walked into the store, he didn't see the saleswoman. A man greeted Mitchell. His nametag read Mr. Taft, the manager.

"I'm looking for Mrs. Avon."

The sadness on the man's face caused Mitchell to brace for unfavorable news.

"Mrs. Avon died in her sleep early Sunday. When she didn't show up for her shift, I called. A neighbor at her house answered." He shook his head. "She was such a sweet lady and a top seller here. She'll be missed by staff and customers."

Mitchell took a moment to mourn as his heart sunk. Mother's Day hadn't been promised to Mrs. Avon. He thanked the manager and left after assuring him there weren't any problems with his recent purchase. His footsteps were heavy as he returned to his truck—the new one. His old one had been declared a total loss during the shooting.

He started the engine but didn't pull off right away. Twice now, Mitchell had been in the presence of death recently. Mrs. Avon was taken yesterday, and weeks ago, he had been spared. Mitchell drove the speed limit on autopilot to his modest home in Richmond Heights, a suburb of St. Louis.

There were two places Mitchell considered his comfort zone—the gym he owned and his home. The story-and-a-half fixer-upper was his baby, which he'd had plans to sell during the hot housing market, but then he'd fallen in love with the location and neighborhood. He stayed.

The comfort was void as Mitchell stepped into the living room his mother decorated with the intent of creating an inviting vibe. He flopped on the sofa, numbed. Confusion filled his head. Why did he have to meet the sweet lady days before she died? Mitchell stared into the darkness because he had yet to turn on a light.

His large flat screen waited for his voice command to do his bidding. Instead, Mitchell welcomed the quietness until the solitude began to torment him. He needed to vent the madness to someone. First, his stomach growled. Leftovers from the restaurant where his father and two brothers took their mother beckoned him to the kitchen.

Omega's name came to mind as he ate. Had she experienced similar things since the robbery? He grabbed his phone and found her number, then debated if calling her was a wise move.

He finished eating, then took his chances and reached out to Omega. She sounded as down as he felt. "This is Mitchell Franklin. Did I catch you at a bad time? I can call you back," he said out of politeness when he really wanted to talk to anyone who would listen and understand.

"No. I'm glad you called. I haven't been the same since the shooting."

"Me either." Mitchell didn't know if he was glad they had that connection or not.

"Right. How are you feeling? How's your shoulder?"

"As long as I take it easy, it will heal and I'll be one hundred percent again," he said and rotated his shoulder. "But there's something else that I can't explain. It's like God is showing me things."

"You too?" Omega's voice became animated. "It's this burden for others.... "

"Yes. I'm glad we ran into each other. I wanted to say thank you for visiting me in the hospital and saving my life."

"Huh? I think it's the other way around." Her chuckle was soft. "You took the bullet for me, remember?"

"I remember that night well and every day after that. I've had vibrant and fascinating dreams, so I don't want to wake up. It's as if I'm getting a glimpse of Heaven. One night, God let me know if I hadn't tried to save you, I'd be dead. My vehicle was bullet-ridden and undrivable. I was right in the line of fire if I'd stayed where I was."

"Wow." She paused. "In my mind, I'd been killed if it hadn't been for you."

"Sounds like a thesis for which came first, the chicken or the egg." He had an appetite for dessert now, so he reached into the freezer for his favorite, French vanilla ice cream, and got a hearty serving.

Omega laughed. It was deep and throaty instead of a soft giggle. "Well, I'm glad both of us are alive. While God is giving you dreams, it seems like the Lord is showing me people targeted for death and people who *are* dead, and I'm not talking about séances. My coworker, Yolanda, made an appearance in the office, but she was already dead. She had died in a car accident hours earlier."

Mitchell stopped his spoon of ice cream midair. "What? Seriously? I'd have freaked out on that one. If you repeat I said that, I'll never admit to it. My nephew thinks I'm not scared of anything."

This time, Omega did giggle, and he smiled. "It's strange that only four of us saw her. The other staff are clueless about what happen. One coworker seems unfazed, the other two are still processing it whether it was real or not. I know that vision was God sent."

"My life would have been forever changed," he sampled the scoop, "like what we witnessed on the night of the robbery. My outlook on life is different."

"I know this might sound like a cliché, but it's our destiny to do something. I mean, not together. You have yours, and I have mine…." Omega's voice faded. "Honestly, I wish I could hide in my closet because I'm afraid of what's going to happen next or who the Lord will reveal is doomed."

"That's deep." Their entire conversation was strange. Mitchell finished eating, rinsed the container in the sink, then placed it in the dishwasher without missing a beat of what Omega was telling him.

Returning to his living room, he grabbed the remote and pointed toward the screen but kept the volume muted. Mitchell rested back on his sofa. "The dreams aren't as strange as the words coming out of my mouth. I surprise myself."

Without realizing it, the two of them tried to one-up the other.

"Is God speaking in heavenly tongues to you too? Do you recognize what you're saying?" Omega didn't hide her excitement.

"Ah, I wouldn't call it heavenly, but I feel my words are God-inspired, not something I would say."

"Maybe God is teaching you to be like my neighbor, Mrs. Helena, a retired schoolteacher. She seems to have a personal connection with God as if she's Moses." Omega laughed. "I know I'm giving her too much credit, but on the morning of the shooting, she said to me, 'May God send angels to protect you.' She had never said that to me before, then look what happened."

"*Hmmm*. Thank God your angels protected me too."

Being victims of crime had made them kindred spirits. He doubted the news reporter who still called for an interview would want to hear about angels and demons.

Talking to Omega had created another comfort zone for Mitchell. "What do you think about us joining forces and becoming partners in crime—seems like God paired us together."

Omega didn't answer right away. "*Hmmm.* I'm new at this. I'm going to introduce you to Mrs. Helena, and she'll have insight into what you're experiencing."

Finally, Mitchell would know his purpose. That made him grin.

"She invited me to visit her church, and when I did…wow. I was in great company. Pastor Rodney didn't have to ask me twice if I wanted to be saved. I had to repent of my sins and be baptized. I saw more angels stirring in the water. The most unforgettable thing was when God's heavenly language exploded from my mouth. *Whew.* Don't get me started on that. I may start praying and praising God on this phone."

"Don't mind me." He chuckled and unmuted the volume on his TV to listen to the commenter's remark about a baseball pitch. "You're making me hungry for what you've experienced. It can't be any stranger than what I've gone through."

Mitchell rotated his arm. "But I'll be fine. I'm a trained physical therapist, so I know the ranges of exercises to do. Plus, I invested in a gym franchise. The weights can help me build up my strength at a steady pace."

"I'm impressed."

Yeah, most women were when they learned his credentials. Farrah certainly had been.

Omega yawned. "I'm sorry. It's been a long weekend and a draining day. I need to get some rest."

"Of course." Mitchell sat straighter. He wasn't ready to say goodbye. "How selfish of me. Please don't forget to mention me to your neighbor. I want to prepare myself for what God has up His sleeve."

"I'm sure she'll have some insight. Plus, I need to talk to her about something else."

As Omega was about to end the call, he stopped her. "You now have my number. Call me if you feel over your head or something."

"Over my head? You mean like trying to change people's life goals. Slow them down, so they won't be so eager to approach their death date. What's to feel over my head?" Omega gave a dry laugh and ended the call.

Mitchell didn't know if she was being sarcastic or joking, but he liked her sense of humor and couldn't wait to meet her neighbor.

All day Tuesday, Mitchell went through the motions of a proud, happy business owner when his thoughts were lingering on Mrs. Avon. He hoped she hadn't mourned herself to death. It was an uneasy feeling to see a person one day and the next, they were gone.

Whew. He rubbed the back of his neck. A slight pain radiated from his injured shoulder. Although solid muscle, his bulk didn't stop a bullet from penetrating his body. "Here today, gone tomorrow."

You do not know what will happen tomorrow! Life is a mist that appears for a little while and then vanishes, God whispered. *Study My Word. Read James 4:14.*

So sad. The saleswoman was sweet enough to be Mitchell's grandmother, great-aunt, or a neighbor who lived a few doors down from him. Until he heard from Omega, Mitchell would start to read his Bible.

Outside his gym, Mitchell walked toward his truck. A homeless man sat on a nearby curb eating a sandwich with gusto. In the four years Mitchell's business had been at this location, he had never seen anyone who seemed out of the ordinary.

Kings and Queens Fitness was in a middleclass neighborhood where residents had the means to live comfortably. *I guess it's a good place to beg.*

After the robbery, Mitchell became leery of folks and more on guard.

However, fear wasn't part of his emotions as he approached the man. "Brother, is there anything I can help you with?" Mitchell reached for his wallet.

"Stop, Mitchell. The woman you mourn is resting with Jesus. The harvest is plentiful, but the laborers are few."

Mitchell's breathing paused as he stared at the man who was no longer eating his sandwich. How did this man know his name and thoughts? And what did he mean?

Before he could ask questions, his phone alerted him of a text. He read it.

Bro, you stopping by this evening?

Yep, he texted back his younger brother. Quinn wasn't letting him off the hook for hanging out on Tuesday nights to watch sports at his apartment.

Since Nathan was married and had a family, Quinn boasted he and Mitchell would be bachelor brothers to the end. He smiled, then looked up. The man was gone.

Mitchell blinked and did a three-sixty of his surroundings. There was no trace of him, his backpack, or food wrappings. Vanished before his eyes. This was not a vision like the night of the robbery. Not only did he see the stranger but spoke with him too.

Bewildered, Mitchell walked toward his truck and looked over his shoulder once, then twice. Who was that man?

My messenger, God whispered.

Mitchell appreciated that God saw the sorrow in his heart for the woman he had met once. He never had this personal relationship with Jesus that revealed the Lord was listening to him and that his hurt mattered.

A level of comfort hugged Mitchell as he started his engine and drove off for his barber. Soon, he parked in front of Antoine's Cutup Barbers.

Walking inside, he nodded at unfamiliar patrons and slapped hands with regulars.

"What's going on, man?" his barber—the owner—Antoine asked. "I haven't seen you at the regular hangouts. You alright?"

"I'm good." Mitchell took a seat. "Taking a bullet changed my whole perspective." He stared at the floor, wondering where his life was heading.

His friend and barber had heard about the shooting, then learned Mitchell was one of the victims when he came in with his arm in a sling.

"Like what?" a man asked, waiting for services for his uncombed hair and out-of-control white-and-gray spotted beard.

"How short our life is." Mitchell rubbed his hand over the waves in his hair. He was a few weeks overdue for a fade. "A new day isn't promised, so I don't plan to waste it."

A boisterous patron laughed, drowning out all the chatter in each barber's station. He was a thin-framed man well-dressed down to his unscuffed shoes but who could benefit from weights training for beginners. "If my time is running out, I better get wasted tonight and if I live tomorrow, I'll do it all over."

"Be careful. God's patience might run thin, and there might not be a tomorrow for you." Mitchell stunned himself by saying that.

"Man, you're doom and gloom. Ain't nobody trying to hear that." The patron never said another word.

Neither did Mitchell as he prayed that man wouldn't lose his life anytime soon like Mrs. Avon, regardless of his own stupidity.

Chapter Eleven

... for we know not what we should pray for as we ought: but the Spirit itself makes intercession for us with groanings, which cannot be uttered. —Romans 8:26 KJV

Mrs. Helena agreed to meet with Mitchell at her house. "You come, too, so we can discuss what God told you about the young man at your job."

Omega arrived first, walking to the corner of her cul-de-sac where her neighbor lived in her townhouse, five houses away.

She had been reading and listening to the church sermons on social media, but she was still unsure how to help Caylee, and now Bobby.

Although Mitchell hadn't made it, there was no doubt in Omega's mind that he would show up. She rang the doorbell. Mrs. Helena welcomed her with a warm smile and invited her inside. The first thing Omega noticed was the dining room table was set with Bibles and a notepad instead of place settings.

"Have a seat, Omega. I'm just preparing a light snack," Mrs. Helena shouted from the kitchen as the doorbell rang. "That's our other guest. Will you let him in?"

"Yep." Omega opened the door and sucked in her breath. "Wow. You clean up good."

The crisp shirt and dress pants made the man more handsome—if she was interested. His hair was lined with a steady hand. He stepped inside. Her "bodyguard" towered over her.

"I left the gym early to go home and change. First impressions matter." He grinned, stretching a thin mustache that outlined his mouth.

"You must be Mitchell." Mrs. Helena walked up behind Omega.

"I am." Mitchell handed her neighbor the flowers he held behind his back. "Thank you for agreeing to meet with me."

Flowers? He was crushing the first impression thing. Mrs. Helena blushed. It was a sweet gesture. Omega wished she had done the same.

"Let's have a seat at my table in here. I made lemonade and chicken wraps. I hope you have a little room for both." Her eyes twinkled as she placed a platter in the center.

Mitchell patted his stomach and grinned. "I think that can be arranged."

She and her neighbor chuckled as Mitchell held the chairs back for Mrs. Helena and Omega. Seated side by side, they faced Mrs. Helena like a teacher in a classroom.

Mrs. Helena gave thanks for the snacks, then encouraged them to help themselves. The wraps were tasty, popping with ranch dressing.

While they ate, Mrs. Helena asked Mitchell about his job, family, and relationship with the Lord.

Dabbing his lips with the fancy cloth napkin, he nodded. "I'm a franchisee of Kings and Queens Fitness. I have a background in physical therapy, but when the opportunity presented itself to become a business owner, I jumped on it. I stopped working as a PT last year to put all my energy into my business." The pride in his voice was unmistakable. "I'm the oldest of three sons and have one nephew."

Mrs. Helena extracted more information from him than a machine squeezing lemons for lemonade. Omega was impressed.

She never thought to ask those questions. To her, Mitchell was solely a brave man.

"I've never felt the presence of God like I do now. It's mindboggling." Mitchell frowned. He shared his experience with people, including his family, since the shooting.

"Yes, it is," she mumbled, and Mitchell acknowledged her statement with a nod.

"My most recent strange encounter was with a man outside the fitness club I own. I thought he was homeless, but I think he was God's messenger. Now I'm on the lookout for angels who look like people. How do I know?"

Her neighbor's smile was faint. "An angel does the work of God or delivers His messages. They're dispatched to help us all the time. Sometimes they look like ordinary folks to deliver a message; other times, the Lord Jesus allows us to see their angelic state."

Omega rubbed her forehead. "Instead of an angel talking to me, God is telling me people will die. What am I supposed to do?"

"Pray, pray, pray without ceasing." Mrs. Helena opened her worn Bible, which had colorful note tabs marking sections. She found a passage. "Find the Book of Acts, chapter two in the Bibles in front of you."

She waited as Omega and Mitchell flipped through the pages.

"It's in the New Testament," her neighbor said gently.

Mitchell found it first, then helped Omega. Embarrassed, she whispered her thanks.

"Now," Mrs. Helena began, "in Acts 2:17: *'And it shall come to pass in the last days, saith God, I will pour out of my Spirit upon all flesh: and your sons and your daughters shall prophesy, and your young men shall see visions, and your old men shall dream dreams.'* This same quote is foretold in the Old Testament in Joel 2:28, which means the Scriptures are coming to pass."

"Wow." Mitchell bit his bottom lip. "So many questions are in my head now. I don't know which to ask first."

"We're in the last days on earth?" Omega sucked in her breath. Her heart pounded with mixed emotions.

"That was one of my questions." The concern on his face matched hers.

Mrs. Helena stared past them. Her head tilted as if she considered her answer. "The warning signs are happening now, but Jesus said this is the beginning of sorrow. The Lord is sending angels to help you."

Mitchell nodded. "Help us do what?"

"Win souls for Christ." She gave them a stern expression that would put the fear in misbehaving students. "That is your assignment. It hasn't changed since He rose from the dead thousands of years ago. Witness for Him, especially you, Omega, because you have received the power of His Spirit a few weeks ago, and you're growing in the Lord. The battles you two have described in separate visions are a spiritual war that's already been won. The world doesn't realize it, so people act defeated. That's the devil's strategy to distract you with demonic attacks, paving the path for anxiety that can lead to sickness, suicides, and aggressive behavior."

Omega didn't hide her frustration. "Mrs. Helena, how do I save Caylee? Somehow her life is tied to her sister's aspirations. And Bobby is gearing up for a big celebration. He's got no idea a target is on his back too."

Mrs. Helena pointed to the notepad next to the Bible on the table. "Take it and begin to write the names God brings to your mind and those who ask for prayer. In the morning, at night, and throughout the day, call those names out to the Lord. Prayers change situations, conditions, and people."

A notepad. Omega had recalled seeing one in Yolanda's things that Reba had packed up. It was made out of colorful rich fabric with bits of jewels. Did that contain Yolanda's prayer list? Was Omega's name in it?

"Omega," Mrs. Helena called her name, looking directly at her, "we have to battle for the souls of family, friends, strangers, even enemies. James 5:20 tells us that if we can *'convert a sinner from the error of his way, we shall save a soul from death, and shall hide a multitude of sins.'* Only God can save them through their repentance and baptisms, but you are to be a witness. You must fast and pray and take every opportunity to tell people about Jesus." She closed her Bible. "There are so many treasures God has for us—a crown, rewards…"

The more she spoke about Jesus, the more empowered Mrs. Helena became. She began to pray, then prophesized to Mitchell that God would draw his mother to Him, then save her soul. "It's by faith you should praise God for that. When you speak in the name of the Lord, it will come to pass, and you will know it was God."

Something within Mitchell must have snapped. He began to praise God, rejoice, and confess his sins. Omega joined him in praise and prayer. Suddenly, it felt like the house shook as if there was an explosion within it. There wasn't.

God spoke through Mitchell, and his heavenly language was different from hers. Then she heard Mrs. Helena's. It sounded different too.

This Upper Room experience would stay with her always.

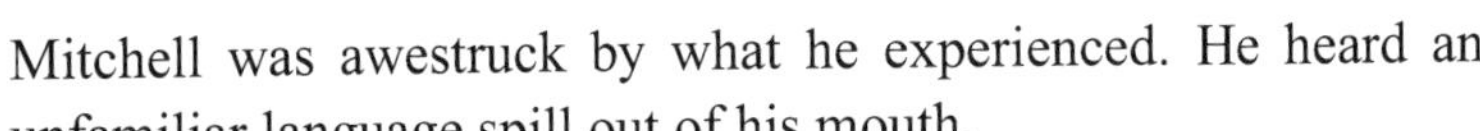

Mitchell was awestruck by what he experienced. He heard an unfamiliar language spill out of his mouth.

His lips trembled.

His arms lifted involuntarily.

What was happening? Mitchell didn't realize he was crying until he felt wetness on his cheeks. Mrs. Helena's prayer was powerful.

"Jesus, Jesus…" were the only words Mitchell could utter as God's presence filled the room.

The magnitude of God's presence calmed the atmosphere around them. Mitchell hugged Omega, then Mrs. Helena without concern about crossing the line. "I felt it. I heard it. The Holy Ghost is real."

Mrs. Helena smiled. "Yes, it is. You've already received the baptism of His Spirit since you've repented. All that is left to complete your salvation process is the baptism in water in the name of Jesus."

Exhausted, Mitchell nodded. He was weak as if he had completed a high-intensity workout. When he heard Mrs. Helena say that God would save his mother, Mitchell lost it and began to thank God. "Is it okay if I get baptized at your church on Sunday?"

"Now, you're trying to make this old lady get up and shout. The more, the merrier." She winked and turned to Omega. "You can invite Caylee and her sister too. Whatever you can't explain to others about God, Pastor Rodney can pick it up from there, so invite, invite, invite."

Omega grinned.

Mitchell went through a couple more rounds of praise. It seemed like God had a conversation with him in a heavenly language.

After an hour, Mrs. Helena reminded him and Omega that they had to work the next day, and if they wanted to stay and praise God, they were welcome. "However, you can praise God in your own home."

"Hint: Go home." Omega laughed, and Mrs. Helena walked them to the door and thanked them for visiting.

"No, thank you for taking the time to answer my questions and pray for us." Mitchell couldn't stop himself from hugging her again.

"That's my job, young man. I'm glad you're the other half of the team." She pointed from Omega to him.

Omega shook her head and said matter-of-factly, "Oh, no. We're not a team."

Mitchell disagreed and mumbled, "That's what you think. We're in this together, intercessor."

Slipping his hands into his pockets, he walked out alongside Omega until they were on the sidewalk. He looked up into the night sky. The moon hung there so peacefully. "It's hard to believe all of this will be destroyed."

Omega glanced up too. "It is. While people are sleeping, working, or playing, the devil and his demon cronies are plotting to kill us."

"We can't let that happen now that we have a glimpse into the spiritual realm. This is all so weird," he admitted, and she agreed.

"I know. I'm glad Mrs. Helena prayed with us, and the Lord filled you with His Spirit." Her eyes sparkled under the moonlit sky.

"Whew. I've got to get home so that I can pray again." He laughed. "I never thought I would hear myself say that, but I never thought I would experience what I did tonight."

She stepped forward as if she wanted to hug him but moved back, realizing their boundaries. He had crossed earlier with no thought. Instead, she smiled. "It's real, isn't it?"

"Yes." The tranquility surrounding him inspired Mitchell to take a closer look at his new prayer partner. He thought Omega was pretty, but now, Mitchell saw a beauty more profound than skin tone and physical assets.

He glanced around the court. "This is a nice neighborhood."

"Yeah. I like it and my neighbors."

"Do you want an escort?" he teased, knowing she lived in one of these townhouses or condos. "I have a shiny new truck for you to ride in."

"That's right." She strolled to the curb and did a closer examination from bumper to bumper, rubbing her hand along the way as if checking for dust. "Again, sorry you had to get a new one."

He shook his head and slipped his hands into his pants pockets. "But I'm not sorry for where the experience led me. So how about that free ride home, and you can check out the interior." He was being pushy. When had he worked so hard to get attention?

"I believe you." She wrinkled her nose. "Nah. I've got Jesus."

"I'll follow for backup."

Omega laughed again and pointed. "I'm five houses down in that condo."

"Come on, woman. Let me walk you to your door so that I can get home. I want to read some of the Scriptures before bed."

That's when she consented. At Omega's door, she said goodbye and went inside.

Spinning around on his heels, Mitchell retraced his steps to his truck and drove home. Blocks from his house, God spoke to him again.

Your wound will heal. The scar and pain will be gone, the Lord Jesus whispered.

Mitchell blinked. He heard it. God said it. "And I believe You."

When Mitchell entered his house, he broke out in a happy dance. This was getting good now.

Chapter Twelve

Rejoice always, pray without ceasing, give thanks in all circumstances; for this is the will of God in Christ Jesus for you.
—1 Thessalonians 5:16–18 KJV

The next morning, Omega received an unexpected wake-up call before her alarm.

"This is not a prank call." Mitchell's deep voice stirred her from her sleep. "I want to pray this morning with you."

There was nothing funny about his request, but Omega laughed anyway. "Of course. Give me five minutes." She turned off her alarm, jumped out of bed and headed to the bathroom. Sounds silly, but she wasn't about to talk to God with an unwashed face and bad breath.

Ten minutes later, she phoned Mitchell back. "You're late. I barely slept last night because Jesus and I had a conversation going."

She smiled, understanding the excitement of their salvation. "Okay. I'm kneeling and ready." She closed her eyes and waited.

"Jesus," he began, "thank You for my—our—salvation. Thank You for waking us up and giving us spiritual discernment today to defeat the devil. He's going down, in Jesus' name. Amen."

"Amen," she repeated. "I had expected at least an hour's prayer."

"Oh, it's coming, I'm sure. Have a good day and thank you for letting me meet Mrs. Helena."

They said their goodbyes, and Omega showered and dressed. She reflected on what Mrs. Helena told Mitchell about his mother. What about her family? Omega wanted to ask but became distracted. She grabbed her keys and headed out the door.

She waved at Mrs. Helena, who was on her post at the corner of the cul-de-sac, encouraging neighbors with inspirational send-offs.

The day at work was uneventful. When Omega crossed paths with Bobby in the hall or breakroom, she didn't want to think about what God had said about him. She prayed that Bobby would want Jesus in his life more than anything. Whatever his decision, his soul depended on it.

Omega and Mitchell had started an evening routine, texting each other about their day.

By Friday, Caylee had survived a week at Hathaway Health, and Reba had no complaints. Omega treated her to lunch at a nearby Imo's Pizza. With Caylee's back to a large window, Omega faced it and admired the spring colors blooming from the trees and gardens on the street.

"How's April's job hunt going for a New York modeling agency?" Omega asked out of politeness while she prayed for the opposite to happen.

Caylee huffed. "No bites yet, and she's working so hard to reach her dream."

"Is there anything else April would like to do?" Omega was hopeful. "I've learned that God's will is perfect."

"Modeling is April's dream. I'm pulling for her, so I told her I'd help with research for more agencies this weekend." Caylee shivered as if someone had ushered in a cool draft.

Omega looked behind Caylee out the window, and that's when she saw a faceless dark figure outside, like a shadow. "Jesus," she said with authority.

"What's wrong? I didn't know you swear." Caylee gave her an odd look.

"Oh, I don't. There's power in His name." *The demons fear God's name. I had to get them away from you.*

"Maybe I should call on Jesus when I get these random calls for stripper gigs." She lowered her voice.

"Yes, please. Reba says you're catching on. After three months, you'll get a raise, so it's worth hanging out with us."

Caylee grinned and rocked in her chair. "I like the atmosphere here. Everyone is professional."

After lunch, the two returned to the building and their work. Closing her office door, Omega began to pray, throwing out all the Scriptures she had learned the devil didn't like. "At the name of Jesus, you demons tremble. Every knee shall bow and tongue confess that Jesus is Lord…." Heavenly tongues filled her soul as she spoke to the Lord, calling out Caylee's name and Bobby's.

On the drive home, Omega reflected on what happened. The devil wanted Caylee bad. Why? What was it about her that made her his target? She stepped up her prayer time, but was it enough if the people God spoke to Omega about were going to die anyway?

God spoke passages He wanted her to read.

It was going to be a long night.

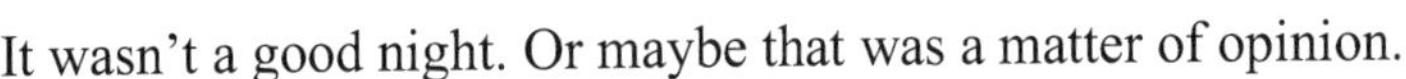

It wasn't a good night. Or maybe that was a matter of opinion.

While Omega slept, something woke her. She sensed a presence in her house, worse, in her bedroom. The alarm hadn't sounded, but Omega felt she was being watched. Whoever or whatever it was seemed to be encamped around her, ready to attack. She sat up and scanned the room—no one.

She didn't own a gun.

Omega began to pray. Closing her natural eyes, her spiritual eyes opened and zoomed in on beast-like creatures hanging in the corners of her ceiling. She aimed spiritual darts as if her finger were a loaded pistol and picked them off. "Jesus…one down. Jesus…another. Jesus…" She continued until her atmosphere felt at peace

I'll never leave you alone, God whispered.

Believing the Lord, Omega slid under the covers, then drifted back to sleep.

The following day, she wondered if she had been dreaming. "How would I know if last night was real, Lord?" she asked as she prepared breakfast.

Jesus was silent.

After she tidied her kitchen, she walked into the living room and grabbed the study Bible Mrs. Helena had given her. "Lord, show me what to read. She flipped through the pages and paused at Proverbs, the third chapter. Her heart pounded when she read verse twenty-four. The Scripture answered her question: *When you lie down, you shalt not be afraid: yes, you shalt lie down, and your sleep shall be sweet.*

Omega grinned as her phone played her sister's ringtone. "Hey, Dell. What's up?"

"Whoa. You're in a good mood for a Saturday morning."

"Yep. My sleep was sweet." She lifted her hand in praise.

"So, what ya doin' today?"

After yesterday at work with Caylee and last night's attempted peace disturbance, Omega wanted to check on the Prince sisters. "What's up?" she asked instead.

"Want to see a matinee since I'm being passed over for Sunday brunch?" Delta didn't hide her attitude.

Omega rolled her eyes. Since the shooting, Delta had accused Omega of going Jesus on her. That much was somewhat true as she tried to understand this spiritual realm.

"I prefer to go to church first, then we can go out, whether you come to service or not," she corrected her sister, but missed spending time with her. "What are we going to see? Where, and what time?"

The movie Delta chose was a suspense thriller. Any other time, Omega would have been eager to see it. Now, she would rather sit this one out. But only by spending time with her sister and family could she talk to them about Jesus and the safety net of His salvation. In the back of her mind, she wondered about God's plans for Mitchell's mother's salvation.

One thing for sure, Omega planned to visit Caylee and April today, even if it were five minutes. She had yet to invite them to church. There were too many demonic sightings around Caylee.

As expected, Delta enjoyed the thriller, while Omega picked apart the demonic influences on the characters and situations.

The highlight of their outing was seeing their brother with his longtime girlfriend, Tally, entering the mall as the sisters were leaving.

Delta shouted to Randall, and the couple turned around.

Tally smiled and welcomed the sisters' hugs. She was a good fit for their brother. Where he was guarded, she taught him to trust his feelings. The result: they fell in love.

Omega looped her arm through Tally's and pulled her away from Randall.

"Hey," he protested. "She belongs to me."

Tally blew him an air kiss, which he caught with his fist and never took his eyes off her.

"You've got the Big Bad Wolf wrapped around your finger." Delta laughed. "I love it."

"Me too." Tally giggled. Her sultry eyes sparkled, and soft dimples appeared. She was pretty and sweet, and a welcome addition to the family if the couple decided to take their relationship to the next level.

"Did my brother tell you my big news?" Omega doubted he did, but she needed an open door.

"No, O. What I miss?" Tally's excitement matched Omega's.

"I got baptized and spoke in a heavenly language. It was amazing."

"Really?" Tally's brow lifted with interest.

Before Omega could say more, Randall came to Tally's side after Delta waved him over.

"Don't bore my baby with that church stuff." He wrapped his arm around her waist. "Babe, can you believe I just found out she survived the robbery at that gas station last month?" He gave Omega a scolding frown. "I should've been one of the first to know, not the last."

"And I'm just now finding out about it?" Tally gasped and patted her chest. "You weren't hurt, were you?"

"No. That's a long story—"

"That you're not about to tell her anytime soon. We're here so my baby can look for a dress for an affair. She doesn't want to hear about that church stuff, sis."

"But I do." Tally playfully scrunched her nose at Randall.

Omega loved it when Tally put her brother in his place. She couldn't stop grinning.

"O, I want to hear all about it. The robbery. Baptism. Everything. Call me. You have my number, right?"

"You better give it to me again." Omega tapped it in her phone.

Delta and Omega exchanged hugs with Tally and Randall, then the couple linked hands again and went on their way.

"Do you have to tell everybody about Jesus?" Delta said in a hushed tone.

"Yep. As a Christian, I'm supposed to tell people—family, friends, strangers—about Jesus' love and warn them about Satan's game plan to kill them."

"Sis, you are so over the top." Delta rolled her eyes and munched on the remains of the popcorn from the theater. "I guess that means you're not going clubbing with me tonight either. It's been a while."

"Nope. I have one more stop to make before I'm in for the night so I can get ready for church tomorrow."

"Girl, you act like that's a big deal. The highlight of your week." Delta *tsk*ed.

"It is. Things changed for me the night of the shooting, for the better. God has shown me His mercy and second chances."

"You are so no more fun." Delta pouted as they crossed the parking lot to their cars.

"Honestly, I get it, you were scared. I was scared, too, at the thought of losing my sister, but the drastic not-missing-church-thing on Sundays and reading your Bible when I call you, is what I don't get. But I'm sure you'll pray for me." Delta hugged her.

"You know it." Omega parted ways when they spotted their cars.

Omega loved her sister—they were close, unattached, and spent a lot of time together— but Omega was giddy to have dumped her so she could do the Lord's work.

"Will you open it, already?" Caylee pointed at the email from a New York modeling agency in April's inbox.

"I'm nervous." She gritted her teeth.

"Come on, sis. I'm tired and hungry." Caylee stretched her legs before she tucked them under her on the sofa after a thirty-minute bus ride back to their apartment.

Caylee's phone rang, and she recognized Omega's number.

"Hey. I wanted to stop by and see you and April, and I can bring sandwiches."

"Yummy, how fast can you get here?" Caylee laughed, then ended the call. "Omega's on her way over and bringing food."

"Then I'll wait for Omega to get here to open it." April paced the room, too excited to sit.

Caylee admired how graceful her sister moved. It was an art form. People often pegged her as the oldest with her seductive eyes and pouty lips. Caylee wasn't jealous. She was proud.

Twenty minutes later, Omega arrived with sacks of goodies: sandwiches, chips, and drinks.

Although they worked together, the two usually only saw each other in passing. Caylee was determined to show Reba and the others that what she lacked in skills for accounting, she made up for it by being a diligent, thorough, and determined worker. Plus, if she made the cut and was hired on permanently, she would be eligible for tuition reimbursement and Caylee could finish school.

"I'm not going to stay long," Omega said as she washed her hands in the kitchen sink. "I came to invite you to church tomorrow, and I'll even pick you up, so no bus ride."

She joined the sisters at the table and pulled a Penn Station sandwich out of the bag. "I'll say grace."

April smiled. "And while we're praying, we've been waiting on you to open an email. Pray it's good news about a job in New York City."

Omega's expression was unreadable. No mention of 'Let there be good news from New York,' but only God's will for them.

"Yes, Lord, please let this be a life changer for April—us," Caylee chimed in after Omega blessed the food.

"I can't eat. I'm too nervous," April said after one bite. She grabbed her phone.

Caylee and Omega put their sandwiches aside while April clicked on the email. Her face said it all as her eyes moved across the lines.

Caylee's heart pounded. Bad news. She could feel it.

April slumped and twisted her mouth. "They loved my comp picture, but I'm not the face they're looking for now. *Blah...blah...blah.*" She picked at her sandwich. "Maybe we should go to church tomorrow because my prayers aren't being answered."

"Yeah." After the night Caylee had had, she could use some peace herself.

A somber mood settled around them. April bounced back and suggested seeing what was on Netflix. Once fearless, Caylee would watch anything from scary movies to ridiculous comedies.

They weren't ten minutes into the movie when Caylee pointed to the screen. "That thing was in my room last night."

"Huh?" April and Omega said at the same time.

"What thing?" Omega asked first.

"That demon." Caylee scrunched her nose, remembering a figure decomposing but alive and nasty. "It looks like that—bulging eyes, wild hair of thorns or something. It growled as it tried to strangle me in my sleep. I cried for help, but no one came." They looked worse than what she'd seen at the strip club.

April frowned. "I was up late last night and didn't hear you. Now I'm going to have to sleep with the lights on. I think this place is haunted."

"Sorry. I hadn't planned to say anything until I saw whatever that was on the screen. It reminded me of last night. It wasn't human. I called for God to help me. Suddenly, I was released. We're not renewing our lease." Caylee shuddered.

"Well, you're not alone. I had similar demonic beings in my bedroom," Omega said.

What did all this mean? Caylee's eyes widened in fear. "They tried to kill you too?"

Omega had the nerve to grin over this scary stuff. "Nope. I called on Jesus." She snapped her fingers. "They vanished, then I got me some good sleep."

“Caylee, that’s what we need to do. If I move to New York before this lease is up, break the lease and get out of here.” April frowned.

“Or, until then…” Omega paused. She had their attention. “You need the power of the Holy Ghost. Demons flee at the authority of Jesus’ name.”

“You make that sound simple.” Caylee bit her lip, thinking. “I have been tormented recently, and I don’t know why.”

Omega didn’t look surprised at her admission. “I invited a friend to church tomorrow who is getting baptized. Come with us and let the Lord’s will be done in your lives. I’ll pick you up.” She looked hopeful.

Since Caylee had met Omega, good things had happened to her. “When the church doors open, count me and April in.”

All three exchanged a high five. It was a done deal. Satan was going down.

Chapter Thirteen

Put on the whole armor of God so that ye may be able to stand against the devil's wiles. —Ephesians 6:11 KJV

The number of Omega's guests for Sunday morning worship was up to plus four. She did a happy dance. "Thank You, Jesus!"

Her sister called while Omega was getting dressed. She had to allow an extra twenty minutes to get the Prince sisters, so she didn't have time for chitchat. "Give me one reason you can't add church to your Sunday calendar with brunch afterward again."

Delta *hmmmphed.* "I don't want to feel guilty. Okay. We're living…Well now, it's I'm living my life the way *I* want. I don't need to hear that I'm going to hell for that."

"You may hear that God loves you despite that."

Silence.

"Okay. I'll come this once, only because Randall and Tally have something to do today, and I don't do brunch by myself." When Delta paused, Omega started another praise dance, then stopped when Delta added, "If I'm not feeling it, I'm warning you not to ask me again. Church is not my thing."

That last comment hurt. Her sister had no idea of the spiritual sabotage the devil plotted on this earth. As sisters, it wasn't the first time they agreed to disagree, but it never stifled their relationship to do stuff together.

"I've heard people busting out in a song and dance, but praying? For real?" Delta continued her rambling while Omega watched the time.

"I can't help it. When an overwhelming urge hit me to pray for somebody or about something, my Holy Ghost responds." Part of the prayers was for thanksgiving that God didn't reveal any demon activity around her siblings. She had enough to deal with thinking about Caylee, April, and now her coworker Bobby.

"I'm telling you right now," Delta said, "I'm not converting, so don't get your hopes up. Text me the address. I'll see you there. Bye."

Heavenly praises exploded from Omega's mouth. She was surprised she made it to Caylee and April's apartment on time, considering she couldn't stop rejoicing for small victories.

Christ For All Church was on fire—literally. When Omega, Caylee, and April arrived, firefighters were on the scene, responding to a fire in the church's adjacent building.

"I see church is canceled," Delta said as she appeared at Omega's side. "Too bad." Her voice lacked disappointment.

Onlookers stood in the parking lot and watched in dismay.

"The devil is a lie," a congregant shouted from the crowd.

Others murmured the same sentiments.

"We can have an open-air service." Another person voiced his solution.

The members were eager. So were Omega and her guests, aside from Delta. Caylee and April were hungry, too, for the same spiritual victory Omega had.

"Hey, ladies," Mitchell greeted, then leaned closer to Omega. "Does this mean service is canceled?"

"I hope so," Delta mumbled.

Omega shot warning daggers at her sister. Why was she so hostile? "Mitchell, you remember my sister, Delta." He nodded. "And this is Caylee. She recently started working with me at Hathaway Health Management, and her sister, April, is an aspiring model."

He shook hands. Mitchell's facial expression gave nothing away about what Omega had said, about the visions concerning Caylee.

"Praise the Lord, everybody!" Pastor Rodney garnered the crowd's attention with a microphone. "Sorry for the distraction. A fire started in the kitchen after Sunday school but is under control, and the fire marshal has cleared us to go back inside and have worship service in the sanctuary. The other part of the building is off limits until it's restored."

"Praise the Lord!" Cheers erupted around Omega and her guests.

She snickered at Delta who rolled her eyes.

Omega and her guests fell in line with the others. She spotted Mrs. Helena. "There's my neighbor." She pointed and hurried to introduce them.

Like Mitchell, Mrs. Helena's facial expression didn't reveal her knowledge of Caylee and April's fate.

The kitchen fire was extinguished, but God's presence was sizzling in the sanctuary. Although Omega wasn't familiar with all the songs, her spirit connected with the worship. She danced in the aisle along with the others who rejoiced.

"Lord, You drew Caylee and April here today. Please turn their situation around," she said softly.

When the praise team yielded way for the pastor, he maintained the energy that jumpstarted service. "Let's begin with Ephesians six, verse eleven."

Omega's friends read the Scripture from the large monitors while Omega opened her Bible. She liked to scribble notes in the margins and highlight passages that confused her.

"We check the oil in our cars, balance our bank accounts, and schedule annual checkups, but do you check your armor?" Pastor Rodney began his sermon with that question.

"What is he talking about?" Delta whispered while Mitchell, April, and Caylee waited for the explanation.

"My dear friends," the minister continued, "every day when you leave home, dress to slay—and I'm not talking about a fashion statement. The Bible says the devil is the prince of this earth. He influences people to take their lives and kill others. He wreaks havoc, pain, and suffering. The Bible describes him as a crook in John 10:10: *'The thief comes only*—keyword—*his sole purpose is to steal, kill, and destroy*.'"

Omega had experienced that firsthand. She exchanged knowing nods with Mitchell.

"This is creepy." Delta shivered. "I expect a church to be a happy place."

Before Omega could respond to her sister's sarcasm, Pastor Rodney pulled her back in.

"Whether you are at home with family and friends or out running errands or at work, you need to suit up with the armor of God," Pastor Rodney shouted into the microphone, which made Omega's ears pop. "That's the only way we can stand against the cunning tricks of the devil. In verse twelve, it reads, *'For we wrestle not against flesh and blood, but against principalities, against powers, against the rulers of the darkness of this world, against spiritual wickedness in high places.'* High, high places. This is serious."

"See, I saw that darkness once when you were at our place," April leaned over Caylee and whispered.

"How do you dress for spiritual warfare? Your attire…gird your loins with truth—that means to wrap up or bind your sexual desires to protect against lusts because the truth that only comes from God has set you free." He paused and nodded. "Yep, I said it. The lust of sex will get you in trouble, but that's another sermon."

Pastor Rodney cleared his throat and returned to his passage in the Bible. "Next, we're to wear the breastplate of righteousness. On your feet, be ready to take the gospel of peace everywhere you go. For those who like superhero movies, you'll like this one: Take the shield of faith to quench the fiery darts of the wicked. Helmet of salvation and the sword of the Spirit, which is this." He lifted his Bible. "The Word of God."

Swords had kept Omega and Mitchell alive the evening of the shooting. She glanced at him, and he must have thought the same when he gave her a slight nod. Then they shared a smile.

"And lastly, saints, we must pray and submit to the Holy Spirit, and we'll win our battles."

"Whew." Delta nudged Omega. "I'm glad he gave a solution to all this doom and gloom."

"Shhh." Omega bumped her back.

"If you want this power, come. Come to the altar today with repentance in your hearts. Tell God you're sorry and have the ministers pray for you." Pastor Rodney closed his Bible. "Like people who sign up for the military, we all have to sign up to be in the Lord's army. After you repent, ask to be baptized in the name of Jesus to wash away your sins. Some sins are invisible to man, but God sees them all. The same blood that Jesus shed on the cross will wash your soul white as snow. Then our ministers will pray with you to receive God's gift of the Holy Ghost." He raised his arm. "Come on."

"I've been waiting for this part." Mitchell grinned and stood. He walked toward the altar in confident strides. Omega smiled to herself.

April got to her feet. "I'm ready too."

Caylee was hesitant, but after a few moments, she followed her younger sister.

Yes! Relief washed over Omega as she turned to Delta, who didn't budge.

"Ain't happening today, sis." Delta shook her head and folded her arms. "This sermon is deep, but I think I'm cruising through this world okay for now."

Omega couldn't sway her sister to reconsider.

Let them take the water of life freely, God whispered. *Read, my child, Revelation 22:17.*

Soon, the water in the baptism pool stirred as the women candidates donned white gowns and socks while the men changed into white T-shirts and pants. Two by two, they stepped into the water.

Judging by the line of candidates, dozens wanted God's armor. The ministers in the pool didn't seem tired as they baptized each candidate in Jesus' name:

"My dear sister and brother, upon the confession of your faith, and the confidence you have in the blessed Word of God concerning His death, burial, and grand resurrection, I now indeed baptize you in the name of Jesus Christ, for there is no other name under heaven by which we can be saved, for the remission of your sins, and you shall receive the Holy Ghost. Amen!"

Rejoicing intensified throughout the sanctuary with each baptism, even as Delta sat watching. Now that Caylee and April were committed to starting their salvation journey, Omega wondered if this would reverse God's decision about Caylee's life.

Chapter Fourteen

If the Son, therefore, makes you free,
ye shall be free indeed. —John 8:36 KJV

It was a done deal. Mitchell was sealed with salvation as he rejoiced in the water and continued to the dressing room.

Without a doubt, Mitchell saw an angel stirring the water at the same moment God's heavenly language exploded in the pool. He would never question what God showed him in the spiritual realm again. The pain from his shoulder, which had been aching since he woke had dissipated.

Mitchell was at peace and felt carefree as he returned to the sanctuary. He was pleased to see Omega among others who waited for loved ones who were baptized or in the prayer room until God's gift of the Holy Ghost filled them.

Omega stood to greet him with outstretched arms. "You've completed your salvation. Now, we have to do our best to encourage others to come."

He clung to her. "Amen, sister." Mitchell never considered himself a churchgoer, but after today, and surrounded by others who were excited to worship Jesus, he wouldn't miss a Sunday if it could be helped.

"My shoulder was bothering me this morning. Not now." Mitchell rotated his arm to prove it, then glanced around. "Where is your sister?"

"Out of here." Omega thumbed toward the exit. "Too much rejoicing, I guess. I hope the Lord will save my family, friends, and anyone else close to me. According to Mrs. Helena, your mom is on God's radar to save." She mumbled, "But what about mine?"

"She will come." Mitchell squeezed her arm, then realized he had become too touchy, so he stepped back, still amazed at all this. "I can't wait to share this experience with my family. I wonder what assignments God will give them." He scanned the auditorium.

Tilting her head, Omega twisted her mouth. "You know, I never thought about other people having assignments too." She nodded. "That makes me feel better that the pressure isn't only on you and me."

"Us." Mitchell lifted his brow. "We're in this together. Say, where's Caylee and her sister?"

Omega craned her neck. She smiled and pointed. "Here they come now."

Their glow revealed they had experienced what he had—the Holy Ghost. April's hands were lifted as her soul worshipped God. Caylee guided her to a nearby pew to sit where they continued to praise the Lord.

Before long, members gathered around the sisters in praise and dance. They only exited the sanctuary when the lights flickered.

"Let's celebrate. My treat," he said to the ladies.

Omega looked at Caylee and April. They agreed and met at Kobe Steakhouse in Westport Plaza. He learned more about the woman he had protected by listening to the things Omega shared with the sisters. The trio chatted like old friends. Mitchell wondered what God had in store for them.

Their assigned chef at the hibachi steakhouse was engaging as he teased Mitchell about having an entourage of beautiful ladies. They all blushed, including Omega. He learned that

Omega hadn't been in a relationship in more than a year, Caylee wasn't interested as she wanted to focus on herself, and April, with her exotic looks, had a lot of prospects.

"Men want to flatter me but not support my dreams." April jutted her chin. "I guess I'll get married when I'm old like Omega," she teased.

"Hey, just because I'm thirty-four, I'm old enough to be a big sister, not your mother."

Caylee and April double-teamed Mitchell, wanting to know all about him. He obliged and answered their questions. The ladies were impressed that he owned a gym, so he offered them free passes. "No expiration date."

The conversation flipped back to the service in between the cook joking with them at the grill, tossing pieces of chicken, shrimp, and steak to see who could catch them in their mouths without using their hands. Only he and Omega played along while the sisters laughed at them. Omega missed all three times. Mitchell was the winner. He didn't believe in wasting a meal, even if it was a small portion.

"I'm excited that God's in my corner, and I heard some say He will give me my heart's desires." April grinned with a camera-ready smile.

"Delight yourself in the Lord, and He will give you the desires of your heart," the chef said while cleaning his station.

The group stared at him.

Was he a practicing Christian?

"What did you say?" Mitchell squinted.

"Have a good evening." The chef shrugged, gathered his culinary utensils, and left.

"Didn't you hear him say, 'Delight in the Lord?'" Omega was the first to ask.

April and Caylee nodded. "I heard that too," April seconded.

"But he seemed clueless." Omega frowned. "What do you think, Mitchell?"

Considering he had one encounter with an angel, could the chef be another? Before he could give his take, the Lord filled his mouth. *"Be not forgetful to entertain strangers: for thereby some have entertained angels unawares."*

"An angel?" Caylee repeated. "Cool. Finally, a good one."

Mitchell was quiet as he processed what God had spoken through the man and now him. How many angels did God have anyway?

They parted ways not long after Mitchell paid the tab, praising God for what they had experienced and encountered that day.

"Text me when you make it back home, Omega."

"I will."

But she didn't. Thirty minutes later, Mitchell called her. "The cook seemed clueless about what he had said. Do you think the cook was really an angel? He looked human to me…" She rambled off more questions and commentaries, amusing him.

Mitchell stretched out on his sofa with his arm anchoring the back of his head. "I don't think God would have spoken that to me otherwise.. Plus, I found it in Hebrews 13:2 when I searched my Bible app. He didn't disappear like the homeless man I saw, so I don't know."

"That would have been creepy. Wow. I guess angels are among us, and we would never know." Awe was in Omega's voice.

They spoke a few more minutes, then said their goodbyes. When the phone rang again, he answered. What had Omega forgotten to tell him?

"Hi." It was Farrah, his ex, instead.

He should have blocked her number, but that would only encourage her to stop by uninvited. "How are you?"

"Sad and lonely without you. How was your day?"

"The best day of my life. I got baptized!" He couldn't contain his excitement for the Lord.

"Wow. You really did flip. I mean, you've completely gone to the other side. I had no idea that you were that shaken up."

Farrah didn't get it. "The robbery was a wakeup call for me to get my life together."

"*Hmmmph.* What does this mean for us? I said I was sorry I upset you the day we had dinner, but you won't forgive me so we can move past this."

Mitchell didn't hide his frustration, but he tempered it with kindness. "Farrah, there is no us anymore. We're two different people now. I forgave you because Christ forgave me of my sins. I'm not looking to be in a relationship. If I were, she would be a church-goer, Bible-reading, and a praying woman." He waited for her to respond to that.

"That's not me, Mitch. We both enjoyed the sex. Don't you miss it?"

He reflected on the message about the armor of God and containing his lust. "It's not going to happen anymore, Farrah. I don't need or want that from you. Unless you want to go to church and build a spiritual life with Christ, please don't call. I won't answer." There, he said it.

"I'm not desperate for you." She spew a string of profanities and ended the call.

Mitchell pitied her. He prayed longer than usual to experience the spiritual high of the Holy Ghost and for Farrah before he climbed into bed. The presence of the Lord was strong. Without being injured during the robbery, no telling when he would have surrendered to Christ.

The next day, two men approached him as he was about to enter his gym. They were shorter and thin frames—not gym rats—and young, in their late teens. Something about them warned him to be on alert.

"Hey, man, can you give up some spare change?"

Never show your hand when you're outnumbered. He sized them up. Mitchell could take both. When he caught a glimpse of the guns in their waists, he had to rethink that strategy.

Not again, Lord. Shot twice within thirty days—no. Mitchel remained calm. *Okay, what is the plan?* The two seemed to grow impatient.

Give them My Word, God whispered.

Mitchell would rather fight than talk about Jesus now. *Excuse me. I want to interrupt this holdup to tell you about Jesus.* "I think you two need to walk away." Mitchell hoped it was a better response.

Bad miscalculation. They pulled out their guns. "Give us your wallet, phone, and keys," one of them said.

Are you kidding me? I have never been robbed in my thirty-eight years. I give my life to Christ, and I'm about to lose it to thugs?

Do as they demand, God whispered.

Mitchell huffed and began to comply. "No worries because the Lord says vengeance is mine, and He will repay. If you take from me—or anyone—God will take from you—your life, home, or loved ones. Think about that. Jesus died for you not to go to hell, but the devil has reservations in your names."

The shorter one's hand became unsteady with his gun.

Mitchell gave them his truck keys. "Here's my phone. I hope you read the daily Scriptures, and here's my wallet. I hope it will buy baby formula."

"How you know I got a baby?" one asked, and the other shoved him.

"I didn't. God knows. If you shoot me, I forgive you and hope you'll repent before someone kills you."

Their eyes widened, and fear draped their faces. They dropped his items and their guns in haste and took off running. Mitchell relaxed and exhaled. That had been close.

After collecting his things and disabling the guns, he turned around. An angel stood with his sword drawn. "Thank You, Jesus, for sparing my life." Mitchell began to praise God and worshipped Him in heavenly tongues. When he composed himself, the angel was gone. He recalled the sermon from yesterday. The sword of the Spirit is the Word of God.

As he was about to go inside, two police cars pulled up. "Sir, are you okay? That man over there flagged us down."

Mitchell looked in that direction. The same homeless man stood afar off.

It wasn't funny, but Mitchell laughed as the officers took his report. He had thought his bold words had put fear in the two thugs.

No. I sent backup for your protection, God whispered.

Which one? Mitchell wondered if it was the homeless man or the angel with the sword. Didn't matter. God knew what he needed.

Chapter Fifteen

And everyone that hath forsaken houses, or brethren, or sisters, or father, or mother, or wife, or children, or lands, for my name's sake, shall receive a hundredfold and shall inherit everlasting life. —Matthew 19:29 KJV

All was quiet on the spiritual battlefield for the rest of the week for Mitchell. Omega said the same for her and the sisters.

"Yep. My mission has been accomplished. I brought Caylee and April to the Lord. My attention is now on Bobby, but this coworker might be a hard sell."

"We'll pray for each other."

Mitchell looked forward to telling his family in detail about his salvation experience and the angels that protected him when they gathered on Memorial Day.

His heart pumped with anticipation. knowing his mother would accept the Lord's salvation as foretold by Mrs. Helena. Mitchell praised God from his house to their front door.

The aroma of barbecue drew him through his parents' house straight back to the grill on the deck. He shook hands with his dad and kissed his mother and sister-in-law, Patrice, Nathan's wife.

Their son, Justin, gave him a high five and pulled back the sleeve of his T-shirt. "Look, Uncle Mitch, I have muscles."

"They're coming."

Nathan "Nat" and Quinn gave Mitchell hearty pats on his back.

"Nat, watch out for your brother's shoulder. You know he was injured." Marva Franklin scowled at her son.

"This big old hunk. He can handle it." Nat grunted.

"Does it still hurt, Uncle Mitch? Can I see it?" Justin asked.

Rolling up his T-shirt sleeve, Mitchell tried to find the indentation the bullet had caused. "*Hmmm.* I don't see it."

"Nonsense," his mother said, angling his upper body. She scrutinized the front and back, then squeezed his shoulder. "It's gone. That was a deep wound. It's too soon for your surgical scar to have faded as if it was never there." His mother frowned, still perplexed, and examined his shoulder again. "Did you have plastic surgery?"

"Funny, Mom. If you don't see it either, then God did it." Mitchell realized he hadn't experienced the slightest muscle ache in the morning or random sharp pains. He excused himself to the bathroom.

Mitchell locked the door, then pulled his shirt over his head to see for himself. There wasn't a scar. He blinked and jabbed his skin for sensitivity. Flawless. "Jesus, I thank You, I praise You."

His nephew banged on the door. "Uncle Mitch, Grandma says come on so we can eat. I'm hungry."

His worship ended. Mitchell washed his face, tugged his shirt back on, composed himself, and walked out.

Another miracle. He couldn't wait to share this news with Omega.

At the table, his father bowed his head to say grace before his family fixed their plates. "Lord, thank You for the family You've given me. Please bless the food we are about to receive and our service members, in Jesus' name. Amen."

"Amen," Mitchell repeated and grinned.

"Who were you talking to in the bathroom, son?" His father squinted.

"I praised God for healing my shoulder," Mitchell said.

"I can't understand it," his mother said, shaking her head, "I saw the wound and the bandage. It's as if you were never shot."

"Trust me, I was." Mitchell bit off the meat on his rib and chewed. After he swallowed, he told them about the angels, the heavenly tongues they heard him speak from the bathroom, the baptism, everything. He held nothing back.

"I didn't realize God had healed me until now. This is a testimony of God's power. This is a miracle. I hope it's enough for you all to come to Christ too."

"We believe in God. That's enough." David Franklin scooped up a helping of potato salad and slid it into his mouth.

The shocker: His mother agreed with her husband. That wasn't supposed to happen.

Quinn, his younger brother by three years, chuckled. "I see the prankster is back. I don't know how you did it or what they did, but you got us, bro."

"I believe you, Uncle Mitch." Justin's hero worship was unfazed.

Mitchell rubbed his nephew's head. "Thanks, buddy."

The others didn't, and that hurt. His family respected him, and his brothers looked up to him, but this time they thought he was joking.

His mother fanned her hand. "Son, some things in life can't be explained. I'm glad you're into the church, and if you love it, I'm happy for you."

"Thanks, Mom." Her words weren't comforting, and his appetite was waning, but he would get over it. These were the best ribs he'd ever tasted.

In a more somber mood when he returned home, Mitchell wasn't in the mood to text Omega. Confusion plagued him as he walked into his kitchen and slid the plate his mom had fixed into his refrigerator.

What happened? Mrs. Helena said God had said He would save his mother. Mitchell braced his hands on his sink and stared out the window at nothing. Now he wondered if God had healed him. "Nah, that was real." He had felt for the wound himself.

Wasn't that evidence enough for his mother and family to worship God? His younger brother called his healing fake. Mitchell didn't know disappointment could feel this heavy. Sulking for the rest of the night, he couldn't bring himself to read his Bible before climbing into his bed after praying.

The following week, Mitchell noticed his business was slower than usual. Gym visits slacked off during the summer because his members got their exercise through sports and fun activities, but where were his bodybuilders? They didn't skip a beat. So far this week, they were missing. Was this God's punishment for questioning Him?

Mitchell's Good News he shared with his parents had caused them to be at odds over how to respond to him. His father called his salvation unnecessary church theatrics. His mother wanted to know more about his spiritual experience.

It got worse. His brother, Quinn, opted to leave Mitchell out of his plans to hang out at a sports bar. That was their thing—the single brothers spending time together.

"I don't want to be the one to cause you to backslide with the ladies, liquor, and a warm bed in case the urges hit you. That gas station robbery really changed you, and I don't know if it's for the better," Quinn had explained.

"My salvation isn't keeping me from hanging out with you. Who knows, somebody might need to hear about Jesus."

"And there lies the problem. I don't. Got to go." Quinn ended the call seconds later.

Family meant everything to Omega, especially not knowing if they would accept the Lord's salvation. That concerned her.

Would the Lord show her the devil had a mark on their backs before they had a chance to repent?

Her siblings had put some distance between her. Whenever Omega wanted to discuss church, Randall and Delta shut her down. Her brother continued his grudge about Omega withholding the robbery from him, and Delta lost interest in doing some things together.

By mid-June after two other gas station robberies that didn't result in fatalities, Randall forced Omega's hand to tell their parents, so she set up a family Zoom meeting.

The tension was thick with her siblings after she asked to open their meeting with prayer.

Omega's mother, Glenda Addams, was the first to speak. "I'm not against prayer, but did you have to make it that lengthy? So how are my babies?"

Delta groaned. "We're all adults, Mom."

"Who aren't married with *babies*," she reminded them.

Randall cleared his throat. "Omega has something she wants to say." He lifted his brow in a challenge.

Not really, but she took a deep breath. "A few months ago, there was a gas station robbery—"

"I read about that, not far from you, right?" Her father frowned. "I'm glad my baby girl wasn't there."

"But she was, Dad." Randall had no shame to be a tattletale.

Her parents reacted at the same time with questions. "What! Why are we just now hearing about this?" her father demanded.

"I didn't want to worry you." Omega shrugged.

"But she worried me, and I had to get her and bring her home." Delta rolled her eyes.

Wow. Her sister had betrayed her trust.

Omega had done as Delta requested and toned-down sharing church-related topics while silently praying for her sister's salvation.

She muted everyone as they tried to get their point across at once, then she spoke. "This is old news. I'm alive and well. As Delta knows, it took me a while to process what happened. Praise God, I wasn't killed, and my life was spared, thanks to an innocent bystander named Mitchell Franklin. That reason alone is worth us celebrating my life, not death, and me serving the Lord."

Once Omega had her say, she unmuted the others and waited for the first person to speak.

"I pray to God that never happens to you again, or Delta or Randall, but if it does, we want to be the first to know," her mother scolded. "We would have come to the rescue."

Her father's brows were etched together with concern. "I don't like it you were in harm's way. Although we enjoy the Texas weather, we'll move back to St. Louis in a heartbeat." Eric Addams didn't bluff.

"No," Omega and her siblings answered in a harmonious chorus.

Before the Zoom meeting ended, Omega asked her siblings to stay on after their parents left.

"Dell, church isn't for you—now. I respect that, sis." Omega tried to be as gentle with her tone as possible, "but as you saw firsthand, the night of the robbery, I was in shock—"

"A hot mess," Delta countered.

"That, too, and it changed my life. I'm eager to learn more about the activities at Christ For All Church to strengthen my faith, so there may be times we have to reschedule our get-togethers not only on Sundays, but throughout the week." She paused and prayed for understanding. "Work with me on this, sis."

Delta twisted her mouth as she gave some thought to what Omega said. "Okay. I forgive you, but heads-up, I don't want Caylee and April always tagging along with us. They should have their own life."

Yeah, and for Caylee, those days were numbered. “Understood. Bye, sis. Love you.”

That left Randall. They engaged in a stare-down before he spoke. “Don’t keep me out of the loop when something like that ever happens again. Let me be a big brother.” His feelings were crushed.

“I’m sorry. I am, but you’re known to go overboard with the big brother bear act.”

“And that’s a problem? You’re my baby sister—”

“No, Delta is.”

“Same thing—younger. Until Pop and I hand over the protection torch to your husband for safe-keeping, we’re your bodyguards.”

How many times had she heard the bodyguard declaration? *Lord, please don’t let me marry a man like my brother.*

Done.

Omega smirked. She didn’t expect God to answer.

“Oh, one more thing. Tally’s going to call you for lunch one day this week. Do not talk to her about Jesus, speaking in tongues, or anything. Repeat—do not. Do we have an understanding?”

His threatening expression didn’t work on her. Like their father, Randall didn’t bluff much, but Omega had a stubborn streak too. “Understood.”

When they ended the meeting, she praised God that He wouldn’t let her fall for a man like her brother.

Chapter Sixteen

Watch out! Be on your guard against all kinds of greed; life does not consist in an abundance of possessions... You fool! This very night your life will be demanded from you. —Luke 12:15–20 KJV

Omega couldn't believe it. Bobby Turman had no shame in forming a planning committee from Hathaway Health employees to help make his twenty-fifth party a celebration for the history books, and he was willing to spend a lot of money to make that happen.

Lord, help me to reach him.

Later that morning, Bobby was in the breakroom when Omega strolled in for bottled water out of the fridge. "Hey, you. How's it going?"

"What's up, O. Good." He grinned, bobbing his head. "Finalizing the details for my big, big part-tee next month. You comin', right?"

No way. "I've got an invitation for you too. The church I attend has its annual family and friends' day this coming Sunday. Be *my* guest."

"Yolanda's gone, and..." Bobby twisted his lips as if there was a bad taste in his mouth. "Now you've done gone religious on me."

"Is that a yes?" Omega half-joked to play along.

"It's a naw, not now. Just like you don't want to help me celebrate a quarter of a century, why should I go to church with you?" He folded his arms in a challenge.

"Because God gave us a warning the day Yolanda died. Are you going to ignore that vision?"

He gathered his snacks and stood. "I don't know what I saw. It could have been something in the air vents that caused hallucinations. It didn't scare me. You don't know what you're missing. I think everybody is going, O, but you."

"Everybody? Caylee?" Her friend had surrendered her life to Christ, so what fellowship did light have with darkness? She read that passage in 2 Corinthians 6:14.

"Yep." He walked out, adding an extra dose of swag. "It's going to be big, big, big."

Omega rubbed her forehead. *God, why can't I get through to him?*

Unless something changed, Bobby's twenty-fifth birthday party could be his final one.

Her heart broke as she returned to her office. She was in a somber mood until she got a call from Tally, Randall's girlfriend, which lifted her spirits.

The Addams family liked her and hoped she and Randall would marry.

"Hey, O. I'm close to your office today. Are you free for lunch?"

Omega checked her calendar. She had a meeting this afternoon but was free now. Omega could use some fresh air after butting heads with Bobby. "Yep. I could use a break."

Tally named the place and time, and the two chatted for a few more minutes. "See you then."

Dynasty was a tea shop near Hathaway Health. She and Delta had attended a bridal shower there years earlier. The decor was dainty and very feminine, like Tally herself. She had an engaging smile. Her Pixie hairstyle was to be envied by any woman, regardless of their hair length.

Like sisters, the two exchanged warmed hugs, then picked a table that gave them a magnificent view of a patio garden.

"What brings you downtown?" Omega asked.

She leaned across the table. Her hazel-colored eyes were bright. "I had some business to take care of, but honestly, I could have taken care of it online, but I wanted us to talk in private."

Uh-oh. Something is wrong. Omega sucked in her breath. No demon sightings, so that was a good thing.

"Last month, when Randall and I ran into you and Delta at the mall, you mentioned a salvation journey. When I asked Randall about it, he brushed it off and said the shooting he didn't know about put the fear of God in you."

She paused when the server placed their menus on the table and gave them the lunch special.

"I'll take the strawberry poppy seed pecan salad. Yummy." Tally's eyes sparkled.

"Me too."

The server disappeared, and Tally patted her hands on the table. "I want to hear about your experience with Jesus."

Omega grinned. She was happy to testify about the Lord.

You promised your brother not to bring up Jesus with his girlfriend, a tiny voice reminded her.

Better to obey God than man, a louder voice edged her on.

Plus, it wasn't a promise. Omega had said, she understood. "Randall will get mad at me for sure."

Tally waved her hand. "He doesn't scare me with his roar, and I know you're too strong-willed to care." She winked, and the two giggled.

"Right. Mitchell, whom I didn't know at the time, shielded me from a bullet. We both hit the ground, and as I lay there helpless from Mitchell's weight, I thought I saw two angels shielding Mitchell and me from the bullets the gunman aimed at us." Omega told her about Yolanda and other things, leaving Caylee and Bobby out of the conversation since they were still missions in progress.

When Omega finished, they both were surprised to see their salads on the table and the ice melting in their glasses.

Tally's lips formed an "O" before she said, "Wow."

Omega said grace, and they preceded to munch on their salads.

"Then I guess what I experienced isn't crazy," Tally mumbled more to herself than Omega.

"What do you mean?"

"A few months ago, I spent the night at Randall's, and I woke up in the middle of the night screaming and crying." Tally exhaled as if she had taken a puff of a cigarette. "I saw myself standing on the planet Earth. Fire raged all around me. There was no escape. I was about to be burnt alive. I was so scared."

"Oh no." Omega sucked in her breath. She could imagine how real that must have felt.

"I woke Randall. He wrapped his arms around me and whispered repeatedly that I was safe. That quieted me, so he thought I fell back to sleep. But I couldn't, not after what seemed so real to me. I knew that night I wanted to be saved from Hell."

Omega didn't interrupt.

Tally continued, "Since then, I haven't slept with your brother again. He thinks it's something he did and..." She smiled. "He's been trying to do little things to make me happy. But none of that stuff does it for me anymore. I want a balanced life with the Lord."

"I don't think my brother is ready for a Jesus commitment."

"I know." Tally anchored her elbows on the table and rested her chin. She stared at the remains of her salad.

"What are you going to do?" Omega was hopeful her sister-in-law-to-be was ready to surrender to Christ. Her lips curled upward.

"I'm breaking up with him." Tears filled her eyes.

Omega's smile vanished as her jaw dropped. Randall was going to kill Omega because he loved him some Tally Gilbert. She handed Tally some tissues from her purse and waited as Tally blew her nose.

More composed, Tally straightened her shoulders. "And I want you to show me the way to Christ. Nightmare or not, I felt the heat from those flames."

Omega practiced her breathing exercises as she would need them to shield herself from a headache that was sure to come from her brother. "Perfect timing. Sunday is family and friends' day at the church I'm attending. You can be my guest."

Tally's smile brightened her face, erasing the worry wrinkles that had appeared earlier.

"I can't wait!" They discussed Scriptures about heavenly languages and the gifts of the Holy Ghost.

Tally never mentioned Randall's name again. Had she already severed ties? Omega would find out soon enough.

God is faithful, even when men aren't. That Bible truth held Mitchell together as he saw his clientele decline.

Mitchell prayed. He joined a men's prayer group at church because he loved hearing God speak through him. Omega was praying for him, too, so why was his successful business failing?

With a handful of members in his gym, Mitchell used the slow day to make phone calls to patrons, most of which defaulted to voicemails. Next, he updated his email list to send out a newsletter.

Some of his female patrons had their memberships on pause or canceled them. They didn't feel safe because of increased robberies and assaults in the area. Great. He thought back to the day he was almost robbed. Security was an option if it would lure them back. Mitchell would have to crunch the numbers for the additional cost to his payroll.

For the men, it was all about their vehicle safety after a rash of car break-ins. Both setbacks were beyond his control. King and Queen Fitness was a facility in a good neighborhood. He liked his location. These pop-up crimes could happen anywhere, even in broad daylight.

He consulted with Pastor Rodney. "I don't understand. I'm a child of the King. Blessings are supposed to follow me. I did everything according to the Scriptures, but my livelihood isn't prospering."

"Brother Mitchell, this is part of the journey. In James one, verses three and four: *'Knowing that the trying of your faith works patience. But let patience have her perfect work, that ye may be perfect and whole, wanting nothing.'* Your faith in God is being tested. The devil can't touch your life, so he's going after your possessions. Remember, God can recover whatever the devil steals and more. Be faithful and trust God to send the people to your business."

Mitchell nodded Amen with a tear in his eye that he refused to let fall. After the phone call, Mitchell grabbed his Bible to take to the front counter while he babysat his spacious facility. During this time of day, he usually had thirty-plus in his gym. Today, there were between twelve and fifteen—he might have counted a few twice.

As a licensed physical therapist, Mitchell had made good money. He was set for life with a career he enjoyed until this opportunity offered him another avenue to help others keep a healthy body while he enjoyed Black ownership.

Mitchell paid into the franchise. At first, he worked part-time while building his business. His father loaned him the money as a down payment on the building and renovations. The business had boomed, and Mitchell had been able to pay him back earlier than expected. When he said goodbye to his fellow therapists, Mitchell never thought he would look back with regret.

Until now.

Now his clientele was half of what it was at the peak.

The trying of my faith works patience, Mitchell repeated over and over. He needed to make calls, update his website, and send emails. He couldn't even read his Bible without distraction.

“Bye, Mitch,” a longtime patron, Sallie Cole, called out and waved as she was about to leave.

Mitchell hadn’t realized how long he had been reading the same passage in his Bible until he glanced up.

Stop her, God whispered when Sallie was almost out the door. *Say these words to her.*

“Sallie, instead of going straight home, stop at the store.” Mitchell was clueless as to what to say next. “They might have some specials, or you’ll see something you need...” he rambled.

She squinted at him with a bewildered expression. “O-okay. If you say so, Mitch. See you tomorrow.” She walked away, then gave him a backward glance.

Mitchell rubbed his forehead. It would help if the Lord would give him a heads-up.

I am God, and God alone. I am not subject to man’s will, but they are to Mine, was loud as thunder, but no one else could hear.

Chastened, he repented and would never question God again when he heard His voice.

Later that night at home, Mitchell watched a video of a fire that gutted an apartment building on the local news. He said a prayer for the families impacted before getting ready for bed.

The next day, Sallie hurried into the gym. She raced to the counter where Mitchell had seconds earlier ended a call. She babbled until tears flooded her eyes. “Mitch, my life was spared. My daughter and I…stopped by the store as you told me to check out the bargains. There weren’t any…We lost everything when our apartment caught on fire, but we’re alive.”

Sallie broke down, and he came from behind the counter and comforted her while she outwardly praised God. This was why the Lord had Mitch stop her. The building he saw on the news was charred.

She sniffed and wiped her eyes before looking up at him. “There was a gas leak, and the building where we live caught fire. How did you know for me not to go straight home?" Her eyes searched his.

"I didn't." Mitchell shook his head. "I said what God told me—well, except for the last part about the bargains."

"It doesn't matter." Sallie, a petite woman, hugged him with all her strength. "You're a hero."

He chuckled. She sounded so much like Omega. He missed talking to her, but again, he couldn't take the credit. "No. God is." Mitchell proceeded to tell her about Jesus' goodness and salvation. "He's already proven that He loves you. Surrender to the Lord and seek Him while you have this opportunity."

"You're right." Sallie's eyes were bright. "I will. I will." She exhaled, then hurried toward the bike area, telling the handful of gym patrons who would listen about what happened to her. Sallie was so animated that she couldn't stand still.

Behind closed doors, Mitchell worshipped the Lord for His unmatched power and love for Sallie. He was humbled for obeying the Lord when it didn't make sense.

He hid in his office for as long as he could to worship God in the spiritual realm. His soul worshipped the Lord. He was amazed that the miracles from the Bible came alive. As he composed himself to return to the front counter, God spoke.

Your work isn't done. There are many more. The harvest is plentiful. You must be a laborer for Me.

Mitchell nodded. Outside his office, he spied a few on the treadmills. Sallie was on her bike of choice in an intense discussion with some other gym friends. Looking over her shoulder, she pointed at Mitchell. The other ladies turned his way, grinning and waving.

Lord, let You get the glory out of this, not me, Mitchell prayed.

Omega came to mind again. He couldn't wait to give her an update about what was going on with him. He grabbed his phone. Instead of calling, he texted in case she was in a meeting.

How about dinner tonight? I have news to share with you and Mrs. Helena! Mitchell added happy face emojis.

Me too, but the devil is busy. I'll explain later. See you at 7, she texted back.

Chapter Seventeen

For whosoever will save his life shall lose it: and whosoever will lose his life for my sake shall find it. —Matthew 16:25 KJV

That evening, Omega paced the foyer in her condo, waiting for Mitchell to arrive. Her emotions were a mix of chaos: happy, scared, and sad.

Omega was glad when Mitchell wanted to catch up over dinner. She could use the company of someone who understood what she was facing.

Mitchell parked his truck in her driveway. When he stepped out, a bouquet was in his hand. That made her smile. Mrs. Helena would love the flowers.

She opened the door before he rang the bell. Mitchell pulled her into a hug before she could speak. His surprise gesture calmed her nerves.

When Omega stepped back, she blushed. "Didn't realize I needed that." She hugged herself to recapture the warmth his embrace had brought her. She grabbed her keys and was ready. "We'll go to Mrs. Helena's first, then come back here for dinner…oh, and you're going to spoil her bringing her flowers."

A slight frown crossed his face. "These are for you."

"Me?" Omega patted her chest in surprise. "Why?"

He folded his thick arms. "Number one, you're supposed to say thank you. Number two, I didn't hear your voice, but your text shouted you needed pampering."

Omega was speechless, then stuttered, "Thank you. Let me get a vase. Have a seat."

He trailed her. "What?" Mitchell gave her a clueless expression. "I'm having a seat in your kitchen."

His goofiness made them both laugh.

"God knows I needed to laugh too." Omega admired the flowers as she filled a crystal vase she had never used with water, then added the flowers. She arranged them as if she were tending to a garden. "They're beautiful," she whispered.

Mitchell anchored his elbows on her counter and rested his chin on his fists. He studied her with an intense expression. "Was it that bad?"

His concern was touching. "Walk with me, and I'll tell you."

She punched in the alarm code while he waited on her porch, then they left. "It was a great day. It's the fallout that worries me."

Mitchell took her hand and squeezed. "We're in this together." He didn't let her hand go, and Omega didn't try to shake it free. His presence and understanding made her feel that she wasn't alone in this assignment. What about when he wasn't available? Maybe, if she joined some groups at church, she would have other saints to share her burden. Until then, this was nice to have Mitchell's concern and encouragement.

Mrs. Helena found their hands still connected when she opened her door. He squeezed her fingers before he released them. As soon as Omega stepped inside, a delicious aroma made her stomach growl. She had prepared pasta, garlic bread, and a salad, but it didn't compare to whatever Mrs. Helena had whipped up. "Something smells good."

"It sure does." Mitchell patted his flat stomach.

"You're both in time to eat. The gumbo is ready."

"I can almost taste the spices." Omega's mouth watered. "But I'd already cooked."

"Then you'll have leftovers." Mrs. Helena's smug look dared them not to accept.

Neither Omega nor Mitchell put up much fuss as they washed their hands and sat at the table. Minutes later, the blessings were said, then the trio helped themselves.

"Omega, what has your spirit so troubled?" Mrs. Helena asked, adding another side dish to the table—three-cheese cornbread.

"Well…" she said, dabbing the corners of her mouth, "I invited Bobby from work to family and friends' day on Sunday. He turned me down. That was a bummer. The pick-me-up is my brother's girlfriend invited me to lunch because she wanted to hear about my salvation experience. She wants to be saved and is coming to church this Sunday."

"Praise God," Mrs. Helena said.

"Hallelujah," Mitchell added.

Omega bobbed her head. "Yes, I thank God for that… Has God shown you any of my family coming to Christ?" She gave Mrs. Helena a hopeful expression. "Tally is going to break up with my brother because she wants a balanced life with Christ. Randall wants nothing to do with church and something tells me he'll blame me for her decision."

She shook her head at the absurdity of that accusation. "As a matter of fact, he didn't want me to talk about Jesus at all. He'll go ballistic because he loves her. My family will ex-communicate me too. We all have been waiting for her to be a part of the family. Why is this so hard? We have free will, yet nobody respects it."

Mitchell squeezed her hand. Mrs. Helena patted both of theirs with hers.

"You'll make enemies winning souls for Christ. Sometimes they come in the form of family and friends. I know it hurts to think of it that way, but it might not be as bad as you think. Tally could draw your brother to Christ if he loves her that much."

"I never thought of that." Omega perked up. "She could be my reinforcement."

"Exactly." Mitchell grinned. "I got news too. God used me to spare my patron's life."

Omega listened as Mitchell talked about his business declining. That had him down, then a woman named Sallie listened to the voice of God through Mitchell.

They ended the night at Mrs. Helena's house praying, praising, and reading their Bibles.

On Sunday morning, the pews were packed at Christ For All Church. Pastor Rodney called another annual family and friends' day a success.

Omega had saved a seat for Tally on the row with Mitchell, Caylee, and April. Tally seemed to soak up the environment.

"I feel at home, O, for the first time in a while." Tally bumped Omega, and the two clapped with those around them.

Once the singers quieted, Pastor Rodney returned to the pulpit with his Bible. "Family and friends, you are here today because someone loves you. You accepted because your soul wants to taste and see that the Lord is good. Before I get to my text, I want to ask you a question: What's stopping you from joining the Lord's side? Whatever your reason, my next question is, is it worth your soul?"

"No," Tally leaned over and whispered. "Nothing!"

The pastor continued, "My congregation knows I teach them a balanced life in this world with Christ..."

"A balanced life," Tally whispered and mouthed to Omega, "See."

"You have to take all the good Christ has for you and all the blows the devil tries to get it back. Second Timothy three and verse twelve says, *all that will live godly in Christ Jesus shall suffer persecution.* But guess what?" The excitement rose in Pastor Rodney's voice. "In Revelation twenty-two, verse twelve, God says, *And behold, I come quickly, and my reward is with me, to give every man according as his work shall be. I am Alpha and Omega, the beginning and the end, the first and the last. Ooo-weee…*" Pastor rejoiced before he could announce the altar call.

It was as if visitors knew it was their time as they rushed to the altar to be saved. Tally was among them.

Chapter Eighteen

When I say unto the wicked, Thou shalt surely die; and thou gives him not warning, nor speaks to warn the wicked from his wicked way, to save his life; the same wicked man shall die in his iniquity, but his blood will I require at thine hand. —Ezekiel 3:18 KJV

Omega's life had never been so complicated. Before the gas station robbery, she was carefree with her sister, unaware that danger lurked in the shadows on that April evening.

Now, she braced for Tally to follow through with her determination to break up with her brother. It had been two weeks, and all was quiet in the Randall Addams camp.

Whenever she spoke to Tally to talk about the Scriptures or how things were going, Omega kept Randall's name out of the conversation and focused on encouraging Tally in her new relationship with Jesus.

"She needs you more than you realize, Omega," Mrs. Helena admonished her more than once, referring to the passage in Luke, chapter thirteen that was described as the Parable of the Sower. "Pray and intercede on her behalf. Her spiritual seed must take root in God's Word. The devil is ready to steal it from her. Don't let it happen."

At her desk, between making business calls, Omega grabbed her phone out of her purse and scanned the prayer list she had stored in her Notes app: parents, sister, brother, Tally, Caylee,

April, Bobby, Mitchell and his family, the man at the dry cleaners, the homeless lady sitting outside the dollar store, and more.

She assessed those on her list. Caylee had thrived at Hathaway Health, and by the end of the month, she would complete her probation period and receive a raise.

April was a spitfire for God, unshakeable in building her faith to believe God would give her that modeling career in New York. She was clueless that her blessing would release the Death Angel, and Omega had no idea how to steer her away from that dream. "God, in the name of Jesus, please redirect April's focus." It was the same plea Omega had said throughout the day and night before bed for months.

Bobby was next on her prayer hit list when she overheard him talking near her office on his cell. "Yeah, Mr. Sly. I'm Bobby Truman, and my coworker, Zach, referred me to you after my deejay backed out for my birthday celebration. He says you're a radio performer, which I guess is similar to a deejay.."

It was as if Bobby's birthday bash was an unofficial company holiday.

She had begun to add fasting to her prayers for God to intervene. "Lord Jesus, cancel out the devil's plans for Bobby's soul. Satan, I rebuke you in the name of Jesus to release your hold."

Omega pushed pause on her petitions to God. She turned around as Bobby stuck his head in her doorway. "Hey, O."

"What's up, Bobby?" Omega wouldn't have minded if her coworker overheard her praying for him.

"In case you change your mind and don't wait until the midnight hour to decide to come, you'll have more time to RSVP because I had to change the date for my birthday extravaganza."

Yes! Omega sat straighter. "Is something wrong? Party planning has a lot of moving parts, and it's expensive. I'm sure you can throw down at thirty. I like the sound of that better. Thirty close friends..."

Bobby gave her a side-eye. "What? I'm not cancelling nothin'. I said change, not cancel."

Wishful thinking. She sighed.

"Instead of Fourth of July weekend, I'm pushing it back to the following Saturday." He grinned and rolled back on his heels as if he had accomplished an insurmountable feat.

"Oh." Omega waved Bobby inside. "Close the door." Once he was settled in the chair facing her desk, she asked him again about the vision of Yolanda.

He threw his arms in the air. "Why are you stuck on that? Okay, it spooked me, but that's all. I'm over it. I've got more important things going on in life than freaking out over a dead person."

"What about what she said, warning us to get our lives together with Christ?"

"What's not together? I'm a good person, treat folks right, and" he said, lifting a finger, "I've upgraded my association of friends, so I'm not running with the wrong crowd anymore." Bobby frowned. "Why you hatin' on my party?"

She gritted her teeth and searched for the right words. "I don't call it hatin'. When alcohol is involved, fights break out, and weapons could be packed. If the vision of Yolanda didn't spook you, it spooked me for you. Cancel the party. I know that's asking a lot, but I'll reimburse you." What was she saying? Desperation was talking if she practically begged him to call her bluff and drain her savings. His soul was worth it.

He stood. "You act like I'm going to die or something."

"Or something. Let's suppose tomorrow is our last day on earth. Wouldn't you want to make sure your slate is clean with the Lord?"

Bobby chuckled. "I'd make sure I celebrate, so I don't feel it coming. Gee, O, you're a party crasher without showing up at my gig. My guests are classy. If it will make you feel better, I'll have security. Happy now?"

"Not at all." She punctuated each word as he walked out of her office.

That night, instead of Omega calling Mitchell, he called her minutes after she walked through the door. "Hey, prayer partner. I haven't talked to you in days. Everything okay?"

She sighed. "I'm still on the battlefield, and I'm not gaining ground with Bobby on my job. I hinted the best I could that his party might be the death of him. I think if I had said God is coming after his soul, he would've laughed."

"People are desensitized to Jesus and death. The devil has done an excellent job of keeping people blindfolded with their eyes open." Mitchell huffed. "But hey, I have some encouraging news."

"I'm listening, tell me." Excited, Omega giggled while she changed out of her clothes.

"Remember Sallie, the one the Lord had me divert to a grocery store before going home?"

"Yeah." She walked into her bathroom and began removing her makeup.

"Sallie's been spreading the word about what Jesus did for her through me. Some patrons have asked for prayer, and I've been able to tell them about Jesus. It's like a chain. I pray for one person; they tell someone else, then more come." He paused. "I need this spiritual boost because my business is down."

"I'll bump you up on my prayer list."

"That's not necessary. We know God will take care of us," Mitchell said in a less-than-convincing voice. "We'll pray for each other. See you this weekend?"

Omega smiled. "I look forward to it." She yawned, and they said their good nights.

Minutes later, she answered another call. Randall was angry. "Tally broke up with me tonight with an ultimatum after attending your church—"

Good for her! Omega silently cheered, then braced for her brother's wrath.

"She said for me to get my life right with Jesus, or there's no future for us." Omega imagined his nostrils flared as he continued, "I warned you, O, not to talk to her about Jesus or any church stuff. We were fine the way we were. But no, you went behind my back and had lunch with her. Yeah, she told me, and you invited her to church anyway. Now, I've lost the only woman I love and my favorite sister. We're done."

Favorite sister and *done* caused Omega's heart to break as she sat motionless on her bedroom chaise. Randall had never called her his favorite sister. Both were headstrong, but never had a disagreement where one hung up on the other, even growing up. This wasn't good. The fallout had begun. The only people in her corner were Mrs. Helena, Mitchell, the Prince sisters, and now Tally.

If I'm for you then no man can be against you, Jesus whispered.

Closing her eyes, Omega shook her head. "Lord, please fight this battle head-on. Please."

Sunday mornings were Mitchell's favorite day of the week. Church, sermon, music, and the crew, which now included Tally. She was a sweetheart, and Mitchell hoped Omega's brother got his act together and surrendered to the Lord. Some of the brothers had already been eying her.

Mitchell gave them a look, and they backed off. He chuckled to himself. Sallie, a couple of other gym patrons, and some of her friends were now attending his church. Like Omega, he had a yearning for his folks to surrender to Jesus.

For weeks, his family steered away from any conversation they thought Mitchell could spin to include Jesus.

Marva Franklin stated, "I'm coming this Sunday to ensure my son isn't mixed up in a cult." There wasn't a hint of a smile when she said it.

So now, he rubbed his hands as he waited. One last glance at the sanctuary door made his heart skip a few beats.

His mother was there.

Alone.

Mitchell bit back his disappointment.

Meeting her halfway, Mitchell hugged his mother as if he hadn't seen her in years instead of a couple of days ago. He led her to his pew, and his crew made room for her as the singers finished their last song.

"Can you feel it?" was the first thing Pastor Rodney said as the praise team yielded him the remainder of the service. "I know I'm supposed to say good morning and welcome and all the preliminaries, but first, I ask one more time, can you feel it? The presence of the Lord is here!"

He pounded his fist on the podium, which seemed to detonate an explosion of Holy Ghost power. Mitchell leaped to his feet along with many others and lifted his hands to worship God for his mother being there.

Mitchell humbled himself before the Lord as he uttered things for the Lord's ears only. Tears trinkled down his cheeks unchecked when he sat.

His mother rubbed his back.

"Son, are you okay?"

He opened his eyes to see her worried expression.

"Yeah, Mom. God's presence is real. There's no way you could not feel His power." He wiped the tears from his eyes with a tissue Omega handed him.

It was a bit embarrassing—a big man crying with his mother trying to soothe him—but Mitchell wasn't alone as other men submitted to the Lord. Even the pastor wiped his eyes.

Omega's eyes were watery too. "You better be glad I had an extra tissue."

He nudged her shoulder, and they shared a smile.

"*Awww*. Isn't a praise break refreshing?" Pastor Rodney gathered the congregation's attention.

"Yeah," many shouted back.

"Whew! Now, visitors, welcome to Christ For All Church. We aren't ashamed of the gospel of Jesus Christ because it is the power of God for our salvation, but only to those who believe. Jews, Muslims, Christians…"

"Son," his mother said, leaning into him, "who's your friend?"

Her question interrupted his focus on the service. "Oh, Omega. I'll introduce you after service."

"Omega? The woman you saved in the gas station robbery?" Her eyes widened in recognition.

Clearly, his mother was more interested in gossip than in the gospel.

"And you're both here together in the same church. Interesting." Marva wasn't discreet about her scrutiny. "She's pretty."

Mitchell cleared his throat. "She can hear you, Mom."

"Tell her thank you." Omega giggled as Pastor Rodney opened his Bible. "Question: Why did you come to church today?"

Shouts mingled throughout the sanctuary, but Sallie's response was most audible. "To get saved."

Those around them applauded and yelled, "Hallelujah."

"I hear some good answers. At some point, we come because we're stressed, depressed, and sick—mentally, spiritually, and physically. The gospel is called the Good News because God has whatever we need. In the Book of Matthew, chapter eleven, verses twenty-eight through thirty, Jesus tells us to *'Come unto me, all ye that labor and who are heavy burdened, and I will give you rest. Take my yoke upon you and learn of me; for I am meek and lowly in heart: and you shall find rest unto your souls. For my yoke is easy, and my burden is light.'* The last part is the most important to remember. The Apostle Paul said that the sufferings in this world can't be compared to the glory which shall be revealed in us."

Pastor Rodney's message was simple. It was better to walk with Christ than with the world. Forty minutes later, Sallie and her crew had repented and were about to be baptized in water as Mitchell's mother looked on and asked many questions.

He was hopeful that this was the day that it would come to pass for his mother's salvation. Instead, she grabbed her purse and told her son she would give his father a good report. "I'll visit again." She smiled. "Will Omega be here?"

"Yes, Mrs. Franklin," Omega answered with a blush.

Hiding his disappointment, Mitchell walked his mother to her car. He had hoped she would ask about the message. Instead, she wanted to know how close he and Omega were. Were they dating? And more.

"No, Mom. We're friends." Mitchell huffed and slipped his hands into his pants pockets.

She stopped in her tracks and stared at him. "Then something is wrong with you. Do you think God had you save her for no reason? Open your eyes and see your gift."

Dumbfounded, Mitchell said nothing as he opened his mother's door.

"I am glad I came, son. That shooting really affected both of you. I'm glad she's here with you." She started her engine and drove off.

Mitchell groaned out his frustration. His mother completely missed the point. Why wait for something bad to happen to surrender to the Lord like in his and Omega's case? Like the Lord, Mitchell wanted his parents and family to come freely. With mixed emotions, he strolled back inside the church.

Chapter Nineteen

Then Agrippa said unto Paul, Almost thou persuade me to be a Christian. —Acts 26:27 KJV

Omega and Tally waited at the Kingside Diner in the Central West End for Delta to show up for brunch. This would be the first Sunday brunch with her sister since Omega started attending church.

Only Tally knew how to pull the sisters together because they loved her as their own. She was a year older than Omega. "There she is." Tally smiled and waved Delta to their booth.

Delta strutted their way as if she were working a runway like April. She grinned at Tally and squinted at Omega.

The enemy was written on her face.

"She hates me," Omega mumbled.

"No. She's a little sister who has the upper hand on ya right now." Tally reassured her that everything would work out.

"Hey." Delta hugged Tally. "I'm so glad you dumped my brother. You can do better."

"You traitor." Tally scooted over as Delta bumped her into the seat. "I love your brother, and you know it. This is not about bad-mouthing my boyfriend—or ex. I have to get used to saying that." Her expression was mournful, but she bounced back. "I happen to love my soul more."

Omega nodded and squeezed Tally's soft hands, which were smooth and always freshly manicured, courtesy of her brother, who loved to pamper his woman.

Their waiter approached the table, introduced himself, flirted, then rambled off the buffet and brunch specials. Tally ordered chicken and waffles. Omega and Delta shared a secret smile when they both ordered St. Louis cheesy spinach omelets.

"So, my dear sister brainwashed you, huh?" Delta cut her eyes at Omega as if she were a little girl instead of a grown professional woman. Omega also glimpsed Delta's sadness because Tally's lifestyle change didn't include Randall.

As far as Omega's family was concerned, she was the bad person for sharing the Good News about being freed from the yoke of sin. The more Tally tried to draw Omega into the conversations about travel, work, and lessons learned from her relationship with Randall, Delta would cut Omega off.

Wounded, Omega held her peace. She was content to spend overdue time with her sister.

"Granted, I was there the night my sister was in shock from the robbery, and I can almost understand her wanting nobody but Jesus." Delta gave her a sympathetic look, then turned back to Tally and shook her head. "You, I don't understand. You've got everything going for you. My brother loves you. He looks pitiful. Mom and Dad said he's drinking, and Randall can't hold his liquor."

A tear fell from Omega's eye as Tally began to sob. "I love him so much, and I'm sorry I hurt him." She sniffed. "But liquor is a temporary coping skill. He needs to run to Jesus. I want us together because you know I love me some Randall Addams, but I had to make some choices that included the well-being of my soul."

"*Hmmmph*. I'm sure some of them hussies will try to snatch him up." Delta frowned.

While Delta gave Tally something to consider, Omega silently prayed. She was sure the lure to fall back into the same lifestyle with Randall was tempting, but Omega would stay in the prayer gap until her brother surrendered.

When Tally sobered, she gave Delta a pointed look. "This is not a kiss-and-makeup breakup. I know what I saw and experienced while I slept next to Randall. I can't erase that. I tried to convince your brother to read the Bible or come to church with us. When we both said, 'I love you' before we ended the call, I wanted us to pray. He told me, 'Don't bother,' and hung up. That hurt, but I know I did the right thing."

"You did." Omega offered an encouraging smile.

"I'm not so sure," Delta countered with a warning look.

That evening before bedtime, Mitchell texted Omega a quote for inspiration: **Be strong in the Lord and in the power of His might (Ephesians 6:10).**

How did he know she needed that? She had called him, and they prayed together.

Monday morning, Omega woke refreshed and well-rested. She waved at her neighbor as Mrs. Helena yelled, "God bless you, Omega! It's a good day."

"I hope so. I need it."

The brunch with the ladies the previous day had Omega still raw with emotions. Delta felt betrayed by Tally's decision to leave her brother under Omega's religious influence.

Mid-morning, Mitchell called as she sat in her office. It had become a habit when he had downtime at the gym. "How's your day going?"

"Busy. I've been juggling requests to coordinate transportation for residents to doctor visits until the end of the month. How's it going with you?"

"Slow," he sighed, "but I trust Psalm 50:11, that God will supply all my needs according to His riches in glory, and we know our Father in heaven is rich."

Omega couldn't argue with that. The psalm was a constant reminder that the Lord owned everything. "I'm praying hard that God will increase your business."

"Thank you. Want to hear something funny?"

"Sure." She laughed as if it were a prerequisite.

"My mother thinks you're cute. I corrected her that you're pretty."

"Oh, she's sweet. I'm glad she came." Omega blushed. Whenever Mitchell mentioned his family, she couldn't help but wonder when the Addams would visit, but Randall had bad-mouthed Omega to them, blaming her for his breakup. Her brother could be "over the top" on stuff—like now. God had called Tally, not Omega.

"Since she knew our history with the robbery, my mom told me she met my dad by accident, and *blah, blah, blah*. I told her it wasn't the same thing."

Omega chuckled and glanced at the doorway. Bobby stood there, seemingly flustered.

"Let me talk to you later." She ended the call, offered him a seat, and linked her hands on the desk. "Is something wrong?"

"Yeah." Bobby pointed. "O, you got into my head last week and all weekend. You know how to ruin a brother's celebration." Bobby slapped his leg.

She frowned and studied him. "So, you're canceling or postponing your party?"

"No!" He rubbed his shaved head. "I've already changed the date once, and half of the staff has helped me plan it, so they're invested in it too. I think they would be disappointed if I backed out now."

"They'll get over it. I told you I'll foot the expenses."

Bobby whistled as if it were the first time she'd told him that. He rubbed his shaven head.

Another knock on the door brought Caylee to her office. “Oh, hey, Bobby. I’ll come back.”

“No, we’re done here.” Bobby stood, squinted at Omega, then strolled out.

Caylee took the seat he vacated. “I’ve got great news.” Her excitement was contagious.

“Come on, tell me.” Omega smiled. She could use some good news.

“April signed a contract yesterday with a New York modeling agency. She leaves in August.” She snapped her fingers in jubilation.

Not good news. One tear fell, then another, until Omega was overcome with emotions.

Caylee jumped up and hurried behind the desk to her. “I know you love us like real sisters, and I’m going to miss her too. But this is a good thing. We’ve been praying for this, remember?”

This is not a good thing for you. Tell her, Lord. Tell her. Omega sniffed. The saying, “Be careful what you pray for, because you just might get it” came to mind.

She had not been able to sway Bobby’s decision or Caylee’s situation. Omega was a terrible intercessor. Her day went downhill from that moment. Mrs. Helena was wrong. Omega wasn’t having a good day.

After talking to Omega, Mitchell smiled as he strolled through Kings and Queens Fitness, chatting with familiar faces.

Pray, God whispered.

“Pray?”

Pray My will for your life and this place.

With each step, Mitchell did as he was told. *Lord, if it’s Your will, bless everyone who enters—*

"What's up, Mitch?" a patron spoke as he headed to the locker room.

Mitchell nodded his greeting as he walked the perimeter a couple of times. *Jesus, let them feel Your presence. Let their souls prosper as their bodies prospers from exercise and healthy lifestyles. Lord, bless me to be the light and testify of Your saving grace.*

Sallie entered the gym in a trot, and when she saw him, it turned into a jog. "Mitchell, Mitchell, you're never going to believe what happened." She was crying and laughing at the same time, so he didn't know which emotion to believe.

He folded his arms and gave Sallie his attention.

"Praise God! Prayer works. In my Bible, I read in the Book of Mark that signs follow those who believe…" Sallie started praising the Lord in a heavenly language.

The anointing touched Mitchell, and he had to usher Sallie into his office so they could worship God in private.

"'In My name shall they cast out devils; they shall speak with new tongues, which I already did when I received the Holy Ghost—and they shall take up serpents; and if they drink any deadly thing, it shall not hurt them; they shall lay hands on the sick, and they shall recover.' I believe, I believe!" Tears filled Sallie's eyes.

"My nephew got ahold of some of his grandmother's medicine. It stopped Jeffrey's heart. My sister started screaming when he stopped breathing. I began to pray and laid my hand on his chest. I believe! I believe! His heart started to beat again." Sallie jumped up and down as if she were jumping rope or preparing for a lift off.

"*Whew*. He recovered. He recovered," she repeated. "When the paramedics arrived, he was alert, breathing, and talking. His speech was slurred. The doctors ran tests but couldn't find any traces of that prescription in his system." She laughed again and clapped her hands. "We showed the doctor the empty pill bottle, and they were amazed. They kept Jeffrey for observation, but he's back to his normal self—busy."

And these signs shall follow them that believe. Mitchell recalled that verse in Mark sixteen.

Minutes later, they exited his office under some watchful busybodies in the gym. He chuckled. If they wanted to know what was happening, Sallie would be more than happy to fill them in.

In the meantime, Mitchell had some more praying of his own to do.

A few hours later, he received a call from another babbling woman. God must be busy today, he thought, then he realized Omega's babbling was near hysteria. "Calm down. I can't understand a word you're saying."

"April's leaving," she said, lowering her voice, "which means Caylee will die. I can't do this right now. I can't." She attempted to stifle her wail.

Mitchell's heart crashed, and he grabbed onto the counter to steady his weight. What? Not the Princes. He had come to look at them as sisters he never had. They both were enjoying Jesus. How could God be this cruel?

I am a righteous judge! The Lord thundered.

Chastened, Mitchell escaped into his office, closed the door, and prayed until his spirit connected with the Lord.

Omega cried with him—or rather, he shared her pain. When his assistant manager knocked on the door, Mitchell composed himself. "I've got to go. Are you going to be okay?"

"I don't know." Omega's voice cracked.

Mitchell opened his office door and couldn't believe his eyes. Sallie had returned with family members who wanted to sign up for gym membership. Not only that, but there was also a line of others that Mitchell had to assist. *Thank You, Lord,* he mouthed silently. In the next breath, he begged God not to take Caylee from them.

Chapter Twenty

But God said unto him, Thou fool, this night thy soul shall be required of thee: then whose shall those things be, which thou hast provided?
—Luke 12:20 KJV

"I'm surprised *you* want to go out," April said as she watched Caylee dress for Bobby's party.

Caylee shrugged. "It's not that I *want* to go. I'm showing up to support a coworker. I left that party atmosphere behind." She huffed as she slipped her feet into her strappy sandals. "I can't wait until I save enough money to get another car. I'm riding with Reba, and she says she's not staying long."

April picked up her beauty magazine. "Omega's not going?"

"Nope." Caylee shook her head. "And she tried to talk me out of going."

Omega had tried to steer Caylee away with a movie or dinner—her treat.

Caylee believed her friend wanted to keep her away from Bobby as if she was one of his office groupies. She wasn't attracted to Bobby or any man. Since committing to Christ, Caylee would rather spend her time at the church's youth night or reading her Bible.

"Why don't you come with me, please?" Caylee clasped her hands together as if she were praying.

"Nah." April flipped through the pages.

"Fine. I should be back early." Caylee admired her sleeveless dress, which flowed to her ankles. A perfect style on a warm night for a celebration explosion, as Bobby described it.

I'm waiting outside, Reba texted.

"Got to go." She hugged her sister and was out the door. As a stripper, she wasn't interested in making friends with her colleagues. Caylee only wanted to do her job and go home. At Hathaway, she loved the lax working environment, the fun personalities, and the pride coworkers took in their projects. This was where Caylee fit in.

"*Ooh*. Don't you look cute," Reba said as Caylee slid into the passenger seat of her car and buckled up.

"Thank you." Caylee blushed. She felt her coworker's sincerity.

Compliments coming from men at the various clubs weren't always genuine. They were meant to feed the lusts of their eyes.

That was her life before Christ. Caylee would forever be grateful to Omega for showing up that day at the bus stop and saving her from death. As soon as her bus arrived, Caylee had planned to end it all. She was done with life's disappointments.

All that changed. Her life with Christ came with benefits like those from her legit job. She had peace, and that was the biggest blessing.

Excitement was in the air as Reba hoped to meet someone special at the party. "You know Bobby is Mr. Popular and has a lot of friends. I'm looking for a good guy."

"*Hmmm*." Caylee didn't comment as she spied the Gateway Arch as the landmark, the lighthouse of downtown where they were headed. Ten minutes later, the strung white lights hung around the party beckoned to them. "Wow."

"Right." Reba circled Market Street, looking for a parking spot. They snagged one a block away.

Downtown nightlife buzzed with a packed baseball game at Busch Stadium and the overflow at nearby Ballpark Village.

Reba struggled in her heels as they took baby steps toward the function. "Girl, how do you walk steady in those shoes? I know April is a model, but you're missing your calling if you can walk in three-inch-plus heels."

"Let's just say I'm a pro." Caylee left it at that.

They could hear live music as they got closer. "A band?" Reba laughed. "I didn't know B had it in him. I think he has a DJ too."

Coworkers welcomed them with hugs, laughs, and whistles. Other guests gathered at cocktail tables, strategically placed throughout, turned their heads at the newcomers. Bobby spotted them. The man had transformed himself into a cover model of African royalty in his distinguished attire.

With Reba and Caylee on each arm, Bobby introduced them to guests, even coworkers. It was amusing.

There had to be about seventy-five people deep. All were having fun. When a few guys asked Caylee to dance, she declined.

Those days were behind her.

"You're a pretty lady." The guy introduced himself as Andre. "I know you've got moves on the dance floor. Let's show them off." His grin was more of a smirk.

"I do, but now I use them for praise dancing to the Lord. God recently filled me with His Holy Ghost…" Her voice trailed as she talked about her favorite subject—her salvation. Andre excused himself. Jesus was her secret weapon to keep men at bay. She loved it.

Left alone, Caylee sampled the food and watched from the sidelines as the attendees took to the dance floor. Hearing a ding, she dug into the bottom of her purse for her phone.

Omega sent a text. **Everything okay? Having a good time?**

Caylee chuckled. **The men here don't want me to talk about Jesus.**

LOL. Call me if you get too bored, and I'll come get you.

Thanks. Caylee looked up when another coworker waved her over. **I'm good. I came with Reba, so I don't want to leave her.**

Four hours later, Bobby's birthday bash was going strong. The food and drinks were plentiful. Stars filled the sky, and the breeze kept the humidity at bay, so no one seemed to be in the mood to leave.

Caylee found a seat, and a nice-looking guy sat beside her.

"Doesn't look like you're having fun." Dennis introduced himself, and Caylee felt obligated to do thc same. He grinned and saluted her with a martini glass in his hand.

"I'm having a great time watching my coworkers enjoy themselves." Caylee glanced in Reba's direction. The woman hadn't left the dance floor. Caylee never knew her quiet and reserved coworker had that much energy.

"Caylee, a pretty name for a pretty lady. Tell me about yourself." Dennis rested his glass on a nearby counter and gave her his attention.

Hairs tingled on her arms before she could respond. Something had changed—what, she didn't know. Distracted, she glanced around, and nothing seemed amiss.

Refocusing, she looked at Dennis who waited patiently for her attention. "Well, I'm in my mid-twenties and I love my job." She shrugged. "The most exciting thing that has happened to me is Jesus. I was baptized in His name, and He filled me with His Spirit. Feeling God's presence was amazing."

There it was again—a presence, but it wasn't God. She glanced toward the dance floor. Not sure what she was seeing, Caylee blinked and then she saw them—the same dark, demonic figures that were in the strip club one night. They intermingled with the crowd. Guests laughed and drank, unaware of the sinister environment encircling them.

Lord, what's going on?

Pray, God whispered.

She grabbed Dennis' hand. "Let's pray. Father, in the name of Jesus, thank You for the cross and the blood You shed. Jesus, dismiss the spirits of darkness from this place and save souls. Save Dennis—"

He snatched his hand back, but Caylee didn't stop praying.

Within minutes, the Holy Ghost moved her feet in a praise dance as her tongues worshipped Him. The more she cried, "Jesus," in her native language, the heavenly tongues overruled, and God spoke.

When Caylee composed herself and opened her eyes, gone were those dark shadowy figures, but she found herself on the dance floor—the only one—like in the strip club, but this time her audience was clapping and cheering her on— "Go, Caylee, go, go"—with smiles as the music played.

Slightly embarrassed and unable to explain what happened, she walked back to her seat with her arms lifted in praise. Dennis was long gone too.

Reba rushed to her side. "You, my friend, stole the show. I've never seen a body move like that. It was as if you were a ballerina on a string the way you twirled gracefully. It was a beautiful expression of art. Whatever you were drinking, I want a sip."

"I was under the influence of the Holy Ghost." Caylee smiled. "If anyone is thirsty, they can go to God where there are streams of living water."

Quiet in thought, Reba frowned. "Girl, you've become so deep. You remind me of Yolanda sometimes. Anyway, I've partied enough for one night and didn't meet any winners. Whenever you're ready."

"We can leave now."

Caylee arrived home in no time. Omega wanted her to call and tell her about Bobby's party. That would have to wait until morning.

Ten minutes later, Reba called in hysterics. Bobby had been shot and killed and four other guests were injured. "What? Not Bobby." It was his birthday.

She thought about those dark figures from earlier that her spiritual eyes had seen. Had they returned? Time to call Omega now.

Omega couldn't sleep long after she and Mitchell had pondered the revelation of Ecclesiastes 9:12, *For man also knows not his time: as the fishes that are taken in an evil net, and as the birds that are caught in the snare; so are the sons of men snared in an evil time, when it falls suddenly upon them.*

Without a doubt, Omega heard God's voice say Bobby would die at his party. That had been scary. She had been happy when she thought he was about to postpone it. The day had come, and Omega fasted most of it for Bobby that God would show mercy, although Bobby hadn't made time for God.

Laying in her bed with her Bible resting on her chest, Omega stared at the ceiling. Her mind ticked as a clock counted the minutes. She was mourning Bobby's life as if his time of death had already come.

The text from Caylee said everything was okay.

She eyed the time on the nightstand clock. It was twelve-thirty. Maybe God had changed His mind and given Bobby another chance.

Then Caylee's ringtone played. Maybe she called to say she'd made it home. Omega considered not answering or sending it to voicemail, but she had to know. "Hello."

"Bobby's dead! He was killed after Reba and I left his party." Caylee bawled.

Omega wept too. She had failed in persuading him to cancel. Would she fail Caylee too? "I'm so sorry." The grief was unbearable. Her breathing was strained, and her head pounded with sorrow that couldn't be contained.

There were no words to console Caylee. God hadn't comforted Omega yet.

Caylee sniffed, then hiccupped. "I felt in my spirit and saw in the spiritual realm dark demons circling the dance floor like a pack of wolves." She explained how God told her to pray and the Holy Ghost manifested Himself.

Both were emotionally distraught to say more. They ended the call. She didn't dare wake Mitchell to tell him, but she couldn't close her eyes, so she endured the memories that flashed in her mind throughout the night.

On Sunday morning, the short drive to Caylee and April's apartment seemed like hundreds of miles away. Last night, Omega had grieved alone. This morning when she called Mitchell, Omega had grieved again with him. What she appreciated about him was he was a strong, very masculine man, even sexy, but he didn't hide his vulnerability as they cried together. He was human.

"I waited for your call through the night. When it didn't come, I was hopeful and drifted off," Mitchell said. "We'll get through this with the help of Jesus."

Omega could only imagine what Caylee was feeling. She was one of the last ones to see Bobby alive. Omega didn't know Caylee's emotional state.

The sisters were ready when Omega arrived. From a distance, nothing was out of the ordinary—until one stepped closer. Their eyes were puffy. Any makeup they wore was gone.

The two collapsed in Omega's arms, and the trio cried together. She didn't rush them. Tears had to be shed.

Once they calmed down, Omega drove to church. There was no music or sniffs. Just an eerie quietness that left them to their own thoughts.

There was refuge inside Christ For All Church. The music was upbeat. Praise was in the atmosphere when they entered the sanctuary, but Omega and her group couldn't release the stronghold of sorrow to relish in it.

Mitchell had saved seats for them and gave each hugs of comfort. He squeezed Omega's hand before she took her seat. "You okay? Are they okay?"

Confused, Omega shook her head, then nodded. "I don't know."

Pastor Rodney stepped to the podium and shouted, "Hallelujah! This is a good day to praise Jesus because He's worthy for nailing our sins to His cross. Because of that, Jesus has given us a promise that the dead in Christ shall rise first, and we who are alive and remain shall be caught up to meet him in the air."

Omega couldn't pinpoint the Scripture, but Mrs. Helena had drilled into her that the rapture was her hope in First Thessalonians 4 and something.

"I know life happens, but don't get drawn into the sorrows of this world as if you have no hope. In Romans 13:11, *And that, knowing the time, that now it is high time to awake out of sleep: for now, is our salvation nearer than when we believed.* We're one day closer to eternity."

Omega tried not to think about Bobby and his eternity. If only people knew the urgency to surrender to Christ. She sighed, and Mitchell gave her a questioning expression and mouthed, "You good?"

"Still processing."

"Understandable. I'm here for you and the ladies." Mitchell smiled, forcing Omega to do the same, even if it was a sad one.

Pastor Rodney preached from various Scriptures to paint the picture of Jesus returning for His church. "Be encouraged today that many are called, few are chosen, and God chose you." He closed his Bible and extended an invitation to those who wanted prayer and salvation. Many answered the call.

As the Mama Bear to Omega and her friends, Mrs. Helena invited them to her house after church where they cried, and she comforted them with prayer and Scriptures. They all stayed until dark. Mitchell offered to drop the sisters at their apartment since Omega was already home in her gated community. She accepted his offer, emotionally drained.

Monday morning, the company owner had sent grief counselors to the office for a second time within months for the few who had struggled to come to work. The others who had attended Bobby's party were in too much shock. Those who were injured weren't Hathaway employees.

Images of the robbery at the gas station resurfaced in Omega's mind. Who and why did anyone want to shoot up at Bobby's party? Tears streamed down her cheeks. Omega sniffed, but it did nothing to stop the flow. Plus, her head ached from the stress of the tragedy.

Mitchell sent flowers to Omega at her office with a note: *We know tomorrow is not promised, but Jesus promised never to leave nor forsake us. Don't forget that's our hope. —Mitchell*

Omega smiled. When did he get so deep? Must have been God-inspired. She walked to Caylee's cubicle. Her friend was there because she didn't want to jeopardize her perfect attendance.

The office resembled a ghost town.

Doors were closed.

No one ventured out.

Even the breakroom was dark and empty.

The silence was haunting. Omega offered to take Caylee home since H.R. would pay the staff even if they took the day off.

"The quiet time will be good for me since April won't be at the apartment," Caylee said, accepting the ride back home and the day off.

But not for me, Omega thought as Caylee's days were now numbered. *God, this isn't fair. Lord, how can I stop her?*

Pray My Will.

Chapter Twenty-one

Consequently, there is no condemnation for those in Christ Jesus.
—Romans 8:1 KJV

A week later, those still grieving the death of their charismatic coworker couldn't bear to attend Bobby's funeral, including Caylee.

Omega, Gerri from H.R., and a few other managers went. Mitchell stayed by Omega's side. Tears fell as friends gave accolades about what Bobby had accomplished in his short life—his volunteerism, artistic abilities, and fun-loving spirit.

The only consolation to his grieving parents and siblings was the police had one of Bobby's former associates in custody for the deadly drive-by. The suspect had said Bobby dumped his homies and turned bourgeois on them.

Caylee had walked away from her past too. How did God pick and choose who would live and who would die? she thought as one of Bobby's friends rambled on.

Only whatever men do unto Me will they receive My reward, God whispered. *Read Colossians 3:23–24.*

Omega grabbed her phone to jot down the Scripture.

Mitchell leaned closer and whispered, "Something from God?" His eyes conveyed he understood.

"Yep."

An hour later, after more than a dozen reflections from friends, the service for Bobby Truman, age twenty-five, ended.

"Whew." Omega fanned her face when she stepped out of Austin Layne Mortuary. She had yet to go to one funeral that wasn't sad.

"You want to go to the burial and repast?" Mitchell's voice was low.

Omega faced him. The tenderness in his eyes made her smile. "No. I did all I could for Bobby—I prayed and witnessed to him. God has set his judgment, so my mission for him has ended. I think I want to be alone the rest of the day." She turned to leave.

Mitchell touched her elbow. "That's not going to happen, Omega. We're on this spiritual journey together. Remember the passage, *two are better than one, because they have a good reward for their labor. For if they fall, the one will lift up his fellow: but woe to him that is alone when he falls; for he hath not another to help him up.'"*

Omega smiled and nudged her shoulder against his. "I love it when God gives you Scriptures. They seem right on time."

Mitchell grinned. "He's awesome. Sometimes when I read my Bible, I stumble upon some Scriptures the Lord has spoken through me. Let me look this one up," he said as they stepped aside for the cars lined up for the gravesite processional. He opened his Bible app and searched the keywords he'd said. "It's Ecclesiastes 4:9–10."

"Okay. I'll let you hang with me today."

His eyes twinkled. "I'm honored. How about a picnic before it gets too humid?"

"Sure." He took her hand, escorted her to the car, and opened her door. "I'll drop off my car at the house, then we can go."

"Sounds like a plan."

When Omega turned into her cul-de-sac, Mrs. Helena was washing off her driveway. Omega parked and stepped out. Mitchell, who trailed her, did the same.

"How was Bobby's funeral?"

"Sad," Omega and Mitchell said in unison.

"As far as I know, he didn't accept God's salvation plan before he was killed. Do you think he went to hell? His obituary said he accepted Christ as a child, but his lifestyle didn't reflect it," Omega added.

"Judgment is up to God, but we know from Isaiah five and fourteen that *hell has enlarged herself and opened her mouth without measure: and their glory, and their multitude, and their pomp, and he that rejoices, shall descend into it."*

They were quiet, reflecting on that Scripture.

"It's sad to think about people dying forever and ever." Omega's heart sank.

"It is, but since Adam and Eve, the wickedness of man has increased, and so has their resting place."

Mrs. Helena patted their hands. "The good news," she said, smiling, which seemed to comfort Omega, "is as long as we walk that narrow way, we have a hope in that first resurrection. Remember what Pastor Rodney preached a few Sundays ago?"

"God says, *Blessed and holy is the one who is in the first resurrection, over these, the second death has no power, but they will be priests of God and Christ and will reign with Him for a thousand years*." Mitchell slipped his hands into his pockets. "I'm never prepared when words spill out of my mouth, and sometimes I have no idea what they mean." He looked from Omega to Mrs. Helena.

"God has given you a gift. You quoted Revelation twenty and six. Continue to read and study, and God will open your understanding. Come on inside for sandwiches and lemonade."

Omega nodded. "There's our lunch."

"Do you always have food on the table?" Mitchell snickered.

"People drop in occasionally, so I like to offer a snack." Mrs. Helena's smile was warm.

Relaxing on her spacious patio, shielded from the sun, Omega's mind was elsewhere. A few times, Mitchell squeezed her hand and mouthed, "You okay?"

She would always respond with a smile, then her mood would change when she thought about Bobby.

"Mrs. Helena, I feel so bad about my coworker. Should I have been more forceful? Should I have told him what God told me? Did I fail God because I lost a soul?" The tears fell, and she couldn't control them.

Mitchell scraped his chair back on the concrete and came to her side to comfort her. Mrs. Helena's voice was soothing as she rubbed her hand.

"Sweetie, God knows the choices *we* will make. Free will is part of life. Many are called, but few are chosen because they aren't committed to Christ. Let your heart be at rest. John six and thirty-nine says, *And this is the will of Him who sent Me, that I shall lose none of those He has given Me but raise them at the last day.*"

Omega stood and walked inside her neighbor's house to the powder room to wipe her eyes and blow her nose. She couldn't help but notice Mrs. Helena had a lot of medication bottles. The way her neighbor moved around, she seemed to be in her forties rather than her mid-seventies.

As she was about to step back on the patio, she overheard Mrs. Helena talking to Mitchell.

"The child carries a heavy burden as an intercessor. God has empowered Omega to pray without ceasing. Her gift is to pray for souls, situations, and blessings. God will release the power of the Holy Ghost to explode around her as a raging fire like on the Day of Pentecost, the Azusa Street Revival that happened in the early 1900s in California, and more."

"What's Azusa Street?" Omega asked as she made herself known.

Mitchell held out his hand to take her seat, then he scooted his chair next to her. "Mrs. Helena says the power of the Holy Ghost will fall."

"It has been recorded throughout history that wherever large groups of God-seeking people have gathered, the Holy Ghost works miracles. I want you to focus on those who want Christ, not those you'll never win." Mrs. Helena gave her the stern teacher face before she smiled. "Now, more lemonade?"

Chapter Twenty-two

The Lord is not slack concerning his promise, as some men count slackness; but is longsuffering to us-ward, not willing that any should perish, but that all should come to repentance. —2 Peter 3:9 KJV

Mitchell was not expecting to see both of his parents at church.

Marva's body language shouted, "I'm not a stranger here." It was a humbling moment for Mitchell to see his mother because he wasn't sure when she would return.

His father, David Franklin, was the opposite. The scowl on his face seemed to match the mood that his black suit represented. He didn't want to be there.

Once his mother spotted Mitchell and his friends, he waved them both over. "I couldn't wait to get here." She flashed that smile that his father said he fell in love with.

"I'm ready." His mother gave him no inkling that she was interested in salvation or had a hunger or thirst for Christ. The only hope he had to go on was what Mrs. Helena said. *Thank You, Jesus!*

"The few sermons I've heard online from Pastor Rodney make me want more. I feel like Peter who begged Jesus to wash his hands, head, and feet so he could have part of the Lord. Yep! That's what I want now."

"Oh, you're talking about what Pastor Rodney preached the last time you were here."

"Yes. I've gotten a glimpse of the sermons online—just to make sure your pastor is legit."

"Ummm-hmmm."

Mitchell asked Omega to scoot down to make room for his parents.

His mother sat erect and eager as a kindergartener on the first day of school. "I know how this works, but do I have to wait until the end of the sermon to get baptized?"

He gave it some thought, then shook his head. "No. I guess not. I've seen them stop the sermon to baptize onc soul."

"Okay." Marva raised her hand. "I'll be that one soul today." She grinned as she scanned the church.

"Make that two," his father mumbled.

Mitchell couldn't believe his ears.

"Oh, honey." His wife turned around and hugged her husband so tight that Mitchell was sure he would faint from lack of air.

"There's only one problem, Dad. The Bible says to repent and be baptized. You can't get your sins washed away if you don't confess those sins."

Stuffing his hands in his pocket, his father's frown returned. "Then I'll wait."

The light dimmed in his mother's eyes. "*Hmmmph*. With or without you, David, I'm not leaving this church today without going down, in Jesus' name." She jutted her chin.

"Amen." Omega's sweet voice joined Mitchell's. He hadn't realized she had been listening.

"Hold on, and I'll get an usher to get a note to the pulpit."

The pastor tapped his shoe to the praise music and had his arms lifted in worship.

Mitchell watched the handoff of his note from one usher to another, then to a minister on the pulpit, and finally to their pastor. Minutes later, once he read the message, he walked to the podium and had the musicians silence their instruments.

"I understand Brother Franklin's parents are with him today, and his mother wants salvation now," the pastor said, grinning. A roar of praise erupted in the building as powerful as an earthquake. "Brother Franklin, escort your mother down the aisle. This moment is open to anyone else who can't wait for salvation. You can come now too."

His mother pumped her fists in the air and glided toward the altar without the aid of her son as if she was a game show contestant.

Mitchell's father glanced around and looked bewildered. "These people are that excited about my wife getting baptized?"

"Yep." Mitchell patted his dad's shoulder. The following words that came out of his mouth weren't his. "The angels in heaven do rejoice over one sinner who repents."

"Really?" His father seemed skeptical. "How do you know that?"

Mitchell didn't but hoped God would whisper the answer in his ear.

Read My Word in Luke fifteen.

"It's in the New Testament, Dad, in the Book of Luke, chapter fifteen." Mitchell would have to read it for himself, too, later.

After his mother repented of her sins and the minister prayed for her, the church mothers, including Mrs. Helena, guided her to the back to change her into white attire. Two teenage girls wanted the same thing and followed his mother.

Omega elbowed him. "Isn't this exciting to see your mom surrender to the Lord's salvation?"

"It is." Bobbing his head, Mitchell grinned. He still couldn't believe it.

When the lights flickered on in the pool area for the candidates, Mitchell stood, folded his arms, and prayed. Omega stood beside him. Caylee and April were absent to witness this life-changing moment for Mitchell. They had committed to a modeling gig.

A minister stepped into the water and extended his hand to guide his mother down the stairs into the pool. Suddenly, his mother's arms lifted in praise and worship. The crowd went crazy.

Mitchell didn't realize tears fell until Omega handed him a tissue. He accepted it but didn't wipe his eyes, fearing he would miss something.

A beam of light seemed to pierce the roof and spotlighted his mother. Suddenly, the power of the Holy Ghost exploded from his mother's mouth. She didn't stop speaking to the Lord. The minister held his mother as steady as possible for her baptism.

The voice of one of the ministers in the water boomed as a hush covered the sanctuary.

Mitchell heard Omega's soft prayer. He unfolded his arms and put his left arm around his father's shoulder and his right around Omega's.

"My dear sister, Marva Franklin, upon the confession of your faith and the confidence you have in the blessed Word of God concerning His death, burial, and grand resurrection, I now indeed baptize you in the magnificent, holy name of the Lord Jesus Christ for the remission of your sins. For there is no other name in Heaven, on earth, or under it whose name is more powerful for a person to be saved. And the Lord has already fulfilled His promise to you today by filling you with His Holy Ghost power."

His mother was submerged and seemed to break through the water with her hands lifted in praise. Cheers, applause, and "Thank You, Jesus" circulated throughout the sanctuary. To Mitchell's surprise, his father whistled while Omega jumped in place, shouting, "Hallelujah" and "Save my family, too, Lord."

Mitchell's legs weakened until he slid to his knees and began to worship God.

That's one soul I've saved for you, God whispered.

By the time Pastor Rodney preached his abbreviated sermon, his father had followed a handful of others to the altar to be saved.

That's two souls today, God whispered. *The devil none.*

Omega had mixed emotions Monday morning. She remained in awe that both of Mitchell's parents surrendered to Christ's salvation. It wasn't fair. She couldn't persuade one person in the Addams family to budge. Okay, she was being petty.

Tally called while Omega was feeling sorry for herself. "Praise the Lord, sis."

I give you what you need, God whispered.

Omega chided herself for complaining. Jesus had saved the closest person to her family—Tally. "Praise the Lord." She couldn't help but smile. "Hey, I didn't see you yesterday."

"I got there late, but I saw Mitchell had guests there. I didn't sit too far from you. I ran into your brother. It's the first time since I broke up with him." Her voice was sad. "It was hard."

"I'm sorry. Where?"

"The Galleria. I had a craving for cheesecake. He was there leaving the Apple store. We just stared at each other. It was as if we held our breaths, waiting for the other to move, speak, or in my case, break down in tears. *Whew*."

Tally was quiet. Omega didn't rush her friend.

"Randall made the first move with a swagger that still made me swoon. He towered over me and asked if it was worth it to leave him."

"Wow."

"Although he didn't say what 'it' was, I knew he was talking about God. I didn't have to think twice when I answered yes." She sniffed. "He accused me of breaking up with him over nothing. I corrected him and told him Jesus was my everything and would he rather it had been another man."

Omega shook her head. This petite spitfire could hold her own. "So, how did it end?"

Tally exhaled. "Randall walked away from me without looking back. That hurt so bad. Last night, God led me to read the third chapter of Philippians. Those Scriptures ministered to my soul, especially verses thirteen and fourteen. 'Forget my sins behind me and press toward the mark for the prize of the high calling of God in Christ Jesus.' That gave me some comfort."

They were silent until Omega spoke. "Thanks, sis, for being my role model. I've been pouting that Mitchell's parents surrendered and my family hates me."

"Not true. They're frustrated."

"I guess." Omega exhaled.

"One thing I'm learning about in my new life in Christ is not to take rejection personally. I love me some Randall Addams, and I know he loves me, but didn't you tell me this is a spiritual battle? I haven't seen any demons or angels, but I know that Randall's spirit is rejecting God. I'm praying for his soul. One thing I know is Hell is for real. God let me see and feel a taste of it."

Omega thought about the monster-type figures Caylee had seen one night while working in the strip club. "Yes, very much real."

"Oh, we're both praying for our families, and we have each other to depend on, and of course, you have Mitchell. He's a cutie—no, fine."

"Randall would be jealous to hear you say that," Omega teased. "God knows I want my family saved before God pronounces His judgment on the Earth."

Pray for others, and I'll bless you, God whispered.

That settled her frustration as they said their goodbyes.

Chapter Twenty-three

For I know the thoughts that I think toward you, saith the Lord, thoughts of peace, and not of evil, to give you an expected end.
—Jeremiah 29:11 KJV

Caylee stuck her head into Omega's office. A beaming smile captured her face, and she glowed.

"What are you up to?" Omega chuckled. Her friend had become the perfect employee.

Always on time.

Dressed professionally with her limited wardrobe.

Never complained.

Yolanda would have liked her.

"I've got a surprise." Caylee's smile turned into a grin. Her eyes twinkled with a tease.

Omega gave her a side-eye. She rested her pen on her desk and pushed aside the stack of requests for transportation to medical and dental appointments.

"Are you free tomorrow?" Her expression was hopeful.

She and Delta were supposed to have dinner. Tally had helped to weaken the stress between them at the Sunday brunch. Despite the tangible tension, Delta was speaking to her again.

Her sister had a stipulation for Omega to be welcomed back into the sisterhood. Delta didn't want to hear any church stuff because that had been Tally's downfall, according to Randall.

Omega had asked God how she could win Delta over to Christ if she couldn't talk about Him?

Live it, the Lord had whispered. *Show them the peace I give you and what they don't have.*

Those cryptic messages always prompted a phone call to Mrs. Helena who was more than happy to explain.

Caylee called her name again, pulling Omega back into the present.

"Sorry. Can't. I've got plans." She pouted for good measure.

Caylee huffed, crossed her arms, and leaned against the doorjamb. "You can bring Mitchell."

"No. We aren't joined at the hip, you know." She thought about the Scripture God had given Mitchell—two is better than one. "Nope. I'm hanging out with Delta."

"Oh. Bring her." Her eyes widened with anticipation.

That was tricky. How could she tell Caylee that Delta was jealous of their relationship without hurting her feelings? But unless Omega prayed harder, time was running out for Caylee. Her looming death was sure to happen once April's plane took off. Hadn't Hathaway Health suffered enough loss of coworkers? First Yolanda, then Bobby, and soon… Omega didn't want to think about it.

She took a deep breath. "Caylee, will you pray for my sister?"

"What's wrong?" She raced into her office and took a seat without an invitation. Fear held her eyes captive in a stare.

"Our close relationship was severed. In trying to repair it, I want to be assessable when she does want to get together. She doesn't want Christ." Omega refused to cry at that statement. "The only way she agreed to spend time with me is if I don't talk about Jesus—well church stuff as she calls it."

Caylee gasped as she collapsed back in the chair. "That is sad because I like us talking about the Bible and the rapture and the New Jerusalem."

"Yeah, me too, but I want to draw her, so can I take a raincheck on your surprise*?" Please say yes*, Omega hoped.

"I understand with your sister. April and I are close, and if we were ever separated, I would die of loneliness."

Frowning, Omega jumped in her seat. "Don't ever say that."

"What?" Caylee looked clueless.

"Death."

"Oh, got it," Caylee bit her lip. "Sorry. Bad choice of words. Bobby's death is still in the back of my head too. I'm glad two guys have been charged, but it won't bring him back."

"No, it won't." Crime changes everyone. Every time Omega heard about a holdup, her mind goes back to Gus' Gas Mart and how she could have died.

"Anyway, I've saved up enough money for a down payment on a car, and I'd wanted to surprise you tomorrow when April and I go pick it up. I'd hoped you could come too."

Omega stood, came around her desk, then hugged her friend. "Congratulations. I remember the feeling when I purchased my first one."

"Yeah, it's not new, but it'll be mine. No more pickups for church."

A car crash flashed before Omega's eyes, startling her. *No!* she screamed silently before her heart sank as she forced a smile. Things were not going the way Omega had been praying for. On the contrary, they were falling in place for Caylee's death.

"Show me on Sunday when you and April come to church." Omega never thought of herself as fake, but that's the way she felt with Bobby and now Caylee when God revealed their fate to her.

"We won't be there. April's in a fashion show on Sunday. This is the last one before she takes off for New York."

Did Caylee just raise her hand in praise? Omega couldn't stop her eyes from misting. "Don't remind me." This time her pout was genuine.

"I'm going to miss her, too, but we can always fly up to see her whenever she's in the country. I think her first assignment is in Australia or someplace exotic. Cool." She walked out and returned to her cubicle.

April will be so far away when she learns about her sister's death, Omega thought.

The next day, Omega was grateful for the ceasefire with Delta. They met at Plaza Frontenac. They shopped like old times.

It was fun. Carefree. Bonding. And it was all fake—Omega was torn.

The two sisters wound down their excursion with a meal at BrickTops. "Should I dare ask how you are spending your days now?" Delta asked, then sipped on her margarita.

Omega nursed her Botanical Blend hot tea. "Since you asked…" She gave her sister a pointed stare. "My priorities have changed as I put God first."

"Too bad." Delta shrugged. "I met someone that I want you to meet."

"Really? What's his name? What does he do? What does he look like?"

Delta laughed and shattered the tension as she leaned over and whispered as if someone was eavesdropping. "His name is Kyler Mann. He's older than both of us—thirty-seven—good-looking and has a nice physique. He works in the medical field, but not as a doctor."

Omega blinked. "The one who hates doctors is attracted to one in the field. Priceless." She laughed. She held her stomach until it ached. Omega paused her amusement.

Hmmm. Odd that two sisters had met men in the same industry. The difference was she wasn't dating Mitchell. Plus, his focus was his struggling business. "Did you hurt yourself or something?"

"Not enough to be rushed to an urgent care." Delta snickered. "I tripped, and he caught me. Classic 'I fell into his arms.'"

"Classic cliché" Omega anchored her elbow on the table to rest her chin in the palm of her hand. It felt normal again to talk about matters of the heart with her best friend—her sister. "So, how many dates have you two been on?"

Delta wagged one finger like a wiper on a windshield. "One for now. We've mostly talked on the phone." She paused with a dreamy expression that made Omega smile. "Randall met him when I had to give our brother the 4-1-1 on where I was going. It was one of those 'accidental meetings.' He played the over-the-top protective big brother, but beneath the 'I will hurt you if you hurt my sister,' the sadness in his eyes continues to break my heart. Randall's still upset about him and Tally, and he ain't #teamrelationships right now." She paused and took another sip as their waiter brought their plates.

"I explained to Kyler the reason for my brother's foul mood. Now he wants to meet my sister." Delta grinned. "And he can't wait to meet our parents who named us."

She responded to Omega's surprised expression and shook her head. "Nope. We're not that close yet. Mom will start planning a wedding, and Dad will go Papa Bear on him. Nah. I'm not sure Kyler is worth that stress yet."

It had been a while since both sisters had been in relationships. Omega knew when her sister really liked a guy. At the moment, she wasn't certain. "Sure, When?"

"If you can rent a date, then we can double date. Any prospects?" She winked and grinned as the server brought their food.

"You know I'm not dating." Omega bowed her head and folded her hands. "Lord, thank You for the food set before us. Sanctify it, remove all impurities, and thank You for giving me a sister—my only sister—and help us to strengthen our bond, in

Jesus' name. Amen." Tonight, Omega had to focus on her own sister and keep her mind from wandering to April's pending loss—beginning now.

"Amen," Delta mumbled. "Blessing our food is okay."

Omega couldn't stop her lips from curling into a smile. *Thank You, Lord, for little blessings that may increase abundantly.*

As they sampled their food, Delta asked, "What about Mr. Franklin? Mitchell seems to like you."

"You're reading 'us' wrong. Mitchell and I are partners in Christ—get it, like partners in crime. We are brother and sister in the Lord. We're too busy with the Lord's business for romance."

Hmmmph. Delta shifted in her seat. "You've blessed the food, so no more church talk. I feel uncomfortable like you're trying to recruit me for an army or cult."

"You can rest assured it's not a cult. If you don't believe me, read your Bible."

Anyway, there's more between you and Mitchell. I think the church is your front. I'm glad Kyler and I didn't meet during a Western shootout. Anyway, it looks like you've emotionally recovered from the robbery. You had me scared for you that night."

"I was petrified at what I saw." Omega shivered. The images from the robbery were stored in her memory bank, but the visions of the angels overpowered them every time.

"Which is debatable." Delta rolled her eyes. "Well, ask him to be your date in Christ. I really want your opinion of him. I think in a double-date setting, he'll be more relaxed where Randall just intimidated him."

As if he was summoned, Mitchell texted her: **What you doing?**

She chuckled. **Out to dinner with Delta.** She added smiley emojis.

Praise God. Enjoy your time. Call me later.

Will do. Delta wants us to double date with her and her new boyfriend.

Count me in!

"I know that was Mitchell because you're smiling." Delta *tsk*ed. "Our brother used to smile like that whenever Tally called or texted. Do you think she would join us to make it a triple date?"

Omega shrugged. Tally was happy in her relationship with Christ and seemed to have no regrets about her decision.

"Maybe this will be the perfect time to get them back together." Delta ate with gusto as if it was the perfect plan.

It wasn't. Neither Randall nor Tally would be willing to make the other suffer.

As they were about to devour their dessert, a man across from their table caught their attention when he knelt on one knee.

"Look," Delta whispered. "I think he's about to propose. *Wow*. Brother is fine."

Omega twisted her body for a better view. "And he's coming off the market."

"Chelsie Knight," the man began, "I never knew when I surrendered my life to Christ, He had a jewel for me. I was broken, but your love has healed me."

Her sister didn't want Omega to talk about Christ as if they were in a public school, but her sister heard it from someone. *Good save, Jesus.*

The man's proposal was so heartfelt that even Delta sniffed.

"The Bible says he who finds a wife finds a good thing and favor with the Lord, so you're my double blessings. You'll never have to worry about my love, faithfulness, or respect because God will be the center of our home. Will you marry me?"

His soon-to-be fiancée was too emotional to speak, but she nodded.

A man at another table shouted, "It doesn't count unless you say the word."

Many chuckled as Chelsie stood and wrapped her arms around the proposer's neck. "Yes, Ricky. I'll marry you."

Some applauded; others clinked their stemware.

Delta and Omega faced each other again. "*Whew.* That proposal was hot. I want one just like that. Who knows? Kyler could be the one."

"Then you'll need a man who loves the Scriptures," Omega mumbled, then focused on her slice of cake instead of her sister's frown.

"I knew you would make it big." Caylee and April cruised through Forest Park in Caylee's new car. At least her sister had a chance to ride in it before she took off for New York.

April let the wind kiss her face as she rode with the window down. "I wasn't sure after so many rejections. I wish Mom and Dad were here to see what I've become—and you are doing too." April slapped her sister's shoulder. "I'm so glad you're away from that strip club."

Both shuddered and laughed. "Now, I have a bright future ahead of me." Caylee beamed. Her mind was filled with happy thoughts on the drive back to their apartment

Chapter Twenty-four

O taste and see that the LORD is good: blessed is the man who trusts in him. —Psalm 34:8 KJV

"I do not want to be converted," were the first words out of Delta's mouth when she phoned Omega at work a few days after their dinner.

"That doesn't make me happy, so why are you calling?" Omega wasn't in the mood for rebellious spirits. She hadn't been in the mood for much lately. In seven days and counting, April would take a flight to New York and Caylee her heavenly flight.

Omega had Mitchell fast and pray for things to turn around for the Prince sisters, but it seemed like the Death Angel had his clipboard ready to check Caylee Prince's name off the list.

Delta cleared her throat. "I have a question about something I heard—or read. I can't remember, but it's supposed to be biblical. What does the day you hear my voice harden not your heart mean? It's *just* a question, so don't get too excited."

Omega's heart performed an elaborate gymnastic routine. *Yes!* She stood and closed her door then did a happy dance around her office.

"I think it means don't shut God out or shoot His messengers down...like you saying, 'I don't want to be converted.' There's a war going on, and I'm not talking about on foreign land or in our country. It's a tug-of-war between angels and demons fighting over who will get our souls."

"*Hmmm.*" Delta became quiet.

Lord, what is my sister thinking? Are you drawing her? Omega would have to wait Delta out.

Finally, she said, "Okay, that's all I want to know. Talk to you later."

"Well, I love you too." Omega smiled and stared at her phone as they ended the call. Even though she wanted to spend time with Caylee, Omega was happy she had spent time with her sister. "Thank You, Jesus, for planting a seed in her heart. I don't care how small."

Seconds later, Delta called back. "Oh, yeah. What I really called for. Don't make plans for this Saturday, at seven p.m., at Tuscano's. Randall and Tally are coming. Triple date. *Yayyy*," her sister ended in a sing-song manner.

Omega blinked. "Do they both know the other is coming?"

"Yeah. I started not to tell them, but it wouldn't be cool to ambush our brother and Tally, even though she's gone over to the light side. They are doing it to support me."

"Jesus is the light. Okay. I'll let Mitchell know. Bye." She tapped Mitchell's number.

He answered after a couple of rings.

"Hey. You busy?"

"Actually I am." He chuckled. "It's been a long time since I've said that here at the gym."

"Oh. I'll make it quick. Dinner this Saturday at Tuscano's."

"Should I wear my tux?"

She laughed. "Funny. Nope. Come as handsome as you are."

Omega blinked at her loose lips. That was flirty. Hopefully, it went over his head.

"Whoa, compliments. I love it. And for the record, I'm never too busy to talk to my prayer partner. But I'm thankful business is picking up, so I gotta go. Praise the Lord." He was gone.

Pray, the Lord's voice thundered.

Her spirit kicked in on high alert. She thought about asking Caylee to join her in prayer but decided against it. Omega didn't want to jeopardize her position by praying with another employee during office hours. Mitchell was busy—and that was a good thing—so she was on her own.

"Father, in the mighty name of Jesus, I'm coming boldly to Your throne of grace. Someone needs You, Jesus. Whoever is in trouble, dispatch Your angels for protection. Strengthen Your people to recognize and stand firm in Your Word. Protect our minds against depression and distraction, darkness…"

As God spoke to her, tears streamed down her cheeks. She prayed for strength against the lusts and corruption in their bodies. Omega ended with, "Deliver the saints out of the hands of their persecutors and oppressors, in Jesus' name. Thank You for binding on earth what You have in Heaven. Amen."

She sat quietly, meditating on the Scriptures. Her phone alerted her of a conference call. She dabbed her eyes and patted her face. After reapplying her lipstick, Omega signed into the video chat to join the meeting.

Half an hour later, Phyllis Hawkins blurted out as they were about to end, "There's been a horrific bus accident with children on board, returning from summer camp."

The twelve others on the call were silent. Horror and despair clung to their faces.

"I'll be praying for miraculous minimum injuries." When Omega disconnected, she thanked the Lord for allowing her to intercede.

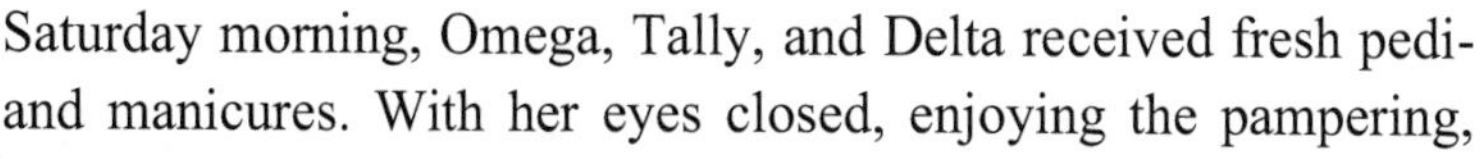

Saturday morning, Omega, Tally, and Delta received fresh pedi- and manicures. With her eyes closed, enjoying the pampering, Delta blurted out, "Are you nervous?"

Omega gave the question some thought. "Not really. A relationship with a Christian man hasn't crossed my mind."

Delta cleared her throat, and Omega opened her eyes. "I was talking to Tally."

Embarrassed, Omega blushed. "Oh. Sorry."

"Don't be. I think it's sweet to be in a relationship with a Christian man interested in your soul first. The attraction between you and Mitchell has been building. I can see a romantic relationship developing. Makes sense to me." Tally snickered.

"Excuse me. This is about Delta and Kyler…and you and Randall if Delta has her way." Omega squinted at the two as her heart pounded. Although she didn't think Mitchell and Farrah were still together, Omega didn't want to pry about the details. He owed her nothing about his private life, even if he had held her hand.

"I've genuinely liked Mitchell from day one. You don't see how he looks at you. And don't forget, the man took a bullet for you." Delta lifted a brow in a tease.

"I'll never forget that. Ever. Everything else about this conversation, I'd like to forget." Omega shifted, careful to keep her feet still.

"Okay, so what are we wearing?" Delta changed the subject to Omega's relief.

Saturday evening, Omega dressed as if she was going on an actual date. Although it was just Mitchell, she still wanted to look and feel pretty.

Omega had the stylist straighten her black hair. Very seldom did she wear more than blush and lipstick. Not this evening. Omega went all the way out tonight—lashes, mascara, liner, brow pencil. She left nothing untouched. Staring in the mirror, she was unrecognizable to herself.

She slipped into a new fitted dress that was a size bigger. She would ask Mitchell about an exercise regimen to shed a few pounds and tone up.

Omega steadied herself in four-inch heels before she took the stairs.

The doorbell rang. She opened it, and the look on Mitchell's face was worth the pampering for their pretend date.

"Wow." Mitchell whistled. "I've definitely got to keep you away from the brothers at church now."

She laughed, blushing. He worked hard to make her feel pretty and she would live in the moment. Omega complimented him too. Not that she hadn't seen him in a suit and tie at church and casual attire. She had even noticed his fresh cuts, but this evening, something was different.

Maybe the fake lashes had obscured her vision. Refusing to entertain romantic notions, Omega set her home alarm, then turned around. Instead of his truck, Mitchell had a driver in a black car.

Her jaw dropped. "You are going all the way out for this not a real date."

Mitchell guided her to the car and opened the back door. He waited for her to slide inside. "Whatever you want to call this dinner—fake, pretend, or real—you, Miss Addams, deserve it." He closed her door and came around and got in on the other side.

During the twenty-minute ride to St. Charles County, Omega brought Mitchell up to date on the bus accident.

"It dangled over a bridge above a creek. There were some injuries, but amazingly no one died. I guess that's why God told me to pray."

Mitchell grabbed her hand and squeezed. "Lord, give O peace in her spirit tonight so she can enjoy her pretty self, in Jesus' name."

He had never called her O before. She stared into his eyes, and no words came to mind to respond to his use of her nickname.

Mitchell winked, and she looked away. He linked his fingers through hers, and his intimate touch felt awkward.

Then familiar.

She relaxed.

When the driver stopped at the entrance, Mitchell climbed out first. He opened her door and held out his hand for hers.

Why did she feel like Cinderella? Mitchell tried to link their hands again, Omega tried to shake free. “I don’t want to give my sister any ideas there is more between us.”

“You know,” he said, frowning, “I like the idea of there being more between us, but I don’t want you to be uncomfortable.”

She playfully nudged his shoulder to ease her wayward thoughts. “Never with you.”

“*Hmmm.* Your hair smells good too,” he complimented and opened the restaurant door.

The others had beaten them there. Tally and Delta had smirks on their faces, which Omega did her best to ignore.

Delta made the introductions. Mitchell shook Kyler’s hand, then extended his to Randall. Her brother hesitated until Tally elbowed him.

Lord, please draw Randall to You for his salvation because he and Tally are perfect together, she prayed as the hostess showed them to their table.

As if it had been rehearsed, the men pulled out the women’s chairs simultaneously.

The dinner was lively with plenty of tales. Tally didn’t seem uncomfortable or frown when Randall put an arm behind her chair. They even laughed together when they shared some fun memories of how they met. On the outside, no one would guess they were no longer a couple.

Randall wouldn’t blink to get on one knee and propose. Tally would hesitate to say yes. For good reason. They were spiritually unequally yoked now. That truth crushed Omega.

While they discussed careers, Mitchell mentioned he owned Kings and Queens Fitness.

“Really?” Kyler recalled going there when he lived nearby. “I thought your face looked familiar.”

After a few hours, no one was in a rush to leave, except Omega when she spied the time.

"Well, it was nice being here with my favorite siblings." She chuckled when Delta said they were her only siblings. "But we have church in the morning."

Mitchell signaled the waiter for their check.

"I got this. My treat," Kyler offered.

"Thanks, but this wouldn't be a date if I let others pay, especially for me and Omega. You understand." Mitchell wasn't going to back down as he handed over his credit card.

Omega wasn't privy to his finances, but she didn't want to be the cause of him overextending himself.

"I better head home too. Thanks for the treat, Kyler." Tally smiled and scooted her chair back.

Randall reached into his back pocket for his wallet and pulled out his credit card. "This is for Tally and me. If anyone is going to treat her, it's me."

Let chivalry live on. Omega and Delta sucked in their breaths and mouthed, *Alrighty now.*

Randall stood and helped Tally to her feet. "I'll trail you to make sure you get home safe."

The expression on Tally's face was nothing less than love. "Thank you."

One by one, they left the restaurant. As the chauffeur pulled off the lot, Omega spied Randall towering over Tally at her car.

"I hope my brother surrenders to Christ's salvation soon because he's miserable without her."

"Imagine how miserable he'll be without Christ on judgment day. We need to pray that Tally can be the light and not surrender to her fleshly desires. If he really loves her, he'll get right with God. As stubborn as my dad is, his love for my mother mellowed his pride so that God could speak to his soul. We've both witnessed that."

"Mitchell, I hope I'm not out of place saying this, but I care about you."

He grinned.

"Your business is suffering, but you wanted to pay the table's tab to call this a date. I'm glad Randall stepped up. Please don't do that again."

"Noted and I appreciate your concern. My business is picking up. It's steady, and I'm thankful it's not declining. Thank you for caring, and all my money isn't tied up in Kings and Queens Fitness. I do pay myself a salary." He paused and bit his bottom lip. "You, Omega Addams, are the type of woman any man would want to impress. End of discussion."

When the driver pulled into her driveway, Mitchell continued his chivalry. At her door, he smiled as he took both her hands. "This was fun. I'll have to thank Delta for making you invite me. Next time, let's do something fun on our own. Since you enjoyed riding instead of driving, how about I pick you up tomorrow for church?"

Omega lifted her freshly waxed eyebrow. "Sure. Don't be late." She kissed his cheek, unlocked her door, and walked inside.

Chapter Twenty-five

As for God, His way is perfect; the word of the LORD is flawless. He is a shield to all who take refuge in Him. —Psalm 18:30 KJV

Mitchell squinted when Delta, Kyler, and Omega breezed through the doors of Kings and Queens Fitness Monday evening. He had spoken with Omega earlier, and she hadn't mentioned she would see him later. Since Saturday evening, they had seen each other three days in a row.

He was generous with his smiles as he greeted his visitors, especially Omega. "What a surprise."

"Do you mind if Delta and I check out your equipment?" Kyler asked. "It might be something we can do together."

While Kyler smiled, Delta didn't look happy about her date's suggestion.

"Do you need a tour?" Mitchell asked but kept his gaze on Omega. Unlike some clients that dressed in flashy work-out clothes to show off their assets, Omega had donned a long T-shirt and leggings.

"And what services would you like to sign up for, my queen?" His lips curled with a mischievous slant.

Tilting her head, she seemed to play along. "I'll need a trainer. My exercise regimen is usually a jog in a park.

His business was steadily picking up, thanks to the word-of-mouth Sallie's testimony had generated. Anthony, Mitchell's recent new hire, came to assist. "I got free time, boss. You can follow me." He waited for Omega.

"I've got this one." Mitchell held out his arm, and Omega slipped her arm through it.

"Tone down the testosterone, Brother Franklin." She snickered and let him lead the way.

Once they were in the stretching room on the mat, Mitchell put her through a series of routines. He knew she was beautiful and had a nice body but seeing the outline of her shape took his breath away.

For all that is in the world, the lust of the flesh, and the lust of the eyes, and the pride of life, is not of Me, but is of the world. God's whisper was thunderous. *Study 1 John 2:16. Your soul depends on it.*

Mitchell almost choked on his breath.

Omega sat up; brows met in a frown. "You okay?"

"Yeah." Mitchell looked down to clear his head, then back at Omega. "Why haven't we dated before Saturday's dinner?"

"That wasn't a real date. It was a setup. Delta is the mastermind behind my being here now. She called me as I left work to say she and Kyler were coming to check out your gym. She knew I would take the bait and tag along too. Besides, I should have come to support you before now."

"I'm glad you did." He spied his regular patron-turned-fellow church member, Sallie, waving and giving him a thumbs-up. Omega's sister wasn't the only one playing matchmaker.

Omega became quiet. She didn't hide the sadness on her face. "April leaves on Friday, and the only reason I'm not there now is they are taking care of business. I'm going after I leave here." She groaned out a sigh. "I'm missing them already."

Mitchell thought about what Mrs. Helena said about Omega carrying the world's weight on her shoulders. As he had her go through several stretches, he prayed for her to accept God's will whether they liked it or not.

"Good job. Now, let's get you on a bike for about ten minutes." He stood beside her like her bodyguard and prayed.

After that, Mitchell adjusted the treadmill speed, set the incline level low for her as a beginner, and continued praying for her peace.

"I feel like I've had a complete overhaul," Omega said forty minutes later.

"It's called a workout." Mitchell grinned.

When Omega was ready to leave, he walked her to her car, and God gave him the words, "*Let not your heart be troubled. The effectual fervent prayer of a righteous man prevails much.* God has heard every whisper, cry, and thought concerning Caylee."

"What does that mean? Will Caylee live or die?" Her eyes were misty as she searched his for the answers.

Mitchell shrugged. "I'm repeating what God gave me."

"I needed to hear that." She stood on her toes and kissed his cheek. "Thank you for being here for me."

"Always."

"I think you should plan our next date." She slid behind the wheel with a flirty smile, started her engine, and drove off.

Rubbing his mustache, he walked back into the gym, shaking his head. "I did not see that coming." So, Omega did want the two of them to go out again. Good to know.

Later that night at home, Mitchell's thoughts were on Omega. Not as his prayer partner, but a woman he did want to date. He mentally tracked every moment they had spent together from the gas station shooting to in his gym earlier. He liked everything about Omega—her passion, vulnerability, and genuineness. Mitchell dozed off as he stretched out on the sofa. Minutes after midnight, Omega's ringtone woke him.

"Hey," Mitchell answered softly as he dragged himself off the sofa and made his way to his bedroom.

Omega bawled.

He panicked.

Mitchell didn't know how to comfort her. Sing a song, quote a Scripture, pray? God said nothing.

When she seemed drained of tears, Omega hiccupped. "Sorry. I held all that until I stepped into my living room, and the dam broke."

"How are Caylee and April?"

"Ecstatic. The glow on their faces made me sniff. I asked April again if she prayed on the decision and waited for God to answer."

"And what did she say?"

"My heart broke when April said, 'this was the desire of her heart, and God gave it to her. She exchanged a high five with Caylee, and they both giggled."

Mitchell debated verbalizing his thoughts. "She'll die in the Lord. That will have to be our comfort."

"Yeah, you're right. It doesn't mean I have to like it." Omega grunted.

Switching the subject, Mitchell steered the conversation about more pleasant thoughts—how beautiful she looked. He made her laugh, giggle, and debate about anything, even Scriptures. That's how he learned to comfort her.

She yawned and Mitchell stifled his. "We better say good night." He didn't go back to sleep right away. Why would God show Omega Caylee's death? Why?

Mitchell's eyelids became heavy, and darkness filled his mind as he waited for an answer.

Chapter Twenty-six

And we know that all things work together for good to them that love God, to them who are called according to his purpose....
—Romans 8:28–29 KJV

This was it. Caylee's life was about to change forever. April would live out her dreams. And Caylee would be her cheerleader. Her emotions were bittersweet—happy and sad.

She tried to put on a brave face at work around Omega. All three had grown close, and Omega was taking it hard too. April would be missed.

At home, Caylee reflected on their lives, which hadn't been without trauma. Their mother abandoned them when Caylee was nine. April was three. Their father was devastated that his wife had a lover who had drawn her away from her family.

When their father died in Caylee's third year in college, she tried to step into the role of a parent and didn't know her self-worth when she took on the role of a stripper. April knew her worth by the time she was a teenager.

Caylee clicked off the TV with the remote. The show had changed, and she wasn't watching the program as her mind wandered.

Closing her eyes, Caylee rested her head on the back of the sofa. She smiled. "God found me when I didn't know where the Lord was."

Opening her eyes, she grabbed her Bible. Caylee flipped the pages and paused at Romans chapter eight. Verse thirty-five spoke to her soul: *Who shall separate us from the love of Christ? Shall tribulation, distress, persecution, famine, nakedness, peril, or sword?*

Her eyes misted. It was a good thing April wasn't there to witness her breakdown. Some of the staff she worked with took her out to dinner to celebrate her sister's accomplishments.

Although Caylee knew nothing could separate her from the love of Christ, it would the separation from her sister that made her heart ache.

Pray, God whispered.

She slid to her knees. God filled her mouth with unknown tongues before she began to petition the Lord. The language was forceful and commanding. With her hands lifted and tears streaming down her cheeks, Jesus showed her a vision as she felt darkness encircle her. It made her shiver but not afraid.

The Lord was with her as she had read in the passage. Nothing could separate her from the love of Christ—no matter what happened. The more she yelled, "Jesus," the more the dark cloud-like figures moved back until they faded out of her vision.

Peace descended over Caylee. She stood, wiped her face, and entered her bedroom to prepare for bed. Everything was going to be alright. God wouldn't let anything or anyone harm April.

When Omega didn't see Mrs. Helena for a few mornings, she stopped to check on her. The brightness in her eyes was dimmed as the two hugged.

"How are you feeling?"

"Like this bronchitis is not going anywhere. It's always like this after a heavy rain." She wheezed as if to demonstrate.

The first time she visited her neighbor, it had stormed for three days and nights, yet Mrs. Helena was outside watering her flower beds as if they would die of thirst.

Her neighbor mustered a smile for Omega's benefit. "Where are you off to this late in the day? You look so cute. If I had your legs, I would wear short dresses too."

Omega gasped and blinked. Huh? Mrs. Helena had never complimented her physical appearance. She harped on inner beauty, and that's what Omega had strived for.

"Thank you, but I've worn this before."

"You have? *Hmmm.* Well, when Mitchell begins to look at you as more than a sister in Christ, remember that he's attracted to more than what's in your heart."

"Mrs. Helena, I didn't know you were a matchmaker. Is there anything I can get you before I go? April is leaving this afternoon, so I took off work, and you know what God revealed to me about this, so I came by for prayer for strength."

"It appears we both need strength." She pointed to her Bible. "Hand me that small bottle of holy oil. We can pray for each other. First, I'll anoint your head, and then you do the same."

Omega took a seat next to her and closed her eyes. Mrs. Helena dabbed her finger on Omega's forehead. "God, in the name of Jesus, I thank You for drawing laborers to Your harvest. You have begun a great work in Omega. Encourage her while Your Word goes forth to accomplish Your Will and won't stop until it gets it done. We know all things work together for good. Let Omega be prosperous for Your Glory and give her strength, in Jesus' name. Amen."

"Amen," Omega repeated and opened her eyes to see the glow and a genuine smile had returned to her neighbor's face. "Thank you."

Next, she did the same as her protégé prayer warrior. "God, in the name of Jesus, thank You for saving me and Mrs. Helena for showing us how to live pleasing to You. We know Your

Word is power, so please speak to the condition in her body and restore her to us again. Thank You. In Jesus' name. Amen."

"Amen!" Mrs. Helena pumped her fist like she was in the ballpark rooting on the Cardinals.

"Wasn't as eloquent as yours—"

"But it got the job done." She stood. "I feel my strength coming back. I guess I'd better go outside and tend to my flowers. Don't fret about the Prince sisters. God's plan is always perfect, no matter the outcome."

Mrs. Helena's encouragement calmed the storm that had been brewing in her spirit. Omega didn't question God about His plan. She was upbeat until she turned on Caylee's street. A dark cloud hovered over the apartment building. It was vibrant as a scene from a high-tech movie against the backdrop of sunny skies with a few clouds.

Her spirit went on high alert as she parked her car but didn't get out. "No, Satan. The Lord rebukes you and your nasty demons. Jesus, dispatch Your angels to fight these creatures. I don't have time for their skirmishes today."

A swarm of angels appeared. Their swords were drawn. Her spiritual eyes gave her an unobstructed vision of the intense battle that ensued. She hadn't seen anything like it, not even the first day she met Caylee.

Whatever you bind on Earth is bound in Heaven, God whispered.

When Omega stepped out of her car, she felt at peace and smiled. "God, I know You never lose a battle."

She rang Caylee's bell, and the door opened immediately.

"'Bout time you got here. April and I were going to leave early for the airport. This is an exciting day!" Caylee did a happy dance.

Rejoice with those who rejoice, God whispered.

Really? Omega had come to accept her sister-in-Christ was going home to be with the Lord, so she praised God for His will.

Soon April joined them. It turned into a farewell praise party.

April's phone chime brought them back to the present. "Oh, it's my alarm. Don't want to be late." She grabbed her phone and squinted. "Wait. I got a text from the agency to call them right away."

Omega and Caylee watched as April punched in the numbers and put the call on speakerphone.

"Monae Clark Agency. This is Sarah." Her voice was monotone, utmost professional.

"Oh, hi, Miss Sarah. This is April Prince."

"Yes, April. Have you left for the airport?" Her desperation was unmistakable.

"Not yet," April said, beaming, "but don't worry, I won't miss my flight."

Omega remained calm and quiet. Not April as she gave Caylee the thumbs up.

"Don't come."

"Huh?" The air chilled as April questioned the woman. "Why?"

"Monae passed away suddenly, and all the assets in her name are frozen. We're waiting on litigation and possibly the dissolution of the business. I'm afraid your contract is void, dear, but you are entitled to keep the signing bonus. No need to come. Goodbye."

April wailed as she collapsed to the floor, reminiscent of a toddler's temper tantrum. Omega and Caylee were at her side and sobbed with her.

Caylee wouldn't die. Omega was relieved as her soul rejoiced. *Thank You, Jesus. Thank You, Jesus.* "Thank You, Jesus."

When she realized the weeping had stopped, Omega opened her eyes and met Caylee and April's frowns.

"Why would you say Thank You, God, Omega? I wanted that job." Angry, she stood and stomped away—temper tantrum in full effect.

"Why?"

Caylee's face was as swollen as Omega's puffed eyes. "In First Thessalonians, it says *in everything give thanks, for this is the will of God in Christ Jesus concerning you.*"

"I know that's a Scripture, but right now, I can't rejoice. I'm mad." Tears spilled and followed the trail down her cheeks. "My sister's heartbroken. How can God let the devil steal our blessings?"

Caylee touched her forehead. "I have a stress headache now. I need to lie down. Maybe when I wake, this will all be a dream."

Dismissed, Omega let herself out. It was bittersweet. God knew what was best for Caylee.

As Omega drove away, she glanced at the top of the building where the battle had raged. A lone angel stood on the rooftop with his arms folded as if it was guarding it, like a mother hen and her chicks.

Omega exhaled. Caylee and April had won this battle. They didn't know it yet.

Chapter Twenty-seven

For the Lord God is a sun and shield: the Lord will give grace and glory: no good thing will he withhold from them that walk uprightly.
—Psalm 84:11 KJV

Caylee's head throbbed as she lay in bed next to her sister, trying to quiet her sobs. Her agonizing moans sounded like a wounded animal begging to be put out of its misery.

"*Shhh*," Caylee cooed as she rubbed April's back.

April hadn't cried this hard when their dad died years ago. Mentally exhausted, Caylee dragged herself into her room and climbed into bed after her sister drifted off to sleep.

How could this happen, and why couldn't the lady wait to die? That sounded selfish, but she would never verbalize the thought that crossed her mind. She closed her eyes and prayed for sleep.

Caylee, God whispered.

She stirred but didn't open her eyes.

God called her name again: *Caylee*.

Startled, she scooted up in bed and glanced around the room. Moonlight peeped through her window, piercing the darkness.

Caylee knew that Scripture read, "*My sheep know My voice*," and she was sure that was the Lord.

Close your eyes and see, God whispered and showed her the wreck she would have been involved in after leaving the airport.

The semi-driver would have plowed into Caylee's new car and instantly killed her.

She gasped in horror. "Oh, no!" April would have been left alone. Now she bawled in thanksgiving that her life had been spared. "I'm sorry, Lord. Please forgive me for being mad at You," Caylee screamed in horror. She opened her eyes and blinked. Had she been dreaming while sitting up?

April rushed into her room and turned on the light, blinding Caylee.

"What's wrong?" Panic was plastered across her face as she jumped on the bed.

As Caylee was about to tell her, the Lord filled her mouth with praise. Shaking her head, Caylee struggled to speak as Jesus' spirit quieted her. "God showed me if you had gotten on that plane for New York, I'd have been killed in a car crash."

April covered her mouth. Her hands shook. April's hug choked the air from Caylee's lungs until she got free from her embrace. "I'd rather have you than that stupid job."

"God spared me!" Caylee was in awe of the revelation.

That triggered another crying binge until they used each other as an anchor to rock from side to side. Soon, Caylee fell back onto her bed. *I almost died.* She was at death's door and didn't know it. "I'm glad I didn't die."

"Me too, but what now?" April asked. "It's embarrassing to go back to that job after I told them I was going to New York. They were so happy for me. I thought God had my back. Since you and I surrendered to Christ's salvation, everything has fallen into place."

"Yeah, I know." Caylee nodded. "Good things were starting to happen for us. I just knew that New York agency was a blessing from God."

Sometimes things aren't as they appear to be. There are false visions. False prophecies. False promises. The devil can appear as an angel of light. God whispered into her spirit to read 2 Corinthians 11.

Suddenly, Caylee balled her fists and fumed. “The devil won’t trick us again. We’re going to wait on the Lord’s voice, cross every T, and dot every I.” Caylee took her sister’s hand and bowed her head to pray. “Lord, help us to know Your will, not ours, and Jesus, show us decoys so we won’t be led astray, in Jesus’ name. Amen.”

Chapter Twenty-eight

Precious in the sight of the LORD is the death of his saints.
—Psalm 116:15 KJV

The Twilight Thursdays summer concert series was set to begin on the lawn of the Missouri History Museum.

Mitchell and Omega were among hundreds stretched out on picnic blankets to enjoy the music of Anita Baker.

He leaned back on his elbows, with Omega doing the same. "You know after what happened with your coworker, I wasn't sure of Caylee's outcome," Mitchell admitted.

"A nail-biter to the last minute. It was like a prisoner getting a reprieve from the governor at the midnight hour to stay the execution. I told you I saw angels and demons fighting above her building."

"*Whew*." Mitchell rubbed his head. "You have to wonder what God has for her that makes the devil want to take her out."

"I know, right?" She smiled, then rested her head against his shoulder, teasing him with her affection in a shy manner.

That was Omega's mistake because he liked when she let her guard down and gave him a glimpse of her attraction. He admired her hair as the light breeze made it dance. She wiggled her polished toes—perfect feet. "Did I tell you how pretty you look tonight?"

"Your eyes did." She playfully scrunched her nose at him. A tease that made him want to kiss her.

"Busted." He grabbed her hand and squeezed. "Have you told Mrs. Helena the good news about Caylee?"

"Haven't had time. I've been going to work early to coordinate transportation for the disabled and disadvantaged for the last quarter of the year. I'm sure she knows." Omega closed her eyes and faced the sky as if she were sunbathing.

The more Mitchell was with her, the stronger his attraction. He identified with her passion but was enamored with her beauty.

He cleared his throat. Mitchell was sure she could feel his eyes on her. "Mrs. Helena will see her on Sunday at church. Any more visions from the Lord?"

"Not as of five minutes ago." She laughed, which sounded more of a giggle, then sobered. "My focus is my family. I want them to surrender to Christ's eternal salvation so bad."

"Someone is praying for them as their intercessor," Mitchell spoke the knowledge God gave him.

"I never thought of that." That brought a smile to her face. "That's encouraging because none of my family is interested in the Lord, although Delta did come to church."

"She might surprise you like my mom." He squeezed her hand. "As saints of God, He'll keep our spirit on high alert for the next assignment. Until then, we need to bear the fruits of God's Spirit…love them no matter what. Be joyful and peaceful around them. Most of all, prepare to be long-suffering because Christ's salvation is a lengthy process for some who fight against God. They're jammin' Anita, so give that burden to the Lord, so you can enjoy our time together."

Omega gave him a salute. "Yes, Sir."

For the next two hours, they clapped, cheered, and surprised themselves that they knew the words to Anita Baker's greatest hits.

With hands linked, Mitchell held her close when the concert ended. "So, I won't lose you in the crowd." He winked. Also, since the gas station robbery, he became more aware of sinister activity around them.

He felt something uneasy before he could identify the cause.

Farrah.

His ex was there with some girlfriends. She had no problem marching up into his face.

"Oh, you're with her now," she demanded as if she had the right.

"It appears so." Mitchell kept walking with the crowd.

When they were in the car, Omega asked, "You didn't break it off with her because of me, did you?"

"Nope. I broke it off with her because of her. She wasn't the one."

Since it was a work night, Mitchell took Omega straight home. He eyed Mrs. Helena's house. It was dark. Omega mentioned she usually retired early.

At Omega's door, Mitchell took both her hands before she reached inside her purse for her keys. "You know I care about you?" He continued when she nodded, looking at him with her beautiful brown eyes. "Do you have a problem with us being more than prayer partners?"

Mitchell could hear his heart pound as he counted the seconds, waiting for her answer.

Tilting her head, she smiled. "I was wondering if you would ever ask. Yes, I'd like—"

He didn't let her finish as he swept Omega into her arms and pecked her soft lips. When she didn't protest, their goodnight kiss was long and sweet.

Once Mitchell regulated his breathing, he grinned. He wanted to sing the childish tune "I Got a Girlfriend" but didn't. "My mom asked me to bring my girlfriend to the barbecue. Since I have one now, will you come?"

Omega laughed. "Your mom had already invited me, but she didn't mention anything about a stipulation that I had to be your girlfriend. Women are always a step ahead. Night."

Just when Omega thought there would be drama with Farrah, Mitchell handled it without much engagement. She respected him for that. But the big story of the night was Omega was in a relationship.

Dating? Really? She couldn't wait to tell Delta her status had changed with Mitchell. The following day, she called her sister and couldn't contain her excitement. "Guess what?" She giggled.

"I already know." Delta snickered.

"You do?" Omega frowned, admiring her manicure, which was holding up nicely. "Who told you?" Gossip didn't travel that fast.

"You and Mitchell are engaged, right?"

"What? Girl, no. We're officially dating." Omega touched her lips, remembering their first kiss. She sighed.

"And it took how long for you two to know that's what you've been doing all along—four, five months? The chemistry between you two was almost as hot as Randall and Tally's."

Omega laughed. "Now you're exaggerating. Their flame has been sizzling for almost two years."

"Speaking of our brother, I don't know how Tally did it, but Randall agreed to attend church with her on Sunday."

What? Omega's words choked in her throat. "What? He told you that?"

"And admit defeat to a pretty five-foot-four-inch woman who is bringing him to his knees for prayer instead of a proposal? Nah. Not our brother."

Her sister did have a point. Randall Addams was alpha male 10.0. He didn't take orders from anyone, which was why he owned his technology firm. He liked to run the show.

"Tally called to check up on me, and she mentioned it. She's been doing a 'well-being check' as she calls it a lot lately. Anyway, she's all excited. Of course, she asked me too. That wasn't happening. I plan to be the last holdout. My relationship with Kyler is getting intense. I don't want to jinx it with religion."

"Religion is meaningless if we don't have Christ. This is about your eternal salvation."

"I've heard this, O." The warning in Delta's voice was clear.

"Okay, okay. So, are we on for brunch tomorrow?" When Delta agreed, Omega asked, "Should I invite Tally?"

"I love Tally, but I don't feel like being outnumbered."

"Bye." Omega whispered thanks to God that she had a relationship with her sister.

By the time she finished dressing for work, Mitchell had called her. "Good morning, my beautiful girlfriend."

Omega couldn't believe he made her blush over the phone. For the months they had been together, his compliments had never done that. "Good morning. Did you sleep well?"

"Of course, knowing that you're off the market."

She laughed. "I think that saying is meant for a woman taking the *man* off the market."

"I'm that too." They chatted a few more minutes before Mitchell wanted to pray for her. "May the Lord watch between me and thee while we're absent one from the other. Please, send angels to protect her today, in Jesus' name. Amen."

"Amen." She was about to end the call.

"Can I get a kiss?" he teased.

She giggled. "Over the phone?" They were going to start that goofy stuff.

"No. Outside your door."

"What?" She jumped and raced to the window in her bedroom. There he was, leaning against his truck. He had on his Kings and Queens Fitness polo shirt, showing off his biceps, with his tan pants. His feet were crossed at the ankles as he waved. "Silly man. I'll be right down."

She grabbed her purse and laptop. Omega locked her door and walked into Mitchell's strong arms for a hug. When she stepped out of his embrace, she looked into his eyes. "I can get used to this."

"Me too." Mitchell wiggled his brows.

"But you work in the opposite direction, so I don't expect you to make this a habit, Mr. Franklin," she said as she punched in her garage code to get her car.

Once in her vehicle, he trailed her out of the cul-de-sac, waving at Mrs. Helena. "Thank You, God, for a praying boyfriend."

The next day, the sisters met at the Peacock Loop Diner in the U. City Loop, not far from The Pageant, considered a top concert venue in the country.

Though it was the two of them, they grabbed a carousel booth that could easily seat six to eight guests. It was a thrill ride for Omega and Delta.

Omega ordered French toast, and Delta, the Loop Slider, a signature dish. While waiting, Delta couldn't resist spinning their table.

"What's the latest with you and Kyler? He seems nice." Omega took a sip of her fruity drink topped with whipped cream.

Delta shrugged. "I like him, but he's too much of an exercise guru. My exercise is a brisk walk in the morning or evening. I'm good. As a matter of fact, he's thinking about joining Kings and Queens Fitness."

"Cool." Omega clapped her hands in a soft applause. "I'm sure Mitchell will appreciate his business. Is that the only turnoff?" She eyed her sister.

"Plus, Mom doesn't get good vibes about him. And you know she's been trying to get all of us married to get grandchildren." Delta scanned the restaurant, where various celebrity life-size cutouts were displayed throughout. They were great backdrops for selfies. She grinned. "Whenever I talk to Mom about men, she thinks I'd be happy with a man like your Mitchell, and she hasn't even met him."

Omega smiled. "He wasn't my Mitchell until after the concert at the history museum and we ran into his ex. He was very diplomatic. No drama."

"*Hmmm*. I like him even more." Delta fanned her hand in the air. "After Mom planted that seed, I started to notice little things. He drinks a little too casually for me. Drunk driving is real. But if I overlook that small indiscretion, he's perfect. Kyler's fine. Charismatic. Doting. But Mom's comments still nag at me."

"They should. Just think, every time you two go out, you'll have to be the designated driver." Omega and Delta had always been picky when it came to men thanks to their dad and brother who drilled into them not to settle for any man with a job and fresh breath.

"Enough about me." She brushed off Omega's assessment. "Tell me everything about the other side of Mr. Franklin." She grinned as the server slid their plates before them.

Omega said grace, then sampled her French toast before giving Delta a detailed description of his words, hugs, and their first kiss. She blushed again.

"Do you think Mitchell could be the one?"

Her sister would have to wait as Omega stalled to indulge in a French toast strip. "It's too early to guess. We have to separate our commitment as prayer partners for us to develop a romantic relationship. I don't know how that will work."

Delta squinted and smirked. "I think you'll both figure it out. If Kyler starts talking about Jesus, it's over."

Omega shook her head. "Girl, a man who loves Jesus—for real, for real—is sexy."

Delta had no comeback as they finished their brunch, left a tip, and headed to shop at the nearby Galleria Mall.

Chapter Twenty-nine

And the Spirit and the bride say, Come. And let him that heareth say, Come. And let him that is athirst come. And whosoever will, let him take the water of life freely. —Revelation 22:17 KJV

Sunday morning, the Spirit of the Lord was high in the sanctuary. It was a perfect celebration for Omega's new relationship, and she spied Randall in the far back row.

"You're not going to go sit with him?" Omega asked Tally, who sat on the same row with the crew. If that had been her family, she wouldn't think twice about sitting with the Addams.

Omega was relieved and thankful God revealed to Caylee His grace that what they had prayed for wasn't God's will. Once Caylee and April got over their disappointment, the sisters were glad they still had each other.

"I can't. Randall would be too much of a distraction. I love him, but I love my soul more. The images I saw in my nightmare will never leave me. Haven't you read in First Corinthians the third chapter about planting a seed? You planted the seed of salvation in Randall. I came along and watered it by showing him I was serious about walking with Jesus. Now, he's here, and my heart is happy, but I'm praying he is attentive, so God will cause the seed to grow." Tally jumped to her feet and began to clap to the beat of the singers.

Omega respected her would-have-been and hope-to-be sister-in-law. Tally walked in God's wisdom. It took strength to leave her brother, knowing how much they loved each other. "I'm praying too."

Tally's eyes sparkled as they misted. "Thank you. Congratulations. I see you and Mitchell have progressed to more than holding hands. The energy between you two is strong. Don't let him go, O. He loves you. Mitchell is a good guy who is sincere about the Lord."

"Loves me?" Omega patted her chest in surprise. "He, me, and we aren't there and may never get to that point." She dropped the subject as Mitchell's parents joined them in the pew.

She scanned the sanctuary and had yet to see Mrs. Helena in the front with the other church mothers dressed in their Sunday white. A staple on Sunday mornings, Omega would check on her after service.

The singers were caught up in a loop of praise. Soon, the sanctuary was set ablaze with God's presence. All around her, saints rejoiced, danced, and praised God. Heavenly tongues filled the place, and she was swept into the vortex. Tears streamed down her cheeks as she worshipped.

Suddenly, movements ceased.

She and Mitchell exchanged looks. Omega wondered if he sensed something was on the brink of happening. Mitchell grabbed her hand and didn't let go.

Mother Kincaid, who usually sat with Mrs. Helena, approached the podium, and spoke to the pastor. He then yielded the microphone to her.

"Praise the Lord, saints of the living God," she greeted them. "While many of us worshipped the Lord in unknown tongues, including myself. God told me to listen to the quietness. I chuckled because there was so much noise of heavenly praise, how was that possible. Then I heard it. God had my ears zoom in across the sanctuary to a faint but powerful voice. She pointed to the opposite side where she sat. "The Lord's voice was clear and distinct. He's got a message for us."

The sanctuary became deafening with applause.

Mother Kincaid closed her eyes. “Jesus said, ‘I’m about to pour out My spirit in a mighty way. Don’t stop praying because I’ll be in the midst of you. Many will be saved.’” She stepped down and returned to her seat as if she hadn’t revealed something so magnificent.

Along with the rest, Omega worshipped God for the message, unsure what it meant. Mrs. Helena would possibly know, so her neighbor’s house would be Omega’s first stop after church.

Pastor Rodney said that since God had already spoken to the congregation, there was nothing for him to add in a sermon, so he made an appeal for salvation. “If you’re here today without Christ in your life, you’ve experienced how real the Lord is. Repent of your sins, walk to the altar for prayer, and complete your salvation with the baptism, in Jesus’ name.”

Omega held her breath. Her heart pounded with hope. She glanced at Tally whose head was bowed. She was praying. Omega took her hand. Mitchell, who hadn’t let hers go, squeezed it. One look into his eyes revealed he knew where her thoughts were. Would her brother make the move?

Men, women, and teenagers flocked to the altar as Omega held her breath. From her peripheral vision, Randall stood. Omega elbowed Tally. They both watched as he walked in the opposite direction toward the exit. He was leaving. Her heart sunk to her feet. The letdown was so heavy.

Omega wanted to cry.

Tally did as her shoulders shook as she silently wept. Caylee tried to comfort her.

Omega couldn’t leave Tally in this distraught state. She would see Mrs. Helena another day. Omega hadn’t seen Tally this emotional since the breakup. It might be a long evening and an even longer night.

Chapter Thirty

I have fought a good fight, I have finished my course, I have kept the faith. Henceforth there is laid up for me a crown of righteousness, which the Lord, the righteous judge, shall give me at that day: and not to me only, but unto all of them also that love his appearing. —2 Timothy 4:7-8 KJV

Omega couldn't find the words to describe the hurt Randall had caused her and Tally by leaving service without speaking to them.

Without committing.

Without wanting prayer.

Be angry at the devil and pray for the scales to be removed from Randall's eyes so that he can see Me, God spoke to her spirit.

After that day after church, Omega and the crew committed to praying nonstop throughout the day.

That meant talking to Jesus as Omega prepared breakfast.

During potty breaks at work.

In her dreams.

Omega's heart broke as Tally became withdrawn and accepted she had lost Randall. "I don't have any regrets, O. I'd rather have Jesus, but the void is agonizing."

They had cried and prayed together over the phone the previous night, then Omega called Delta. "Can you check on Randall?"

"Do I have to? Mom talked to him the other day. He's not only miserable but agitated. It's like cancer is eating him up. I know he loves Tally, but I hope he can bounce back." Even Delta was willing to pray.

Although Omega's heart was heavy, life and responsibilities had to go on.

For the rest of the work week, Mrs. Helena was hit-and-miss watering her lawn. On Wednesday, Omega had planned to stop to speak, but couldn't because she was running late.

On Friday evening after work, Mitchell joined Omega to visit her neighbor.

Mrs. Helena opened her door with a smile that didn't quite reach her eyes.

Omega hugged her first, then Mitchell. The aroma of a hot meal didn't greet them.

Making themselves comfortable in Mrs. Helena's living room, Omega studied her friend. "I've missed seeing you. How are you?"

She chuckled. "Yeah, neighbors have been checking on me all week. Bronchitis is acting up. If it's not the spring allergies, it's the late summer molds. No complaints because it's a sin against God. The Lord is good."

"Amen." Mitchell nodded, then asked, "Are you hungry?" He seemed poise to do her bidding if she hinted she was.

Mrs. Helena waved him off. "Oh no, Brother Mitchell. My neighbors have brought me soup, stews, fruits, and other dishes I won't be able to eat all by myself, but please go in the kitchen and help yourselves. Whatever you find to warm up, fix me a little."

Mitchell stood and did as she asked.

Alone with her Bible mentor, Omega pressed her. "Are you okay, Mrs. Helena? It's not like you to miss church or let much get you down."

"Don't be too concerned, Omega. Neighbors thought I had died because I haven't been out much." She chuckled as if that was a ridiculous assumption. "But from the day we're born, our bodies begin to deteriorate. All my life, I've seen visions about life and death. Recently, God put me in a place where dirty and dingy caskets were lined up. People were in them. It was a dark and scary place. The bodies had disfigured faces. Painful and tormented expressions indicated death hadn't been kind."

Omega shivered. She had seen visions, mostly angels and demons. Never dead people. She sniffed aromas coming from the kitchen as Mitchell appeared in the doorway, listening.

"God told me to keep walking," Mrs. Helena continued, "so I did. It became brighter with each step. My surroundings glowed like the warmth of the sun and were peaceful. There was no fear there. Their caskets were pristine white like pearls. A slight smile resembled their peaceful state."

Omega watched her friend and neighbor as she was reminiscing.

"Death doesn't scare me as it would others who have no hope in Christ. I know where I'm going whenever it's time to go. God has been keeping score and will judge accordingly." Mrs. Helena smacked her lips. "I hope you're not burning Mrs. Stockman's pot roast."

"No, ma'am." Mitchell hurried back to the kitchen from the doorway. Minutes later, he reappeared with a grin. "Dinner is served."

Gathering around the table, Mitchell pulled back their chairs. He said grace, then the trio ate, laughed, and talked about the message from God at Sunday's service.

"What did the message mean?" Omega frowned.

Mrs. Helena rested her fork. "I prayed and asked God about that. I watched the service online, and Sister Kincaid came by to check on me afterward."

"And?" Mitchell asked.

"The Holy Ghost is about to explode when we least expect it. Like the apostles and disciples in the Upper Room, we better wait for it."

Excitement and praise filled Omega's soul. *Let it fall on my brother, Jesus!* "Bring it on."

Mrs. Helena was dead!

Mitchell tried to process that scenario. Omega's call as he was leaving the gym left him stunned. Mitchell froze in the parking lot until a car horn jolted him to move. His feet were too heavy to lift off the ground, so he dragged them to his truck. "I think she was preparing us."

"I guess." Her voice trembled. "One of my neighbors checked on her earlier and noticed Mrs. Helena's door opened, but she wasn't outside. Mrs. Townsend found her in the bed dead. She said it looked as if she was sleeping at first with a slight smile on her face." Omega sniffed. "All the time I've lived here, I never tried to get to know her until after the shooting. I guess it's true, you never know what you have until it's gone." Her voice faded.

"I know, babe. I'll be there shortly."

As he climbed into his truck, he experienced a heavy sense of foreboding. Mitchell was glad he and Omega had taken the time four days earlier to visit Mrs. Helena.

God spoke to him: *Pray for the victims*

When he started his engine, the radio blared the news. Motorists were being advised to avoid an area where a police pursuit was underway. That was the route to Omega's house.

Minutes later, the traffic slowed to a crash ahead. Multiple injuries.

At Omega's, he shared what God had told him to do. "It didn't look good. I'd be surprised if anyone lived."

"Oh no." Omega prayed with him, then they watched for updates online. "I feel we should be mourning Mrs. Helena's death, but it's business as usual with the Lord. Intercessions for others still have to continue."

Mitchell agreed. Later that night, they learned there were two people in critical but stable condition. Several others were injured but either treated and released or listed in satisfactory condition. "But no deaths." He mouthed his praise to God.

Up until her neighbor's funeral, he stayed by Omega's side. Instead of phoning her during the day, he either surprised her at her office with a boxed lunch or took her out. Mitchell missed their Bible mentor too. She had lit a torch within them about God's Word. Now, he and Omega couldn't drop it.

Mrs. Helena Wrighton's homegoing celebration happened that following Saturday.

Caylee and April took it hard. "God spared my life but took Mrs. Helena's. So many people needed her." Her jumbo-sized tears broke Mitchell's heart. He pulled her into a bear hug, then April joined them.

"You heard God's message from a few weeks ago. God's going to use all of us to reach people that maybe Mrs. Helena wouldn't have been able to," Mitchell tried to console them.

April *hmmmph*ed. "Judging from the people packed in here today, she reached the entire St. Louis area."

Mrs. Helena didn't have many relatives, so her neighbors, including Omega, claimed the honor in the procession. She had a distinguished career, which was acknowledged by educators, along with proclamations from various politicians.

Most of those on the program to give brief remarks credited Mrs. Helena with influencing their salvation journey. The shocker was Mrs. Helena's quiet battle with a heart condition.

Mitchell sat between the Prince sisters and Omega. Tally was on the other side of her. He linked his hands with Caylee and Omega. In a sense, he felt like a big brother. The choir sang many of Mrs. Helena's favorite musical selections.

Pastor Rodney's eulogy was brief. "The angels are rejoicing while we mourn our loss because it's their gain. This is a celebration of the lives she touched with words and prayers. She left a legacy of saints who walk with God even today." He quoted 1 Thessalonians 4:16–17 and that ignited the packed church's rejoicing.

Omega leaned over and whispered, "I never knew a funeral could be," she hesitated, "exhilarating."

The ladies climbed into Mitchell's truck for the drive to the final resting place for Mrs. Helena's earthly remains until the Lord's trumpet sounded.

Family and friends didn't need the funeral director's orange stickers for the windshields to trail the hearse to the cemetery. It was obvious they were part of the procession to the gravesite because many had decorated their vehicles with balloons and signs as if they were floats in a parade.

Chapter Thirty-one

The harvest is plentiful, but the laborers are few.
—Matthew 9:37 KJV

How could Omega feel guilty about being happy? Her relationship with Mitchell thrived as well as their spiritual growth.

Life was good.

That wasn't the case for her siblings.

Hope was gone for Tally and Randall's reconciliation.

Delta and Kyler were no longer a couple. Her sister discovered his little drinking problem was major. Kyler suffered from depression. Instead of getting treatment, alcohol became his comforter. Delta said she deserved better. The family agreed with her.

Fast forward to December. While some described Christmas as a magical holiday, Omega understood it as a promise fulfilled.

In preparation for the company's annual Christmas party that night, Omega booked her a manicure, and Delta decided she needed pampering, too, even if she wasn't going anywhere.

Out of the blue, Delta said, "I'm watching you." She pointed her free hand from her eyes to Omega's. "You and Mitchell are a power couple. If it works for y'all, then church might be in my future."

She liked the sound of that phrase. A Pentecostal power prayer couple. Omega smiled to herself. "If *you* want what I have with Mitchell, then salvation is your immediate need. You don't want to face a life-or-death situation before surrendering to God's will as I did. You might not get a second chance," Omega pleaded since her sister had opened the door for a conversation.

"I was talking about the place to find my future husband," Delta corrected.

The door quickly shut. Omega shook her head with a smile. She now understood the Scripture that said no man comes unto God unless He draws them. Omega had to be patient and wait.

Not long after the manicure, she hugged Delta goodbye. "This has been fun. I'll talk to you tomorrow."

"Oh, no. I'm coming to your house." Suddenly, Delta seemed as if she had nothing better to do than to follow Omega home. "You'll need help getting dressed for the Christmas gala."

"What?" Omega side-eyed her sister. "You do know that this isn't my first time attending a company party."

"It is with Mitchell. It's like he's meeting the family."

"Fine," Omega said as they separated in the parking lot, then Delta followed her to the condo. They bypassed Gus' Gas Mart where she and Mitchell's lives changed forever. The owner had upgraded the gas station and it was busy with patrons.

Mitchell made sure she gassed up before the start of the work week, but they both avoided that station if they could.

When Omega felt a twinge of sorrow as she passed the For Sale sign in Mrs. Helena's yard. Who would pray for the neighborhood now? She heard God whisper, *You.* Omega smiled and accepted the assignment.

At her condo, Omega activated her garage opener and waited for her sister to pull into the driveway, then they walked inside. "I don't have much time to get ready."

"Which is why you have me." Delta gave a mischievous grin.

While Omega preferred to indulge in a soaking bath, Delta reminded her she didn't have time, so Omega showered.

Afterward, she stepped into her bedroom where Delta was coordinating Omega's dress and shoes with jewelry.

Shaking her head, Omega was amused. The sisters had found their way back to each other despite their differences. Omega praised God for the mending. She had planted the seed. God would cause it to grow in His own time.

Omega wasn't moving fast enough as far as her sister was concerned, which caused Delta to fuss like a taskmaster.

"Would you hurry up so I can do your makeup."

Her sister was really going over the top for a simple annual party, but it felt good to have Delta there. Once Omega approved her sister's handiwork, Delta helped Omega slip into a new red evening dress, which she insisted Omega needed while they shopped for gifts.

Delta wouldn't let it rest. "With Mr. Franklin escorting you, it's a gala."

Giving in to purchasing the dress, Omega was impressed with her reflection in her full-length bathroom mirror.

"Yep." Delta rubbed her chin. "Just what I expected. Curvy and sexy."

"Not my intent." Omega smiled. "But I like it."

When Mitchell arrived and she opened the door, a slow grin crossed his face. "Omega Addams, you're stunning," he stuttered, biting his bottom lip. "I'd kiss you, but we have an audience."

"Act like I'm a fly on the wall." Delta giggled and slipped on her coat, then waved goodbye.

Mitchell shook his head and exhaled. "I can't kiss you now, O, because I'd lose my sane mind."

The frustration on his face was real and comical. "Then I'll kiss you." She smacked him on the cheek. "Come on, my handsome Hercules." She glanced at the curb. A limousine awaited them. Why was she not surprised? Omega smiled.

The light snowfall created a perfect backdrop for a romantic night as his hand steadied her in heels on the stairs until they reached the door. Inside the limo, Omega snuggled under his arm, then looked up at him. "Why are you so quiet?"

He grunted. "That dress has my thoughts jumbled up. I'm feeling so many things that I can hardly find my voice."

"Should I apologize?" she teased.

"I wouldn't accept it." He brushed a kiss against her lips, then whispered, "Every good and perfect gift comes from the Father above. Thank You, Jesus, for this wonderful gift."

She smiled as his eyes watered before he turned away. Mitchell seemed super sentimental tonight. Something shifted between them, and Omega wasn't sure what would come.

The banquet room at the Chase Park Plaza Hotel was packed with Hathaway Health staffers from two locations and their plus-ones.

Caylee and—her plus-one—April greeted them. Both could pass as models.

Omega had never seen Caylee look so sophisticated. How those two would ever separate was mind-boggling. They reminded her of her relationship with Delta.

"Don't you two look very distinguished." Caylee grinned.

"And you two, so beautiful." Omega exchanged hugs before introducing Mitchell to other staff members who weren't on the dance floor.

When she was about to take a seat at Caylee and April's table, Jay Hicks, the company owner, hushed the audience. "As you know, this has been a devastating year for Hathaway. We lost two of our employees who felt like family. Tonight, we have Yolanda's daughter, Dana, with us, and Bobby's parents, Rodney and Jennifer."

Mr. Hicks asked them to stand. They were greeted with a standing ovation with respectable soft applause.

"We're here for you now and in the future," Mr. Hicks said. "Before we eat, if you would like to have a word, please come forward.

Bobby's parents stood and walked to the front. The room stilled with anticipation.

His mother took the microphone from Mr. Hicks, nodded, and with a soft voice thanked everyone for the calls, flowers, food, and prayers. "It was your prayers that took us through this dark place. Bobby had planned to go to church the day after his party." She sniffed and her husband squeezed her shoulders. "He never made it."

The quietness was thick as Omega's heart ached with pain that she had almost persuaded him.

Bobby's dad guided his wife back to their chairs.

Dana stood from her table and approached. She was more upbeat. "I know there are rumors that my mom came to work the day she died," she paused and smiled. "I guess with God anything is possible, so although I miss her, I'm thankful for the testimony she left us."

Omega exhaled and faced Mitchell. "Yes."

He winked.

Why did he do that? She shivered in response.

As Dana handed Mr. Hicks the microphone, he asked her to bless the food.

Closing her eyes, Dana bowed her head to pray. Instead of saying grace, she boldly shouted, "Jesus!" reminding Omega of the last time she saw Yolanda either dead or alive.

A mist fell, blanketing the room, then a swish of wind stirred up a flame of light resting on many of the guests. Some began to speak in other tongues as others looked on in bewilderment.

Omega had never seen a vision like this.

There were no angels.

No demons.

No battles.

This was a magnificent light of God that moved in a way that held her breathless.

Tears streamed down some faces as they knelt before God. Lifting her hands, Omega worshiped the Lord.

In the last days, I will pour out My Spirit upon all flesh. God's voice faded.

Chapter Thirty-two

Every good and every perfect gift is from above and comes down from the Father of lights, with whom is no variableness, neither shadow of turning. —James 1:17 KJV

Mitchell's eyes were opened the night of the Christmas party. He saw God's Word come to life, pouring out His Holy Spirit in an unfamiliar setting.

God's presence was so tangible. He had experienced the movement of the Holy Ghost at church among believers. But in this room among unbelievers? Maybe there had been a change of heart after seeing the vision of their deceased coworker.

Then there was something else. Love knocked at his door. Omega glowed. He couldn't keep his eyes off her. Mitchell was in tune with her every movement, her words spoken and her smiles. The one. Omega Addams was the woman with whom he wanted to spend his life.

His heart swelled with love, and he planned to profess it before the night was over. As Mitchell contemplated how to say it, when to say it, and what she would say, he spied an older gentleman with Middle Eastern features peeking his head through the door. A younger man beside him made eye contact with Mitchell and motioned to have a word with him.

Mitchell braced for them to complain about their party creating too much noise for many of Omega's coworkers were speaking in other tongues, screaming the name Jesus, and worshiping in song and praise.

"This is the international holiday soirée? We hear someone speaking in our native tongue," the man's interpreter said.

"What you see is the power of God giving His Spirit to willing vessels. The same thing happened on the day of Pentecost in the Upper Room in the Book of Acts."

Omega rushed over to him. Excitement filled her eyes. He couldn't help but admire her beauty. "Mitchell, can you believe what God is doing here? Mr. Hicks and Reba want to know the meaning of this. I explained the salvation process. They and a handful of the others want the baptism in Jesus' name. We better call Pastor Rodney so he can arrange for some ministers to be there to baptize them in the morning."

This was what Mrs. Helena meant when she referenced Azusa Street Revival. When he researched this event, Mitchell learned that the Holy Ghost movement that had exploded in Los Angeles in the early 1900s continued for fifteen years. There were other pop-up instances where the Holy Ghost fell and spread on groups of people.

Mitchell suspected this was the beginning of God's revival of souls before His second coming. "Come, Lord, Jesus, come." He repeated Revelation 22:20.

At the party, the night ended with Omega's boss handing out gifts and Mr. Hicks' excitement about his baptism the next morning. He was filled with such awe about what happened that night that he was beside himself with joy.

At Omega's door, Mitchell ended the night with a soft kiss and professing his love. "I should have said it sooner."

She smiled. "You should have. Because I love you too."

Whispers of love mingled with their soft kisses until Omega said good night.

At Mitchell's home, he slept like a baby. Everything was alright in his world. There were fifteen days before Christmas, and Mitchell had no time to waste. They would be engaged before the end of the year. Better yet, a Christmas present to each other.

Sunday at church, Mitchell gave no inkling of his intentions to propose. As far as the crew was concerned, it was worship as usual. And that distracted him from asking Tally for a favor.

On Monday, Mitchell hoped for another option. Not that he had followed Kyler's routine, but occasionally, Delta's ex showed up. Mitchell would work a double shift if need be to speak with Kyler.

Kyler strolled in late Tuesday evening, and Mitchell was grateful that it wouldn't be another doubleheader. He approached the man, shook hands, and engaged in small talk before he asked for a favor.

"I don't know the details about your breakup with Delta, but I'm working on a surprise Christmas present for Omega and need Delta's help."

Kyler rambled off Delta's number without waiting for Mitchell's commitment, then headed for the weights.

"Thanks, man." Mitchell grinned, said good night to his shift, and headed home. Barely in the door, he texted Delta. **This is Mitchell. Are you with Omega?**

No. Why? Is something wrong?

I'm working on her Christmas present. It's a surprise. I need a favor. Call me when you get a chance.

His phone rang immediately.

"What kind of surprise?" Delta asked without a cordial greeting.

Mitchell hesitated. He knew the sisters were close, and they had resolved their differences, but could she be trusted? "I need to speak with your parents."

Silence.

"Really? They will be here the week of Christmas."

"It can't wait. Is it possible I can have their number to call them?"

"You sure beat around the bush." She huffed. "You better talk to my daddy if you plan to propose to my sister."

Mitchell sighed. "I wouldn't do it any other way."

"Cool. Well, your secret is safe with me if Dad gives his blessing, so you better man up." Delta gave him Eric Addams' number.

They ended their call. Mitchell checked the time. Eight-thirty. Not late, so he placed the call. When Omega's father answered in an intimidating no-non-sense tone, Mitchell introduced himself.

"Yes, young man. You're seeing my daughter."

Mitchell nodded. "Yes, and I'd like to have a word with you, Sir." He exhaled.

"I'm listening."

"In person, please, Sir." Mitchell waited.

"My wife and I will be there the week of Christmas."

"This can't wait, Mr. Addams. I would like to meet with you face-to face before the week is over. Give me a day *this* week and I'll book my flight."

Silence.

Then Mitchell heard muffled voices before Mr. Addams returned to the conversation. "Thursday. My wife and I have other plans this weekend."

Mitchell exhaled. "Thank you, Sir. I'll text you my flight information as soon as I book it."

"Very well. Glenda—that's Mrs. Addams to you—and I look forward to seeing you."

Perfect. Omega would never suspect a midweek trip. He would fly in and out on the same day. Mitchell found a nonstop that would put him in Dallas at noon and return at five-thirty.

Now, he had to pray for good traveling weather in December, no delays, and Omega not finding out. Mitchell made sure he kept his routine with her. They spoke in the morning before work, in the afternoon, and late before bed. A perfect plan.

Except on Thursday, Omega called with a prayer request. A coworker learned she had stage-four cancer, and the doctors didn't give her long to live.

Omega sniffed. "God hasn't given me any insight on her situation, but it's the holidays, and instead of being in the hospital getting treatment, I know she'd rather be with her family. Please help me pray for a miracle for Linda."

"I'm on it, babe. Let's pray now." He led them in prayer and asked for grace, mercy, and salvation for Linda and her family.

"Thank you. I love you," she whispered.

"I loved you first," he teased to lift her spirits.

"No, you didn't. A woman never shows her hand when it comes to her heart," Omega said. He imagined her delicate chin jutted and her hand on her curvy hip.

Mitchell couldn't help the grin stretching across his face. This was one argument he would let her win this time—only this time. "Okay, love of my life. I'll let you go, but I won't stop praying."

After the call, Mitchell grabbed a change of clothes—just in case and two pairs of underwear because his mother drilled into her sons you never leave home for a trip without an extra pair and toiletries in case something happened. Although Mitchell didn't foresee a problem, he added those things to his laptop bag, then drove to Lambert Airport.

Everything was in Mitchell's favor when he got to the airport. The flight was on time and the check-in line was short. The headache came when his plane touched down at Dallas Love Field airport. Once he walked off the plane, he hustled to get his rental car.

With a small window, he paid a higher price to a competitor for a sedan, programmed in the address Mr. Addams had texted him and headed that way. A half-hour drive turned into an hour and twenty minutes. He couldn't miss his flight back home without Omega suspecting something, but he couldn't rush the process of asking for her hand in marriage. *Lord, let me find favor—quick favor with her family.*

Three minutes from his destination, Omega called with an update on her coworker. "Doctors are running tests, but they said she could go home while they wait for results."

"Amen for that."

"Where are you? In the car?"

Mitchell gritted his teeth. He couldn't be busted. "Heading to a meeting. I'll call you later."

"Okay. I hope your meeting goes well. Talk to you tonight."

"Me too." *Whew.* Mitchell's heart pounded. Omega deserved to be surprised, and he hoped to pull it off.

He came to the gated entrance of the Addams family's retirement community. The assortment of shops, stores, and other small businesses ensured residents lacked nothing.

Arriving at the address, Mitchell noted the one-story house looked nothing like its neighbors. Each was unique in design and curb appeal.

He got out and grabbed the flowers for Mrs. Addams he'd picked up in the terminal. Omega's mother opened the door after he barely touched the bell.

"Mitchell, it's nice to meet you. Come in. My husband and I have been expecting you."

Nodding, he stepped inside. "Thank you for seeing me. These are for you, Mrs. Addams." Mitchell handed her the bouquet.

She blushed, reminding him of Omega, and sniffed. "How thoughtful. Your parents reared a respectable young man."

"I'll pass that on." He grinned.

"Hungry?"

He patted his stomach. "I could use a snack. Thank you."

What he didn't expect was a spread of finger foods: chicken wings, sliders, dips, veggies, and more.

"Help yourself." Omega's mother offered.

Mr. Addams appeared, and Mitchell turned to shake his hand, which the man accepted.

"Welcome to our home. After we eat, then you can talk." Mr. Addams said grace, which Mitchell wasn't expecting. They had seemed to give Omega such a tough time about accepting God's will. But he didn't feel any hostility toward him.

China plates clanked as the three of them helped themselves. Mitchell tried to be discreet as he watched his time, but he didn't have the luxury of time on his side.

After twenty minutes, Mitchell wiped his mouth and cleared his throat. "If it's okay with you I would like to tell you the reason for my trip."

Mr. Addams pushed aside his plate and gave Mitchell a pointed look. "You did graduate from college, correct?"

"Yes, Sir." Mitchell nodded.

"What fraternity?" her father asked.

"None."

Hmmmph. Mr. Addams squeezed his mouth. "Alright. You may begin."

After taking a deep breath, then exhaling, Mitchell rubbed his hands. "I love Omega and will until my last breath, and she knows it from the way I treat and respect her. I'm asking for your consent to marry your daughter."

Mrs. Addams smiled, then looked at her husband who bore a straight face.

"When our daughter finally told us what happened, your name came up. But I had no idea you two had developed feelings for each other. You saved my daughter's life the night of the gas station shooting, and for that I'm grateful." Her father choked.

"No, Sir. We saved each other's life. My truck was riddled with bullets as I was protecting her."

"Tragedy brought you two together. What about compatibility, your finances, your relationship with your family?"

"Omega and I became each other's anchor. We both surrendered to God's salvation and have each other's back. I love her passion for life and others. I was a physical therapist before I bought into a franchise, Kings and Queens Fitness Gym, where I encourage my members to stay healthy through proper exercise. My business fell off earlier this year but bounced back, and I've had to hire three additional employees. God opened the door by word of mouth, especially at church, so I can take care of my wife and family."

Mrs. Addams beamed as she clasped her hands. Mr. Addams didn't show his hand.

"Why is the church so important to you and my daughter? I see your religion as divisive."

Here we go. Omega, I hope you're praying for me. "Besides a healthy lifestyle, we had to do a wellness check with God after we were caught in the crossfire. We came willingly to Christ and testified of His mercy and goodness." He paused.

"Our faith—not religion—is to share the Good News about Christ's redemption from the stress in this world. I know she's invited you both to come. The choice is yours, but—and I repeat, but—we will not force your hand."

Mitchell lost track of time as God gave him the right words to draw them. An hour or so later, Mr. Addams' consented and shook hands. Mrs. Addams hugged him with tears in her eyes.

"We want grandbabies as soon as possible." Her eyes sparkled.

"That will be up to Omega, and I'll support her decision," Mitchell said.

"When do you plan to propose?" Mr. Addams asked.

"Christmas Eve, Sir."

"You don't have much time. You'd better not miss your flight back. If you need help, Delta can be discreet."

Mitchell thanked them and hurried to the airport. He praised the Lord for finding favor with the Addamses. He was relieved when he caught his plane and landed back home on time, thankful he didn't need to use his extra pair of underwear.

Chapter Thirty-three

If we believe not, yet He remains faithful: God cannot deny Himself.
– 2 Timothy 2:13 KJV

"This is hard, Omega," Tally told her the week of Christmas, "I've given up all hope that the man I love is going to surrender to Christ."

Yep. It looked that way to Omega, too, but she wasn't going to say it. "My brother is wrestling. The devil wants him in sin, and his soul is fighting for it. The Lord showed me that vision earlier this month. Remember, God doesn't lose a battle."

Tally was quiet. "I was pregnant."

"What?" Omega gasped. "Was?"

"Not a week after I told Randall, I lost our baby. He went ballistic. He was so mad at God for taking me away from him and now his child. I don't see him surrendering anytime soon."

"I'm so sorry. I didn't know." Omega considered the timeframe months ago when Tally seemed to withdraw from everyone. She had been heartbroken when Randall didn't surrender the Sunday he had visited their church. Her friend has suffered in silence. Omega didn't know.

"Sis, do you really think I'm going to let Satan's army win my brother's soul without a fight? I've been praying hard and fasting more. The devil can't have Randall Addams." Omega had on her game face.

Tally sobered and giggled. "Sounds like fighting words to me." She sniffed. "If you can be on the battlefield, then I'll suit up and join you."

"Yeah," Omega roared.

"Yeah!" Tally repeated.

When the call ended, they both were in better moods.

That night, the Lord had Omega read Jeremiah 31:3: *The LORD hath appeared of old unto me, saying, Yea, I have loved thee with an everlasting love: therefore, with loving kindness have I drawn thee.*

Closing her eyes, Omega meditated on that Scripture, then God whispered, *Let patience have her perfect work, that you may be perfect and entire, wanting nothing.*

She had read that in James, chapter one. "Lord, give me patience and peace. Give it to Tally and all the other saints praying for loved ones to come to You."

God had given her peace, and she slept like a baby.

Happy to have taken their vacations at the end of the year, Omega and Mitchell were inseparable as they shopped and attended parties. She finally introduced him to her parents. They were warm to him.

"So, babe," Mitchell said as they wrapped gifts at her place, "what do you think about spending Christmas Eve with your parents at Delta's house, then Christmas at my parents'?"

"Sounds like a plan."

"Right now, it's 'us' time, babe. Let's check out Christmas light displays."

"I love it." She leaned in for a kiss and he delivered.

Early on Christmas Eve at dusk, Mitchell drove to the Winter Wonderland at Tilles Park as light snow began to fall.

"Feel like taking a carriage ride through the displays?"

"Sure. I'm dressed warm." Omega smiled as she snuggled, then closed her eyes.

He kissed her forehead and chuckled. "Babe, you do know that we're supposed to be checking out the light displays."

Opening her eyes, she stared into his. Omega liked his look in the black Fedora and a red scarf around his neck. “I’m content. I don’t care about the displays. Not really. I’m loving this quiet time with you.”

He brushed cold kisses against her lips.

“See, I’m content.” She glanced at the display in passing and became excited at one theme. “Look.” She pointed.

“I can’t. I’m looking at you, wondering if I asked you to marry me, you would.”

Omega blinked. She gulped the chilled air. “Mitchell?” Her mind was too jumbled to say more.

As if on cue, the driver pulled over. Mitchell climbed out, then lifted her and gently placed her on the ground in front of the Cinderella display.

The light snow didn’t stop him from getting on one knee as her heart pounded. She was about to cry.

The tears would dry on her face.

Not a good look, so she sniffed instead.

“Omega Addams, I need you in my life. You’re kind, passionate, gorgeous, and so much more than my prayer partner. I promise to take care of you and be the best husband I can be with the Lord’s help. Spend a lifetime with me as my wife?”

How could she say no to those pleading brown eyes? “Yes, yes. I love you, Mitchell.”

He stood, brushed the snow off his knee and kissed her, then lifted her off the ground. Next, he reached into his pocket and pulled out the diamond engagement ring that flashed along with the lights on display. He helped her back into the carriage. This time when she snuggled up next to him, the only light she noticed was the brightness in his eyes.

Epilogue

I know thy works: behold, I have set before thee an open door, and no man can shut it: for thou hast a little strength, and hast kept my word, and hast not denied my name. —Revelation 3:8 KJV

New beginnings. New blessings.

Everything happened so fast that Caylee and April couldn't believe it. The Monday after the Christmas party, April received a call from a top modeling Agency in Australia.

At first, the sisters were leery of the offer, remembering the fate of Caylee if April had gone to New York. April debated whether she should consider the deal.

"I'm turning it down." April didn't blink an eye.

Caylee couldn't let that happen. This was her sister's ticket into the fashion industry. She asked for Mitchell, Omega, and the pastor to intercede on their behalf.

She also remembered Mrs. Helena once saying that adding a fast to prayer was a must when considering a major life decision. Mitchell paid for an attorney to verify April's modeling contract was legit.

Caylee checked off all the boxes for spiritual guidance.

When God whispered, *Go*, it was on!

Within a week, with the pastor's blessings and a tearful goodbye from the crew, Caylee and April packed up and moved across the world for a new opportunity.

Victoria Jackman at the WINK Models from Darlinghurst New South Wales, Australia, said April needed to prep for the upcoming fashions shows that would highlight clothes for the fall/winter collections. April was ready to work hard.

The woman had heard about April's misfortune with the agency in New York but stated she could further April's career.

Their only hesitation was April's age. At eighteen, they insisted she have a chaperone. Caylee came to the rescue as the adult to accompany her sister.

The Prince sisters were in Australia at Christmastime. It was an incredible sight as she looked out the window from their furnished apartment, and to think they celebrated Christmas fifteen hours before Omega and Mitchell in the States.

Sitting in a small but cozy apartment, Caylee read Christ's birth story beginning in Matthew, chapter one. She reflected on how the WINK Models agency had changed their lives.

Caylee wasn't expecting a gig for herself, but the agency said she had the perfect body type for catalog modeling, so Caylee signed a contract too.

It was exciting and scary. April was groomed for this line of work, not her.

She thought about Ephesians 3:20: *Now unto Him that is able to do exceedingly abundantly above all that we ask or think, according to the power that works in us.*

The sisters earned an unbelievable salary and traveled a lot. They were busy but missed their friends back home. Caylee told Reba, a new practicing Christian, she would stay in touch.

A chime alerted her of a text. **I know it's already Christmas there, and I have an early Christmas announcement: Mitchell proposed, and I accepted.**

"What? Charges for this international call were worth it—at least five minutes—as Caylee tapped her friend's number.

Omega answered, snickering. "Made you call, huh? Merry Christmas."

Caylee laughed. "Merry Christmas to you, big sis, and congratulations to the power couple."

Mitchell shouted in the background, correcting Caylee, "We're a Holy Ghost power couple. When we see demons, we'll slay them in Jesus' name."

Caylee's five-minute call turned into seventeen as Caylee insisted Omega give her an update on everybody, especially Tally.

"Please pray for my brother and Tally. She's given up hope for Randall's salvation. The devil is riding his back, but I got the Word of God for those demons."

The development saddened Caylee. She was so hoping for a happy ending for them. "I'll pray God's will."

"Perfect. Now, we've been on long enough. Kiss and hug April for us. Who knows, Mitchell and I may honeymoon in Australia."

"When?" Caylee laughed. "Come on. Give our love to everyone and Merry Christmas.

She disconnected and sat quietly. Caylee and her sister might be away from the crew, but she had learned how to become an intercessor. Tally treated her and April like sisters. For that reason, Caylee had her back. "Lord, it's time for Randall to go down. What's the game plan? I'm listening."

Author Note

I hope *Day Not Promised* has inspired you to strengthen your prayer life. This story wasn't on my radar for 2022. After I left my prayer closet, God told me to write it, which is different from the Christian romances I enjoy to pen.

My first thought: I can't do it. What was the genre: fantasy or something else? I thought I knew the direction God wanted me to go, so I compiled all the Scriptures about the End Times.

However, when I started writing Omega Addams' story, God wanted me to show His compassion toward us, how He protects us from the danger we can see and those dangers hidden from us.

Jesus loves us. Surrender today, whether your life is in shambles or not.

Please spread the word about this amazing story from the prayer closet to paper and post an honest review.

Much love until the next book in The Intercessors series.

Pat

BOOK CLUB DISCUSSION THOUGHTS TO PONDER

1. What plans have you made that were cancelled turned out to be a blessing?

2. Talk about a time you felt God's presence.

3. Discuss the last time you prayed—not at church—and your prayers turned into praise.

4. What character did you identify with most in the story?

5. Share your salvation experience.

6. Do you have a prayer partner?

7. Describe a time when something happened and you knew it was nothing but God.

About the Author

Pat Simmons is a multi-published Christian romance author of forty-plus titles. She is a self-proclaimed genealogy sleuth who is passionate about researching her ancestors, then casting them in starring roles in her novels. She is a five-time recipient of the RSJ Emma Rodgers Award for Best Inspirational Romance*: Still Guilty, Crowning Glory, The Confession, Christmas Dinner*, and *Queen's Surrender (To A Higher Calling)*. Pat's first inspirational women's fiction, *Lean On Me*, with Sourcebooks, was the February/March Together We Read Digital Book Club pick for the national library system. *Here for You* and *Stand by Me* are also part of the Family is Forever series. Her holiday indie release, *Christmas Dinner*, and traditionally published, *Here for You* were featured in *Woman's World*, a national magazine. *Here for You* was also listed in the "7 Great Reads That Help to Keep the Faith" by Sisters From AARP. She contributed an article, "I'm Listening," in the *Chicken Soup for the Soul: I'm Speaking Now* (2021). Pat is the recipient of the 2022 Leslie Esdaile "Trailblazer" Award given by Building Relationships Around Books Readers' Choice for her work in the Christian fiction genre.

As a Christian, Pat describes the evidence of the gift of the Holy Ghost as a life-altering experience. She has been a featured speaker and workshop presenter at various venues across the country. Pat has converted her sofa-strapped sports fanatical husband into an amateur travel agent, untrained bodyguard, GPS-guided chauffeur, and administrative assistant who is constantly on probation. They have a son and a daughter. Pat holds a B.S. in mass communications from Emerson College in Boston, Massachusetts and has worked in radio, television, and print media for more than twenty years. She oversaw the media publicity for the annual RT Booklovers Conventions for fourteen years. Visit her at www.patsimmons.net.

Other Christian Titles

The Jamieson Legacy series
Book 1: Guilty of Love
Book 2: Not Guilty of Love
Book 3: Still Guilty
Book 4: The Acquittal
Book 5: Guilty by Association
Book 6: The Guilt Trip
Book 7: Free from Guilt
Book 8: The Confession
Book 9: The Guilty Generation
Book 10: Queen's Surrender (To a Higher Calling)

The Intercessors
Book 1: Day Not Promised
Book 2: untitled
Book 3: untitled

The Carmen Sisters
Book 1: No Easy Catch
Book 2: In Defense of Love
Book 3: Driven to Be Loved
Book 4: Redeeming Heart

Love at the Crossroads
Book 1: Stopping Traffic
Book 2: A Baby for Christmas
Book 3: The Keepsake
Book 4: What God Has for Me
Book 5: Every Woman Needs a Praying Man

Restore My Soul series
Book 1: Crowning Glory

Book 2: Jet: The Back Story
Book 3: Love Led by the Spirit

Family is Forever:
Book 1: Lean on Me
Book 2: Here For You
Book 3: Stand by Me

Making Love Work Anthology
Book 1: Love at Work
Book 2: Words of Love
Book 3: A Mother's Love

God's Gifts:
Book1: Couple by Christmas
Book 2: Prayers Answered by Christmas

Perfect Chance at Love series:
Book 1: Love by Delivery
Book 2: Late Summer Love

Single titles
Talk to Me
Her Dress (novella)
House Calls for the Holidays
Christmas Dinner
Christmas Greetings
Taye's Gift
Waiting for Christmas
House Calls for the Holidays
Anderson Brothers
Book 1: Love for the Holidays (Three novellas): A Christian Christmas, A Christian Easter,
A Christian Father's Day
Book 2: A Woman After David's Heart (Valentine's Day)
Book 3: A Noelle for Nathan (Book 3 of the Andersen Brothers)

In *Crowning Glory*, Cinderella had a prince; Karyn Wallace has a King. While Karyn served four years in prison for an unthinkable crime, she embraced salvation through Crowns for Christ outreach ministry. After her release, Karyn stays strong and confident, despite the stigma society places on ex-offenders. Since Christ strengthens the underdog, Karyn refuses to sway away from the scripture, "He who the Son has set free is free indeed." Levi Tolliver, for the most part, is a practicing Christian. One contradiction is he doesn't believe in turning the other cheek. He's steadfast there is a price to pay for every sin committed, especially after the untimely death of his wife during a robbery. Then Karyn enters Levi's life. He is enthralled not only with her beauty, but her sweet spirit until he learns about her incarceration. If Levi can accept that Christ paid Karyn's debt in full, then a treasure awaits him. This is a powerful tale and reminds readers of the permanency of redemption.

Jet: The Back Story to Love Led By the Spirit, to say Jesetta "Jet" Hutchens has issues is an understatement. In Crowning Glory, Book 1 of the Restoring My Soul series, she releases a firestorm of anger with an unforgiving heart. But every hurting soul has a history. In Jet: The Back Story to Love Led by the Spirit, Jet doesn't know how to cope with the loss of her younger sister, Diane. But God sets her on the road to a spiritual recovery. To make sure she doesn't get lost, Jesus sends the handsome and single Minister Rossi Tolliver to be her guide. Psalm 147:3 says

Jesus can heal the brokenhearted and bind up their wounds. That sets the stage for Love Led by the Spirit.

In *Love Led By the Spirit*, Minister Rossi Tolliver is ready to settle down. Besides the outwardly attraction, he desires a woman who is sweet, humble, and loves church folks. Sounds simple enough on paper, but when he gets off his knees, praying for that special someone to come into his life, God opens his eyes to the woman who has been there all along. There is only a slight problem. Love is the farthest thing from Jesetta "Jet" Hutchens' mind. But Rossi, the man and the minister, is hard to resist. Is Jet ready to allow the Holy Spirit to lead her to love?

In *Stopping Traffic*, Book 1, Candace Clark has a phobia about crossing the street, and for good reason. As fate would have it, her daughter's principal assigns her to crossing guard duties as part of the school's Parent Participation program. With no choice in the matter, Candace begrudgingly accepts her stop sign and safety vest, then reports to her designated crosswalk. Once Candace is determined to overcome her fears, God opens the door for a blessing, and Royce Kavanaugh enters into her life, a firefighter built to rescue any damsel in distress. When a spark of attraction ignites, Candace and Royce soon discover there's more than one way to stop traffic.

In *A Baby For Christmas*, Book 2, yes, diamonds are a girl's best friend, but in Solae Wyatt-Palmer's case, she desires something more valuable. Captain Hershel Kavanaugh is a divorcee and the father of two adorable little boys. Solae has never been married and longs to be a mother. Although Hershel showers her with expensive gifts, his hesitation about proposing causes Solae to walk and never look back. As the holidays approach, Hershel must convince Solae that she has everything he could ever want for Christmas.

In *The Keepsake*, Book 3, Until death us do part…or until Desiree walks away. Desiree "Desi" Bishop is devastated when she finds evidence of her husband's affair. God knew she didn't get married only to one day have to stand before a judge and file for a divorce. But Desi wants out no matter how much her heart says to forgive Michael. That isn't easier said than done. She sees God's one acceptable reason for a divorce as the only opt-out clause in her marriage. Michael Bishop is a repenting man who loves his wife of three years. If only…he had paid attention to the red flags God sent to keep him from falling into the devil's snares. But Michael didn't and he had fallen. Although God had forgiven him instantly when he repented, Desi's forgiveness is moving as a snail's pace. In the end, after all the tears have been shed and forgiveness granted and received, the couple learns that some marriages are worth keeping

In *What God Has For Me*, Book 4, Halcyon Holland is leaving her live-in boyfriend, taking their daughter and the baby in her belly with her. She's tired of waiting for the ring, so she buys herself one. When her ex doesn't reconcile their relationship, Halcyon begins to second-guess whether or not she compromised her chance for a happily ever after. After all, what man in his right mind would want to deal with the community stigma of 'baby mama drama?' But Zachary Bishop has had his eye on Halcyon since the first time he saw her. Without a ring on her finger, Zachary prays that she will come to her senses and not only leave Scott, but come back to God. What one man doesn't cherish, Zach is ready to treasure. Not deterred by Halcyon's broken spirit, Zachary is on a mission to offer her a second chance at love that she can't refuse. And as far as her adorable children are concerned, Zachary's love is unconditional for a ready-made family. Halcyon will soon learn that her past circumstances won't hinder the Lord's blessings, because what God has for her, is for her…and him…and the children.

In *Every Woman Needs A Praying Man*, Book 5, first impressions can make or break a business deal and they definitely could be a relationship buster, but an ill-timed panic attack draws two strangers together. Unlike firefighters who run into danger, instincts tell businessman Tyson Graham to head the other way as fast as he can when he meets a certain damsel in distress. Days later, the same woman struts through his door for a job interview. Monica Wyatt might possess the outwardly beauty and the brains on paper, but Tyson doesn't trust her to work for his firm, or maybe he doesn't trust his heart around her.

In *Guilty of Love*, when do you know the most important decision of your life is the right one? Reaping the seeds from what she's sown; Cheney Reynolds moves into a historic neighborhood in Ferguson, Missouri, and becomes a reclusive. Her first neighbor, the incomparable Mrs. Beatrice Tilley Beacon aka Grandma BB, is an opinionated childless widow. Grandma BB is a self-proclaimed expert on topics Cheney isn’t seeking advice—everything from landscaping to hip-hop dancing to romance. Then there is Parke Kokumuo Jamison VI, a direct descendant of a royal African tribe. He learned his family ancestry, African history, and lineage preservation before he could count. Unwittingly, they are drawn to each other, but it takes Christ to weave their lives into a spiritual bliss while He exonerates their past indiscretions.

In *Not Guilty*, one man, one woman, one God and one big problem. Malcolm Jamieson wasn't the man who got away, but the man God instructed Hallison Dinkins to set free. Instead of their explosive love affair leading them to the wedding altar, God diverted Hallison to the prayer altar during her first visit back to church in years. Malcolm was convinced that his woman had loss her mind to break off their engagement. Didn't Hallison know that Malcolm, a tenth generation descendant of a royal African tribe, couldn't be replaced? Once Malcolm concedes that their relationship can't be savaged, he issues Hallison his own edict, “If we're meant to be with each other, we'll find our way back. If not, that means that there's a love stronger than what we had.” His words begin to haunt Hallison until she begins to regret their break up, and that's where their story begins. Someone has to retreat, and God never loses a battle.

In *Still Guilty*, Cheney Reynolds Jamieson made a choice years ago that is now shaping her future and the future of the men she loves. A botched abortion left her unable to carry a baby to term, and her husband, Parke K. Jamison VI, is expected to produce heirs. With a wife who cannot give him a child, Parke vows to find and get custody of his illegitimate son by any means necessary. Meanwhile, Cheney's twin brother, Rainey, struggles with his anger over his ex-girlfriend's actions that haunt him, and their father, Dr. Roland Reynolds, fights to keep an old secret in the past.

In *The Acquittal*, two worlds apart, but their hearts dance to the same African drum beat. On a professional level, Dr. Rainey Reynolds is a competent, highly sought-after orthodontist. Inwardly, he needs to be set free from the chaos of revelations that make him question if happiness is obtainable. To get away from the drama, Rainey is willing to leave the country under the guise of a mission trip with Dentist Without Borders. Will changing his surroundings really change him? If one woman can heal his wounds, then he will believe that there is really peace after the storm.

Ghanaian beauty Josephine Abena Yaa Amoah returns to Africa after completing her studies as an exchange student in St. Louis, Missouri. Although her heart bleeds for his peace, she knows she must step back and pray for Rainey's surrender to Christ in order for God to acquit him of his self-inflicted mental torture. In the Motherland of Ghana, Africa, Rainey not only visits the places of his ancestors, will he embrace the liberty that Christ's Blood really does set every man free.

In *Guilty By Association*, how important is a name? To the St. Louis Jamiesons who are tenth generation descendants of a royal

African tribe—everything. To the Boston Jamiesons whose father never married their mother—there is no loyalty or legacy. Kidd Jamieson suffers from the "angry" male syndrome because his father was an absent in the home, but insisted his two sons carry his last name. It takes an old woman who mingles genealogy truths and Bible verses together for Kidd to realize his worth as a strong black man. He learns it's not his association with the name that identifies him, but the man he becomes that defines him.

In *The Guilt Trip*, Aaron "Ace" Jamieson is living a carefree life. He's good-looking, respectable when he's in the mood, but his weakness is women. If a woman tries to ambush him with a pregnancy, he takes off in the other direction. It's a lesson learned from his absentee father that responsibility is optional. Talise Rogers has a bright future ahead of her. She's pretty and has no problem catching a man's eye, which is exactly what she does with Ace. Trapping Ace Jamieson is the furthest thing from Talise's mind when she learns she pregnant and Ace rejects her. "I want nothing from you Ace, not even your name." And Talise meant it.

In *Free From Guilt*, it's salvation round-up time and Cameron Jamieson's name is on God's hit list. Although his brothers and cousins embraced God—thanks to the women in their lives—the two-degreed MIT graduate isn't going to let any woman take him down that path without a fight. He's satisfied with his career, social calendar, and good genes. But God uses a beautiful messenger, Gabrielle Dupree, to show him that he's in a spiritual deficit. Cameron learns the hard way that man's wisdom is like foolishness to God. For every philosophical argument he throws her way, Gabrielle exposes him to scriptures that makes him question his worldly knowledge.

In *Sandra Nicholson Backstory*, Sandra has made good and bad choices throughout the years, but the best one was to give her life to Christ when her sons were small and to rear them up in the best Christian way she knew how. That was thirty something years ago and Sandra has evolved from a young single mother of two rambunctious boys: Kidd and Ace Jamieson, to a godly woman seasoned with wisdom. Despite the challenges and trials of rearing two strong-willed personalities, Sandra maintained her sanity through the grace of God, which kept gray strands at bay. But there is something to be said about a woman's first love. Kidd and Ace Jamieson's father, Samuel Jamieson broke their mother's heart. Can Sandra recover? Her sons don't believe any man is good enough for her, especially their absentee father. Kidd doesn't deny his mother should find love again since she never married Samuel. But will she fall for a carbon copy of his father? God's love gives second chances.

In *The Confession*, Sandra Nicholson had made good and bad choices throughout the years, but the best one was to give her life to Christ when her sons were small and to rear them up in the best Christian way she knew how. That was thirty something years ago and Sandra has evolved from a young single mother of two rambunctious boys, Kidd and Ace Jamieson, to a godly woman seasoned with wisdom. Despite the challenges and trials of rearing two strong-willed personalities, Sandra maintained her sanity through the grace of God, which kept gray strands at bay.

Now, Sandra Nicholson is on the threshold of happiness, but Kidd believes no man is good enough for his mother, especially if her love interest could be a man just like his absentee father.

In *The Guilty Generation*, seventeen-year-old Kami Jamieson is so over being daddy's little girl. Now that she has captured the attention of Tango, the bad boy from her school, Kami's love for her family and God have taken a backseat to her teen crush.

Although the Jamiesons have instilled godly principles in Kami since she was young, they will stop at nothing, including prayer and fasting, to protect her from falling prey to society's peer pressure. Can Kami survive her teen rebellion, or will she be guilty of dividing the next generation?

In *Queen's Surrender (To a Higher Calling)*, Opposites attract...or clash. The Jamieson saga continues with the Queen of the family in this inspirational romance. She's the mistress of flirtation but Philip is unaffected by her charm. The two enjoy a harmless banter about God's will versus Queen's, who prefers her own free-will lifestyle. Philip doesn't judge her choices—most of the time—and Queen respects his opinions—most of the time. It's perfect harmony sometimes.

Queen, the youngest sister of the Jamieson clan, wears her name as if it's a crown. She's single, sassy, and most of the time, loving her status, but she's about to strut down an unexpected spiritual path. Love takes no prisoners. When the descendants of a royal African tribe on her father's maternal side show up and show off at a family game night, Queen's vanity is kicked up a notch. The Robnetts take royalty to a new level with their own Queen.

Evangelist Philip Dupree is on the hot seat as the trial pastor at Total Surrender Church. The deadline for the congregation to officially elect him as pastor is months away. The stalemate: They want a family man to lead their flock. The board's ultimatum is enough to make him quit the ministry. But can a man of God walk away from his calling?

Can two people with different lifestyles and priorities cross paths and continue the journey as one? Who is going to be the first to surrender?

In *Fun and Games with the Jamieson Men*, The Jamieson Legacy series inspired this game book of fun activities:• Brain Teasers• Crossword Puzzles• Word Searches •Sudoku •Mazes •Coloring Pages. The Jamiesons are fictional characters that put emphasis on Black Heritage, which includes Black American History tidbits, African American genealogy, and strong Black families. Relax, grab a pencil and play along.

In *No Easy Catch*, Book 1, Shae Carmen hasn't lost her faith in God, only the men she's come across. Shae's recent heartbreak was discovering that her boyfriend was not only married, but on the verge of reconciling with his estranged wife. Humiliated, Shae begins to second guess herself as why she didn't see the signs that he was nothing more than a devil's decoy masquerading as a devout Christian man. St. Louis Outfielder Rahn Maxwell finds himself a victim of an attempted carjacking. The Lord guides him out of harms' way by opening the gunmen's eyes to Rahn's identity. The crook instead becomes infatuated fan and asks for Rahn's autograph, and as a good will gesture, directs Rahn out of the ambush! When the news media gets wind of what happened with the baseball player, Shae's television station lands an exclusive interview. Shae and Rahn's chance meeting sets in motion a relationship where Rahn not only surrenders to Christ, but pursues Shae with a purpose to prove that good men are still out there. After letting her guard down, Shae is faced with another scandal that rocks her world. This time the stakes are higher. Not only is her heart on the line, so is her professional credibility. She and Rahn are at odds as how to handle it and friction erupts between them. Will she strike out at love again? The Lord shows Rahn that nothing happens by chance, and everything is done for Him to get the glory.

In *Defense of Love*, Book 2, lately, nothing in Garrett Nash's life has made sense. When two people close to the U.S. Marshal wrong him deeply, Garrett expects God to remove them from his life. Instead, the Lord relocates Garrett to another city to start over, as if he were the offender instead of the victim. Criminal attorney Shari Carmen is comfortable in her own skin—most of the time. Being a "dark and lovely" African-American sister has its challenges, especially when it comes to relationships. Although she's a fireball in the courtroom, she knows how to fade into the background and keep the proverbial spotlight off her personal life. But literal spotlights are a different matter altogether. While playing tenor saxophone at an anniversary party, she grabs the attention of Garrett Nash. And as God draws them closer together, He makes another request of Garrett, one to which it will prove far more difficult to say "Yes, Lord."

In *Redeeming Heart*, Book 3, Landon Thomas (In Defense of Love) brings a new definition to the word "prodigal," as in prodigal son, brother or anything else imaginable. It's a good thing that God's love covers a multitude of sins, but He isn't letting Landon off easy. His journey from riches to rags proves to be humbling and a lesson well learned. Real Estate Agent Octavia Winston is a woman on a mission, whether it's God's or hers professionally. One thing is for certain, she's not about to compromise when it comes to a Christian mate, so why did God send a homeless man to steal her heart? Minister Rossi Tolliver (Crowning Glory) knows how to minister to God's lost sheep and through God's redemption, the game changes for Landon and Octavia.

In *Driven to Be Loved*, Book 4, on the surface, Brecee Carmen has nothing in common with Adrian Cole. She is a pediatrician certified in trauma care; he is a transportation problem solver for a luxury car dealership (a.k.a., a car salesman). Despite their slow but steady attraction to each other, neither one of them are sure that they're compatible. To complicate matters, Brecee is the sole unattached Carmen when it seems as though everyone else around her—family and friends—are finding love, except her. Through a series of discoveries, Adrian and Brecee learn that things don't happen by coincidence. Generational forces are at work, keeping promises, protecting family members, and perhaps even drawing Adrian back to the church. For Brecee and Adrian, God has been hard at work, playing matchmaker all along the way for their paths cross at the right time and the right place.

Lean on Me, Book 1. No one should have to go it alone... Caregivers sometimes need a little TLC too.

Tabitha Knicely believes in family before everything. She may be overwhelmed caring for her beloved great-aunt, but she would never turn her back on the woman who raised her, even if Aunt Tweet's dementia is getting worse. Tabitha is sure she can do this on her own. But when Aunt Tweet ends up on her neighbor's front porch, and the man has the audacity to accuse Tabitha of elder abuse, things go from bad to awful. Marcus Whittington feels a mountain of regret at causing problems for Tabitha and her great-aunt. How was he to know the frail older woman's niece was doing the best she could? As Marcus gets to know Aunt Tweet and sees how hard Tabitha is fighting to keep everything together, he can't walk away from the pair. Particularly when helping Tabitha care for her great-aunt leads the two of them on a spiritual journey of faith and surrender.

Here For You, Book 2. Rachel Knicely's life has been on hold for six months while she takes care of her great aunt, who has Alzheimer's. Putting her aunt first was an easy decision—accepting that Aunt Tweet is nearing the end of her battle is far more difficult. Nicholas Adams's ministry is bringing comfort to those who are sick and homebound. He responds to a request for help for an ailing woman but when he meets the Knicelys, he realizes Rachel is the one who needs support the most. Nicholas is charmed by and attracted to Rachel, but then devastating news brings both a crisis of faith and roadblocks to their budding relationship that neither could have anticipated. This beautifully emotional and clean story contains a hero and heroine who are better at taking care of other people than themselves, a dark moment that shakes their faith, and a well-earned happily ever after.

Stand by Me, Book 3. An uplifting story about embracing love and giving others—and yourself—one more chance. When it comes to being a caregiver, Kym Knicely has been there and done that. Then she meets Charles "Chaz" Banks and soon learns that every caregiving situation is different. Chaz takes care of his seven-year-old autistic granddaughter, Chauncy. Although Kym's attraction to Chaz is strong, she has to decide whether a romantic relationship can survive and thrive between two people at different stages in life. It's a journey with a different set of rules that Kym has to play by if she and Chaz are to have their happily ever after and the faith and family they envision.

About *Waiting for Christmas*,

A chance meeting. An undeniable attraction.

And a first date that starts with a stakeout that leads to a winner takes all shopping spree. It's the making of a holiday romance. While philanthropist Sterling Price believes in charitable causes, he and licensed social worker Ciara Summers have a difference of opinion on how to bless others. Ciara is a rebel with a cause and a hundred reasons why helping those less fortunate is important. Sterling is a man of means who believes there is a financial responsibility that comes with giving.

The Lord will make sure everyone's needs are met, and He has something extra for Sterling and Ciara that can't wait until Christmas.

About *Christmas Dinner*,

How do you celebrate the holidays after losing a loved one? Take the journey, beginning with Christmas Dinner. For months, Darcelle Price has suffered depression in silence. But things are about to change as she plans to celebrate Christmas Eve with family and share her journey. Darcelle invites them via group text, not knowing she had included her ex. Evanston Giles is surprised to hear from the woman he loved after months following their breakup. Seeking closure, he shows up on her doorsteps for answers. A lot can happen on Christmas Eve. Restoring family ties, building her faith in God, and falling in love again are just the beginning of the night of miracles.

About *Taye's Gift*,

Welcome to Snowflake, Colorado—a small town where wishes come true! When six old high school friends receive a letter that their fellow friend, Charity Hart, wrote before she passed away, their lives take an unexpected turn. She leaves them each a check for $1,500 and asks them to grant a wish—a secret wish—for someone else by Christmas. Who lays off someone before the holidays? Taye Thomas' employer did, so instead of Christmas shopping, she's job hunting. More devastating news comes when an old high school friend passed away. Could God be answering her prayers for help when she learns that Charity Hart left a $1500 check? No, the caveat is it's more blessed to give than receive. Taye has 30 days to find someone else in need to bless. To complicate matters, she's lives in Kansas City, which is more than eight hours away from Snowflake and she can't do it alone. Keeping a secret has never been so much work.

About *Couple by Christmas*,

Holidays haven't been the same for Derek Washington since his divorce. He and his ex-wife, Robyn, go out of their way to avoid each other. This Christmas may be different when he decides to give his son, Tyler, the family he once had before they split. Derek's going to need the Lord's intervention to soften her heart to agree to some outings. God's help doesn't come in the way he expected, but it's all good because everything falls in place for them to be a couple by Christmas.

About *Prayers Answered By Christmas*,

Christmas is coming. While other children are compiling their lists for a fictional Santa, eight-year-old Mikaela Washington is on her knees, making her requests known to the Lord: One mommy for Christmas please. Portia Hunter refuses to let her ex-husband cheat her out of the family she wants. Her prayer is for God to send the right man into her life. Marlon

Washington will do anything for his two little girls, but can he find a mommy for them and a love for himself? Since Christmas is the time of year to remember the many gifts God has given men, maybe these three souls will get their heart s desire.

About *A Noelle for Nathan*,

A Noelle for Nathan is a story of kindness, selflessness, and falling in love during the Christmas season. Andersen Investors & Consultants, LLC, CFO Nathan Andersen (A Christian Christmas) isn't looking for attention when he buys a homeless man a meal, but grade school teacher Noelle Foster is watching his every move with admiration. His generosity makes him a man after her own heart. While donors give more to children and families in need around the holiday season, Noelle Foster believes in giving year-round after seeing many of her students struggle with hunger and finding a warm bed at night. At a second-chance meeting, sparks fly when Noelle and Nathan share a kindred spirit with their passion to help those less fortunate. Whether they're doing charity work or attending Christmas parties, the couple becomes inseparable. Although Noelle and Nathan exchange gifts, the biggest present is the one from Christ.

One reader says, "A Noelle for Nathan makes you fall in love with love…the love of mankind and the love of God. You cannot read this without having a desire to give and do more, all while being appreciative of what you have."

About *Christmas Greetings*,

Saige Carter loves everything about Christmas: the shopping, the food, the lights, and of course, Christmas wouldn't be complete without family and friends to share in the traditions they've created together. Plus, Saige is extra excited about her line of Christmas greeting cards hitting store shelves, but when she gets devastating news around the holidays, she wonders if she'll ever look at Christmas the same again. Daniel Washington is no Scrooge, but he'd rather skip the holidays altogether than spend them with his estranged family. After one too many arguments around the dinner table one year, Daniel had enough and walked away from the drama. As one year has turned into many, no one seems willing to take the first step toward reconciliation. When Daniel reads one of Saige's greeting cards, he's unsure if the words inside are enough to erase the pain and bring about forgiveness. Once God reveals to them His purpose for their lives, they will have a reason to rejoice. *Come unto me, all ye that labor and are heavy laden, and I will give you rest. Take my yoke upon you, and learn of me; for I am meek and lowly in heart: and ye shall find rest unto your souls*. Matthew 11:28-29

About *A Baby for Christmas*,

Yes, diamonds are a girl's best friend, but unless the jewel is going on Solae Wyatt-Palmer's ring finger, they hold little value to her. When she meets Fire Captain Hershel Kavanaugh, their magnetism is undeniable and there's no doubt that it's love at first sight. Since Solae adores Hershel's two boys from his failed marriage, she wouldn't blink at the chance to become a mother to them. But when it seems as if Hershel doesn't have a proposal on his agenda, she has no choice but to cut her losses and move on. But Christmas is coming. And in order to win Solae back, Hershel must resolve some past issues before convincing her that she possesses everything he wants.

About *A Christian Christmas*,

Christmas will never be the same for Joy Knight if Christian Andersen has his way. Not to be confused with a secret Santa, Christian and his family are busier than Santa's elves making sure the Lord's blessings are distributed to those less fortunate by Christmas day. Joy is playing the hand that life dealt her, rearing four children in a home that is on the brink of foreclosure. She's not looking for a handout, but when Christian rescues her in the checkout line; her niece thinks Christian is an angel. Joy thinks he's just another man who will eventually leave, disappointing her and the children. Although Christian is a servant of the Lord, he is a flesh and blood man and all he wants for Christmas is Joy Knight. Can time spent with Christian turn Joy's attention from her financial woes to the real meaning of Christmas—and true love? A Christian Christmas is a holiday novella to be enjoyed any time of the year.

Made in the USA
Middletown, DE
04 December 2022

15921526R00150